Sign up for our newsletter to hear
about new and upcoming releases.

www.ylva-publishing.com

Other Books by
A.L. Brooks

The Club
Dark Horse

miles
apart

A.L. BROOKS

Acknowledgements

As always, thanks to the wonderfulness that is Ylva Publishing. You're a dream to work with and your professionalism and support only make me want to try harder with every book I write. In particular, big shout-outs to Astrid, Daniela, Jo, Gill McKnight, and Andrea Bramhall.

To my beta readers, Katja, Erin, and Emma, your comments and insight were invaluable and kept me on the true path of this story, for which I am eternally grateful.

To Glendon, for a wonderful cover.

And to my "technical advisors": my Canadian friends/colleagues who helped ensure any references I make to life in Montreal are as accurate as possible. Any mistakes in that respect are purely mine. All bars, restaurants, and offices mentioned in the book are purely fictional.

Lastly, and by no means leastly, to my own long-distance love, Tanja, for her daily encouragement and support, and everything she does that makes me feel incredibly lucky that she is in my life.

Dedication

For the Lesvos crew

Chapter 1

JUSTINE SMILED WIDELY AS THE woman—she'd forgotten her name already—draped over her from behind. The music was pumping and her latest conquest was thrusting her hips against Justine's in time to the beat. Her body responded in all the right ways and Justine glanced at her watch.

Yeah, this was a good time to leave.

Justine turned to face her. Anna! That was her name. *Thank God.*

"Anna," she said, bending to speak directly in her ear. "Shall we get out of here?"

Anna beamed and nodded, her dark hair bouncing.

Justine smiled and grabbed her hand.

Anna lived only a ten minutes' drive away. Justine didn't let on that her place was closer—tonight she was happier going elsewhere for whatever was about to follow.

Anna fumbled with her door keys when Justine snaked up behind her on the step and nuzzled her neck.

"Oh," Anna murmured when Justine's hands slipped under Anna's thick coat and squeezed her ass.

Justine laughed and let go. "Go on, get that door unlocked."

Anna did as she was told and Justine followed her into the apartment. She barely gave it a glance; she wasn't here for a tour of Anna's home. Just her bedroom.

Justine grabbed Anna and pulled her roughly to her, kissing her fiercely. Her last assignation was a couple of weeks ago, and she was hungry for the release she knew was on its way. Anna moaned and held on tight as Justine plundered her mouth.

Their hands scrabbled at each other's coats and scarves and pulled them away, dropping them on the floor at their feet.

As Justine moved her mouth to the softness of Anna's neck, she let her hands roam. She pulled Anna's T-shirt out from her pants, and there it was—warm, soft skin. Just what she wanted.

"Oh," Anna whispered. "I love your hands on me."

Justine smiled against her neck and continued her explorations, running her hands up Anna's ribs to the underside of her bra.

Anna pushed against her, her own hands digging into Justine's back. "I knew you would feel like this," she said, offering yet more of her neck to Justine's lips. "That connection we had on the dance floor was just too special to ignore."

Justine hesitated ever so slightly. What was she talking about?

Anna pulled back as Justine's lips stopped moving. "You felt it too, didn't you?"

"Yeah. Sure," Justine said, nudging Anna with her hips. "Bedroom?"

"This way."

Anna grinned. Grabbing Justine's hand, she tugged her down the hallway and into a large bedroom. Turning to face Justine, she pulled her T-shirt off, then her bra.

Justine's mouth watered. "Beautiful," she murmured, taking her time to admire the full breasts, their nipples hardening as she gazed at them.

"All for you, baby," Anna murmured.

Justine lunged forwards, briefly kissing Anna again as her hands cupped those bountiful breasts, then dipping her head so she could lick one of Anna's firm nipples. Anna ran her fingers through Justine's curly hair, tightening their grip against her scalp the more Justine's lips nibbled and sucked.

"You and I are going to be amazing. I can just feel it." Anna's words made their way through the desire-induced fog in Justine's brain, and she raised her head.

Anna looked down at her. "Don't stop," she said, pushing herself towards Justine's mouth. "We've got so much to share, and it all starts here."

Anna's words were like ice-cold water being thrown in her face. Justine stood and stared at Anna, who tilted her head, her eyes narrowing.

"What are you talking about?" Justine took a small step backwards.

Anna smiled. "Us," she said, reaching for Justine and pouting when Justine pulled back. "Come on, you feel it too. You know you do."

Oh, holy shit.

Justine took another step back. Her arousal had disappeared entirely. Now all she could think about was getting out of this as fast as possible.

"Look, I think we've got a little problem here," she began, and flinched as Anna's face crumpled. She exhaled. Oh crap, this was going to be... difficult. "I think you want more from this than I do. So I think I should just go."

Anna stared at her, and her expression moved to one of hurt anger. "You mean, you just wanted me for one night?"

Scratching idly at the back of her neck, Justine tried not to laugh. She wasn't normally a callous person, but maybe that was the only way she'd get Anna to understand.

"Well, yeah. That's always all I'm after."

She watched the words hit home and hated herself, more than a little, for causing pain to another person. She'd never had this kind of thing happen before. Normally whomever she picked up wanted exactly the same thing: no strings, one night of fun, thanks and goodbye in the morning.

Anna started to cry.

"I'm going to go," Justine said, backing away.

"Yes, I think you should." Anna's tone was icy and Justine didn't waste any more time. She left the bedroom, retrieved her coat from the floor, and yanked open the front door.

"You bitch!" Anna screamed as Justine stepped back out into the cold air.

She wanted to retort, to defend herself. *No, actually, I'm a nice person who just read the signals wrong. Much like you.* But she knew there was no point.

As she pulled the door closed behind her, she heard a loud thump against it. If she had to guess, she'd say Anna had just thrown a boot at it. She shook her head as she walked down the steps to street level.

How had she got that one so wrong? She was normally so good at this.

She huffed out a breath as she set off for the main road. She'd give herself five minutes to find a cab before calling Lyft. Montreal's winter was already creeping in and she really didn't want to walk home if she could avoid it.

What a disaster the night had turned out to be. This life—one-night stands and going home alone—was the only life she'd been able to stomach since Nadia had taken her world away eighteen months ago. God, was it that long? Sometimes, like now, it seemed it was only yesterday. At least she got out and about these days, and two or three times a month found a warm body to enjoy. But lately it had seemed…empty. Meaningless.

Maybe her heart was finally starting to heal and make room for something that *did* have meaning.

⸺⸺⸺⸻⸺⸺⸺

Justine's phone rang just as she stepped out of the shower. She knew who was calling, and she laughed as she strode across the bedroom to answer the call before it went to voice mail.

"*Bonsoir*, Christina. I know, I'm very late."

Justine was notorious for running late to everything. It always surprised her, as she usually thought she'd timed everything right. But, invariably, she was the last one into the room at meetings, always a few minutes late for appointments, and never on time to meet up with Christina and Sylvie.

Christina snorted with laughter. "Of course you are! But how close are you?"

"Um," Justine said, looking down at her still-damp body and running her fingers through her wet hair. "If I tell you about twenty minutes, will you believe me?"

"Pah, we'll see you in forty, then. We're going to order some starters. We can't wait that long." Christina sounded grumpy, as she always did when kept from her food too long. She was one of those annoying women who was stick-thin but could eat like a horse.

"Go ahead. I'll be as fast as I can, promise." Justine chuckled as Christina snorted again, then abruptly ended the call.

Towelling herself off, she pondered what to wear. It was cold out, the temperature having dropped further since the start of the week. They'd even forecast a light snow. So that meant layers, at least. As long as the base layer was something tight, and sexy, and—

She stopped herself. Tonight was supposed to be just about seeing Christina and Sylvie—no extracurricular activities.

4

She finished drying her hair, pushing her blonde curls around until they fell into the messy just-out-of-bed look she liked to sport outside of work, and looked back at the closet again. Tonight she was just meeting friends for food and wine. No picking up a woman and going home with her. She needed a break from that, needed to regroup. Especially after what had happened on Monday. She shuddered.

She smiled to herself—Christina would be delighted to hear that Justine might be on her road to reform. Christina was her closest friend and had watched Justine's descent into a series of lacklustre one-night stands with open disdain. She would be very happy to hear that Justine felt a need to put a stop to that, even if only temporarily.

So tonight called for jeans and a T-shirt, nothing fancy. Having decided, she dressed, adding a warm sweater, a little jewellery, and pulling on her favourite soft brown leather boots. Grabbing her scarf and jacket along with her wallet, she headed out of the apartment and strode down the street. She only had a ten-minute walk to the bar where she was meeting them.

The one good thing that came out of Nadia ending their relationship was that it forced Justine into moving home. She'd listened to Christina's advice and put herself in the heart of the Gay Village, surrounding herself with a community where she could feel completely herself. Not stuck out on the outskirts of the city in the executive home the status-hungry Nadia had insisted they live in when they got serious about their relationship. As Justine walked down Rue Sainte-Catherine Est, she shook her head, wondering, with hindsight, how she had managed to live in that soulless place for over four years. She'd hated it. She smiled ruefully to herself. *The things you do for love.*

She trotted up the steps of Gabrielle's and pushed open the door. Spotting Christina and Sylvie straight away, she strolled over, laughing at Christina's glare as her friend tapped the watch on her wrist.

"Sorry," she said, leaning down to kiss each of them on both cheeks, then shedding her jacket and pulling out the third chair to sit down. She reached for the wine bottle and poured herself a glass, taking a long swallow before sitting back and smiling at them. Christina was dressed in her trademark all black—T-shirt and dressy pants. Her long dark hair was pulled back in a tight ponytail with a few strands hanging down either side of her face, framing her bright red glasses, her only nod to the colour palette. Some might have called her look severe, but Justine always thought it exuded a sexy classiness. Sylvie, in contrast, was dressed in one of her multicoloured short dresses, her chestnut-brown hair piled up in a loose bun with multiple wild strands falling in all directions around her head. She was a petite woman, with an elfin face. She was a few years older than Justine and Christina's thirty-eight, and most definitely wiser than the pair of them put together. Despite appearing to be so very different from their outward appearances, she and Christina worked brilliantly as a partnership and had been together for over eight years.

"You look...different," Christina said, tipping her head to one side and staring at Justine as if examining a painting in a gallery.

"Different how?"

"Not physically. Something in your demeanour. Something intangible. You seem more relaxed somehow."

Frighteningly perceptive was a phrase Justine had often used to describe Christina, and she wasn't letting Justine down now.

"Very good," she murmured, nodding. "One of the reasons I was late was because I was having a little think about my...lifestyle over the last couple of years."

"Oh, please tell me this is good news," Christina cried, grabbing Justine's arm dramatically, making Sylvie roll her eyes and Justine laugh.

"You will be happy, I think. Given what a disaster my last conquest was, I've decided to cool things off for a while."

"How long is 'a while'?" Sylvie asked, smirking, her eyes expressing her disbelief in Justine's commitment to her declaration.

"I can't put a number on it. And, before you get all excited, I don't know if that means I want to start looking for something more meaningful, or if I just want a break. I'm just going to see how I go, and make sure my nights out are not only focused on getting laid."

"Well, it's a start," Christina drawled, and Justine smiled at her.

"What brought this on?" Sylvie asked, reaching across the table to steal a piece of calamari from the plate in front of Christina, who growled jokingly at the thievery.

Justine shrugged. "I guess I've not been happy for a while but just couldn't break out of the routine of it. It's just too easy to do, you know that."

Christina and Sylvie would know there was no arrogance in her statement; it was just a simple truth. Justine was an attractive, sexy woman. Her blonde curls and pale blue eyes coupled with her lithe body ensured that women were drawn to her on an alarmingly regular basis. She had used this to her advantage for some time now, but she knew both her friends had known for all that time that it never really fulfilled her, no matter what she said. And while she laughed about each conquest afterwards, it was hollow laughter.

"Well," Sylvie said, patting Justine's hand where it rested on the table, "I am glad you are here with us tonight, so let's eat and catch up on everything else."

Justine smiled, grateful for Sylvie's tact in changing the direction of their conversation.

"So," Christina said, leaning in close, "did you hear about Lucile and that butch she picked up last week?"

Justine laughed and relaxed into the evening as Christina launched into a gossip fest.

They parted company a couple of hours—and a couple of bottles of wine—later. Justine didn't linger in her walk home in the cold November air, passing the short journey thinking about the evening. She acknowledged it was the most relaxed she'd felt in a while. She also recalled she hadn't once scoped the room, and she couldn't remember the last time she'd spent a whole evening out without at least one eye on potential bedmates.

Maybe there was hope for her yet.

Chapter 2

The text from Terri made Alex's blood boil—heat of a most unpleasant kind rippled through her skin, her heart rate accelerating along with it.

Sorry. Deal taking longer than we thought. Won't make counselling. Don't wait up.

Before she could filter it, her anger had her swiping open the message and pressing the Call Back icon. She didn't actually know what she'd do if Terri answered or not, but she didn't have to wait long to find out.

"Hey," Terri said, her voice way cheerier than Alex wanted to hear. She wanted remorse and discomfort, and the lack of both in her partner's tone had her free hand clutching painfully at the edge of her desk.

"Seriously, Terri? This is the third time you've cancelled counselling. What am I supposed to do now?" She managed to keep the volume of her voice low, but her words were clipped and spat from between her lips.

"Oh, come on, give me a break! You know what my job's like. You know how quickly things can change in a day." Terri's voice had risen and it sounded incredibly loud in Alex's ear, making her tremble as her anger transformed into agitation.

Confrontation was not Alex's natural style, and she was suddenly struggling with the bad energy between them. Her usual need to smooth things over was overcoming her anger. Yes, she did know how fast-paced Terri's job was, and how her days often careened off-track. It was a big part of what had got them into this mess in the first place. Exhaling slowly, and rolling her head to try to ease the sudden tightness in her neck and shoulders, she paused before speaking again.

"You just don't make this any easier, you know."

There was silence. Then, "I could say the same to you."

The words hit Alex like a verbal slap. She inhaled sharply, but before she could retort, Terri jumped in.

"I don't want to argue. Quite frankly, I don't have time." Her tone held a finality that brooked no argument. "I'm sorry about the counselling. I'll get home as soon as I can, but like I said, don't wait up."

"Fine." Alex hung up before she said something she'd really regret and carefully placed her phone back on her desk. Leaning back in her chair, she closed her eyes.

So Terri was bailing on their counselling again. Alex couldn't stop the acid churning in her stomach at how…coldly Terri had written off their session.

Her teeth ground as she bit back the string of expletives queueing up to escape her mouth. While anger was still her overriding emotion, she opened her eyes as she acknowledged the other strong feeling coursing through her. Relief.

A few hours later Alex slotted her key in the lock with an overwhelming sense of trepidation. Surprisingly, Terri was home already, and Alex had no idea what to expect when she walked into the flat.

She had found the solo counselling session useful, but that didn't really surprise her. Gloria had helped Alex tap into some of her own long-standing issues around relationships. It left her with more questions than answers, but it had purged a little of the anger that still resided deep within her over what Terri had done three months ago. Just not enough. There just didn't seem to be a way to remove that nausea, that twist of anger every time she thought about it. The sessions with Gloria had helped, but it seemed no amount of talking or sharing could quite bring her to be comfortable with where they were.

Breathing in deeply, steeling her bruised heart, she shut the door behind her and locked it.

She shrugged off her coat in the hallway and hung it up, heeling off her shoes in blissful relief as she dropped her bag on the floor.

"I'm home!" she called out.

"In the kitchen," came the muffled response.

Poking her head round the kitchen door, she watched as Terri deftly stirred something in a pan. Terri was in her dark blue track pants, a cotton hoodie over the top with the sleeves rolled up. Her short dark hair was ruffled. Her wire-rimmed glasses were perched on the end of her nose, something she did when cooking to keep them from steaming up too much. She looked adorable, but Alex almost couldn't allow herself to think it. She was still angry with Terri, and thinking nice things about her diminished that anger. Wanting her, desiring her—none of that was good right now.

"You're home earlier than I thought you'd be," Alex said.

"Yep, didn't take as long as I thought in the end." Terri looked up. "Want some soup? I didn't eat earlier and I'm starving."

Terri's casualness irked Alex, but she tried to play nice. "No, I'm good."

Terri blinked a couple of times. Then, "How was the session?"

Alex shrugged and worked hard at keeping her tone neutral. "Okay." She paused. "Get your work done?"

"Yeah." Terri stopped stirring the soup and put the spoon down. "Sorry about earlier," she said quietly. She walked the few steps across the kitchen towards Alex and leaned in for a quick kiss, which Alex returned on autopilot. Alex was aware that she was working very hard not to respond to Terri's kisses, to pretend they didn't move her like they used to. Her mind resented them. Her body—more and more often lately, much to her mind's chagrin—ached for them. But she didn't trust the kisses, didn't trust that Terri truly wanted to kiss *her*. And she wasn't sure she would ever trust that again.

Terri stepped back. "Just so you know, I'm going in early tomorrow. We're having a celebratory breakfast for finally pulling it off."

"We?" Alex asked, before she could stop herself. Terri started and frowned, but before she could speak Alex held up a hand. "Don't. Forget I asked. Sorry." She had promised not to open up old wounds, as part of their path to reconciliation. It was just too hard not to, sometimes.

Terri nodded slowly and breathed deeply, the frown slowly easing itself out.

"So," Terri said eventually, "it looks like I'll be free this weekend. Want to do something?"

Alex took a deep breath. On the way home she'd wondered when would be the best time to tell Terri her news, but now her hand had been forced. She could guess how well—or more likely, not—it would be received.

"Sorry, but I can't. Richard ambushed me at the end of the day—I've got to go back to Montreal."

Terri's emotions played out across her face in stark clarity. Surprise, quickly turning to anger, followed by another attempt to get that anger under control.

"When?" Terri asked, her voice laced with tension.

"This Saturday, back next Friday."

Terri pursed her lips, then turned her back on Alex and walked back to the stove where she picked up the wooden spoon again and aggressively stirred the soup that now bore the brunt of her anger.

Alex took a deep breath and walked over to Terri, slipping her arms round her waist from behind, pulling Terri's resistant body into her own. She rested her chin on Terri's shoulder, knowing her arms weren't fully relaxed around her partner, that she was holding a piece of herself back. Terri leaned back into her.

"I'm sorry, I know you don't like how much travelling I've done this year." Alex's stomach churned. She was apologising again—for being successful, for being good at what she did. It caused a tiny ball of molten heat to ignite in her gut.

Terri shrugged in her arms. "We knew it would be a big part of your new job. I just have to get used to it. Doesn't mean I'll like it, though."

"I know." Alex cringed at her automatic need to make things better for Terri, but she couldn't seem to stop herself. Years of always making everyone else feel better had ingrained this behaviour into her bones—something she'd only just come to realise in her session with Gloria, and something she didn't know how to change. A little voice, far off in the back of her mind, said Terri was being unreasonable, given how many hours Terri put into her own job, the cancelled counselling session being a prime example. But Alex wasn't ready to deal with that voice yet. "I'm hoping this will be the last transatlantic one this year, if that's any consolation?"

11

"I hope so," Terri said, then eased herself out of Alex's arms. "Okay, I'm ready to eat, so if you want to go get changed, we could meet in the living room?"

Alex could see the effort Terri needed to make that sound as relaxed as it did. Gloria had managed to instil in both of them the need to make an effort at key moments. To take a minute to consider, and breathe, and allow for each other's feelings. Some days it worked. Some it didn't. Terri was trying, and Alex had to be thankful for that. Even if all it did was cause that emptiness to gnaw away at her again.

"Okay." Alex kissed her on the cheek and left the room to head to their bedroom.

They sat together on the sofa, not close, watching a detective drama on TV. They each had a glass of wine, something else they were learning to moderate between them. Alcohol had played a significant part in the events that had brought them to this point, and they'd both agreed that Terri, in particular, needed to be aware of how much she now drank. As part of the "deal" they'd done in couples' counselling, Alex never drank more than Terri when at home. Even when, sometimes, all she wanted was to sink into the oblivion that she knew three or four glasses would lend her.

After thirty minutes of silently watching a program she couldn't focus on, she was relieved when her phone rang.

Seeing Danielle's name come up in the caller ID, she hurried to answer.

"I'll go into the bedroom so you can carry on watching," she said to Terri and stood without waiting for a response.

"Hey, you," she said into the phone as she left the room.

"So," Danielle said without preamble, "you *are* alive, then? I have been texting you all day." While Danielle's smoothly upper-class tone sounded pouty, Alex knew that her friend of over twenty years was only teasing. They went back too far, and had shared too much, for Danielle to be that annoyed at Alex not returning a few text messages.

Alex giggled and thrilled at the sound. She hadn't realised she had that left in her today. She walked across the hall to the bedroom and flopped herself on top of the bed. The duvet gave way beneath her with a puff of air.

"I had a very long day, thank you. And found out I have to go back to Montreal this weekend."

"Oh dear, I can't imagine that went down too well at home? Or have you not told her yet?" This time Danielle's tone was acerbic, and Alex knew she meant every bit of that emotion. Danielle, despite thinking what Terri had done was unforgivable, had agreed to support Alex in staying with Terri, when Alex insisted that was what she wanted. But it didn't mean Danielle liked it.

"Yes, I told her. And no, she wasn't happy." The unspoken "of course" hung in the silence after she spoke.

"How have things been?" Danielle asked quietly.

Alex shrugged, even though she knew Danielle couldn't see the gesture. "Okay. Hard. Just…"

Danielle's exhaled breath sounded loud against Alex's ear. "What?" Danielle asked.

Alex's eyes welled up, and she flushed with anger at this weakening of her defences. "Don't," she said. "Don't be nice to me. Not tonight."

There was a pause. "When is your next counselling session?"

"Actually, I had one this evening. But on my own. Terri had to work."

Danielle tutted. "Why am I not surprised," she said. "Do…do they really help?"

Alex couldn't stop the snort that escaped her. "I have no idea," she said. She closed her eyes. She didn't need to get into this with Danielle. Not tonight. She was so tired. "Look, forget it. It's a process. It takes time."

"I understand. But…"

"What?"

"Is this still what you want?" The question came in a rush of words that tumbled over each other, so out of character for Danielle, who usually spoke with a calmness and grace Alex could only envy. "Only I am not so sure it is, quite frankly, and if it isn't, would it not be better to—"

"Don't, Danielle. Please." Alex's voice ached with emotions she couldn't release; the consequences were just too enormous.

Silence fell between them for a moment.

"What about lunch on Friday? Can you manage it?" Danielle's voice had transformed into measured and falsely cheery, but Alex was grateful for the change in direction. Even if it was only a stay of execution until Friday lunchtime.

"I'm sure I could squeeze you in," Alex said, forcing herself to smile as she spoke, to crowbar her own false cheeriness into her tone. "One o'clock, the usual spot?"

"Lovely. See you then. And Alex…"

"Yes?"

"You know where I am. Whenever. All right?"

Alex's throat closed up, and all she managed to squeeze out was a strangled "Uh-huh."

She lay on the bed for some minutes, the phone clutched to her chest. Her emotions were all over the place, but the warmth she felt after talking to Danielle comforted her, even as her friend's question ricocheted around her brain.

"Is this still what you want?"

No, she wasn't sure this was what she wanted anymore. How could she be? She knew plenty of couples managed to survive one partner's infidelity, but right here and now, she had no idea how they did. She'd been trying for over three months and was coming to realise that she wasn't sure she *wanted* them to survive it. They weren't the same people they'd been before that night. And no matter how hard she tried, she couldn't look at Terri and not have an image, however brief, flash up in her mind's eye of Terri with Liz, Terri's boss. Terri had slept with her one night three months ago. A night that had changed everything Alex and Terri had shared for the last five years.

When Terri had guiltily confessed all, a week later, she'd blamed the copious champagne they'd drunk that night as they'd celebrated landing a new client at the bank where she and Liz worked. But Alex had wondered if blaming the alcohol was just the easy way out. She remembered all the references to Liz in the previous few months. That extra little zing in Terri's voice when she spoke about what she and Liz had done during the day. All the niggly little arguments that had started to play a bigger part in her and Terri's daily life, and all the times they simply crossed paths as both their jobs took up more of their time.

The distance that crept between them like a slow-moving fog.

And she remembered all the other late nights, all the other excuses for why Terri wouldn't be home until Alex had gone to bed. Had she and Liz been sleeping together all that time? Terri said it was just one night, but Alex didn't know how to believe her. Or had Liz just been planning it all that time, and the deal, and the champagne that had followed, gave her the perfect opportunity to strike?

As easy as it was for Terri to blame the champagne, it was even easier for Alex to blame Liz. To pretend that Terri was somehow a relatively innocent party in this. But she wasn't. Terri could have said no. She could have resisted.

But she didn't.

Sure, Terri had begged for Alex's forgiveness, sworn it would never happen again, and in her shock, Alex had believed her, for a while. Terri had been consumed with remorse and falling over herself to repent. But it had changed them, as individuals, and it had changed them as an "us".

The couples' counselling had started two weeks later. Alex had insisted on it. She had still been in shock, and although she'd been bitterly angry and upset at what Terri had done, she'd thought what they'd had before that night was enough to be worth rescuing. If they both wanted it enough.

Now, three months down the track, she really wasn't sure if either of them wanted it at all. But that was a can of worms she didn't want to open.

Not yet.

Alex heaved herself upright and walked back to the lounge. She found Terri sleeping in front of the TV.

So much for worrying that Terri would wonder where she'd got to.

She switched off the TV, roused Terri, and they went to bed. After a perfunctory kiss goodnight, Terri rolled over and was asleep in minutes. Intimacy was something they had only just reintroduced into their relationship. For weeks after Terri's affair, Alex had not been able to relax, to believe it was she who Terri saw in front of her and not Liz. From the snippets of information Alex had gleaned over the months, Liz was younger and taller than Alex, bigger-breasted and longer in the legs. Alex had looked at her own body in a new light—breasts still in reasonably good shape, hips maybe a little wider than she'd had before. Her auburn hair was a little dry on the ends and never quite held its style, and her green eyes were constantly circled with dark marks as she threw herself into striving

15

for her promotion. She looked tired, all the time, and lacked energy most weekends for anything other than watching football or heading out to a pub or café for late lunches. Was that why Terri had fallen so easily into Liz's arms?

Still, over this past month, intimacy of a kind had been resurrected between Alex and Terri. Hugs and tender kisses had morphed into deeply passionate kisses and the occasional fumble up each other's T-shirts. Until one evening a fortnight ago, suddenly burning with a desire she'd thought may have disappeared for good, Alex hadn't stopped Terri when her hands slid down inside Alex's jeans. Terri's weight had pressed her into the sofa, and the sex had been hard, and fast, and shockingly delicious. And for those few minutes, Alex had been able to lose herself in the sensations and forget the emotions.

Since then they'd tried a couple more times, but not with the same level of success. She didn't know why, but she couldn't conjure up that same intensity again, that same letting go of emotions. Each time Terri made advances, something shut down inside Alex and she couldn't find a way to turn it back on.

So they were back to where they'd been for the previous three months. Strangers sharing a bed, not even spooning anymore.

She turned her head slightly to look at Terri's silhouette in the darkened room. She was breathing deeply, fast asleep.

Alex tried to fathom why she was still trying to keep this going. Her reasons were a complex mix, and she wasn't sure she had the energy to unravel them, despite the glimmer of insight Gloria had given her. Her age was definitely playing a role, along with the fact she had a series of failed relationships behind her. Her lifelong tendency to loyalty, even if it was to the detriment of her own happiness, was also biting her in the ass. All of these things she should probably face up to and talk to someone about at length. Gloria had offered each of them individual sessions anytime they wanted—they'd had one individual session each in the early days, which was apparently standard practice. Alex had spent the entirety of that first one-hour session in tears. The betrayal had felt overwhelming, and she'd struggled to verbalise what it had done to her. The subsequent sessions she'd had on her own with Gloria had only emphasised how much she needed to deal with, and not just about her failing relationship with Terri.

The fact it was called couples' counselling seemed ironic when she was attending more of the sessions on her own than with her partner.

Partner.

A dictionary definition of the word would suggest sharing or intimacy. Or being together.

She and Terri weren't any of those things right now. Not really.

She wondered if they ever would be again. The distance between them grew ever wider day by day. At the wave of sadness that swept over her, she swallowed back a sudden lump in her throat and rolled over, pressing her face into her pillow and curling into a childlike ball.

———————

"Hey, you're home before me." Terri leaned in to kiss the back of Alex's neck as she chopped salad ingredients.

Alex forced a smile and turned to face her. "Yep. Managed to get out of that meeting I normally have late on Tuesdays and made a run for it. I thought I'd get started on supper as you said you'd be a little late."

Terri beamed, and it cut through Alex. How could she act so...normal? As if nothing was wrong? Was Terri forcing herself to appear happy? Did she really give a shit who cooked each night and why? So much for their counselling helping to improve their communication. Somehow, despite how many sessions they'd had, they seemed worse off than before in that regard. And Alex knew, deep down, that was mostly coming from her. The longer this went on, the more unsure she was. And yet, conversely, the more daunting it seemed to really talk about the mess they were in. To get the truth out.

"So what delights are you serving me?" Terri waggled her eyebrows playfully, and Alex searched her brown eyes for some inkling that it was genuine amusement, not contrived. Nothing in Terri's expression suggested it was anything but real. It tugged at Alex's heart and gut. Was she really the only one who thought this was all turning to crap? Did Terri still think they were going to be okay? Terri's cavalier attitude grated on her nerves.

She glanced away to the food beside her. "Um, well, it's just some grilled salmon, boiled new potatoes, and a salad. And I picked up some of that lime dressing you like so much." She had tried. Really tried. She'd hit the deli next to the station on her way home, determined to make an effort.

She just couldn't help thinking it shouldn't be this hard. Given how long it had been since Terri had slept with Liz, surely she should be past it now, if she truly was committed to Terri. Surely she wouldn't be so exhausted from trying?

"Nice! I love that dressing." Terri leaned forwards and kissed her tenderly again, lingering. This one stirred something, undeniably so. A tightening low in her belly, the barest hint of desire and need and, yes, affection. Surprising herself, she ran with it, clutched at it like a life raft. Then, suddenly, craved it. Deepening the kiss, she let her tongue play over Terri's bottom lip and was rewarded with a long, soft groan from her partner. Kissing Terri had always been her undoing. Her hot mouth, her gently probing tongue, the sound of her ragged breathing. All of it always conspired to weaken Alex, to tear down the resistance she sometimes wasn't even conscious of placing between them.

When they broke for air, Terri's eyes were shining.

"That was…"

"Yeah, it was," Alex whispered. And it was. But just like that, the walls came down again. She didn't want to take it further. Well, her clit, which was now quietly throbbing, wanted to. Badly. But her brain wouldn't let her body go there. Not yet.

She stepped away, exhaling slowly. She smiled as warmly as she could and gestured towards the salad. "Dinner in about ten, okay?"

Terri's eyes dimmed, just a little, but she smiled back. "Sure. I'll just go and get changed."

⋘⋙

Terri slid into bed beside Alex, letting in a small whoosh of cool air as she did. It tickled at the bare skin on Alex's arms where they rested by her head. She was on her left side, facing Terri's pillow. She'd mentally gone back and forth with herself the entire time Terri was in the bathroom.

If I lie on my right side, that puts my back to her, which will only be seen as an insult. But if I lie on my left, that means I'm facing her when she gets in, and will that make her think I want us to take up where we left off in the kitchen? Does she think we'll have sex again? Do I want to if she does? How do I say no if I don't want to?

Eventually, driven to distraction by her own ridiculous roundabout of thoughts, she'd lain on her left, deciding that turning her back was just too harsh. Terri hadn't done anything wrong tonight. She'd been lovely, actually. Almost irresistible. It was what she'd done wrong in August that was still generating the aftershocks Alex couldn't deal with.

"Hey," Terri whispered as she wriggled down into the duvet and gazed at Alex. Six months ago this would have been romantic. Their bedside lights cast a soft glow around the room. The cold evening outside had them both hunkering down into the warmth of the duvet. They'd had a pleasant evening, chatting fairly comfortably over dinner about their days, then watching a movie. Terri had kept a respectful distance between them to begin with, then, as if winning her own mental battle over which path to follow, suddenly she'd snuggled closer and wrapped one arm around Alex's shoulders. Alex hadn't flinched, which had surprised her. And probably surprised Terri as well.

Now, here they were, in bed after that pleasant evening, and clearly Terri wanted to carry on what had started in the kitchen when she'd come home. Her eyes carried a look of desire so intense it almost made Alex wince. Terri reached out a hand. Tentatively, slowly. When Alex didn't move, Terri placed her fingertips on Alex's forehead, just above her eyebrow, and stroked a tantalisingly gentle pathway down around her eye, over her cheekbone, brushing past her top lip, then caressing both lips slowly, from one side of her mouth to the other. Something flared in Alex, but she wasn't entirely sure she was comfortable with it.

"You are so beautiful," Terri said, her voice still a whisper.

Alex closed her eyes. Words like that, words that should make her feel loved, and cherished, and wanted—words like that now just made her disbelieve. How could any of that be possible when Terri had so willingly slept with Liz? Who was she looking at now as she continued to stroke Alex's face? Who did she desire?

The bile rose in Alex's throat and she wrenched her head away. Terri's hand was left hanging in midair, and she dropped it slowly back to the bed, as if she couldn't quite fathom that Alex had pulled back. She frowned, and made to speak, but Alex interrupted her.

"I-I can't. Not tonight."

Terri exhaled and her eyes closed briefly before she opened them again to stare at Alex. "But I thought… Tonight was nice, wasn't it? And that kiss, earlier?" She looked completely bemused, her forehead creased in a deep frown, her gaze darting all over Alex's face, seeking answers.

"It was," Alex admitted quietly. She rolled onto her back, unable to take the intensity of Terri's gaze any longer. "It's just…" God, how could she explain this? At least, how could she do it without causing an almighty row? She'd tried to talk to Terri about this very thing in a couple of the counselling sessions, but Terri just couldn't get it. For Terri, that one night with Liz was all in the past. Done with. Forgotten. Terri had always been good at putting things in little mental boxes. Once she'd felt and dealt with something, she put it away.

Terri reached out a hand under the duvet and laid it carefully on Alex's belly. "Please, baby. Please tell me what it is. I love you, and I want us to fix this. I do," she said earnestly as Alex twitched beneath her hand. "But you have to help me. I need to know how to fix it. What you want me to do."

Alex exhaled, taking her time. All right, she would try this.

She turned her head slightly, her view of Terri oblique. Too face-on and she might not manage it.

"You've said before that you don't understand this. But it's the same problem. A lot of the time, when you kiss me, or touch me, I don't know how to trust that it's really me you're kissing and touching." She didn't understand why Terri couldn't grasp this—Terri who knew exactly what games Jade, Alex's ex, had played on her…

Terri's hand tensed on her belly, then she snatched it back.

"Really?" Terri snapped. "This again? Yeah, you're right, I *don't* understand. I've told you until I'm blue in the face that she's forgotten. That it's all about you."

"It's just not that easy for me!" Alex's voice was more vociferous than she'd intended. "*I'm* the one who was cheated on. *I'm* the one who has to forgive, and find a way to move on. To find a way to trust you again!" She slapped a hand over her mouth. All her pent-up frustration and hurt was threatening to explode and she couldn't do that. Not now. Not this week.

Terri flopped back down beside Alex on the bed.

"Sometimes," Terri said after a few moments, in a voice like acid, "I don't think you ever will."

Nor do I, Alex thought.

"Maybe," Terri said, aggressively pulling the duvet back up to her chin, "it's not such a bad thing you're off to Montreal on Saturday. Maybe a little time apart might be good for us."

Alex exhaled. "Yeah. Maybe."

Something was crawling inside her, something that was gathering force as it churned and swirled, deep down in her belly. Somehow the phrase *time apart* had loosened something, chipped away at more of her internal barriers. Because, suddenly, the idea of being on her own, of having the time and space to really sift through all her feelings without Terri there to distract her, created a yearning that shocked her in its intensity. A week would help, definitely. But it was achingly tempting to think that a much longer period apart might help even more. Scared at the implications of where her thoughts were leading her, she shimmied down under the duvet again.

"Goodnight," she whispered.

Terri rolled over away from her and turned out the light.

Chapter 3

ALEX SMILED. DANIELLE WAS PERFECTLY on time for their lunch date on Friday, as always. The restaurant, tucked behind Holborn Station, was their usual haunt for a lunchtime catch-up, with impeccably swift service and located almost exactly halfway between each of their offices.

Danielle air-kissed Alex and smiled warmly at Alex before sliding gracefully into the chair opposite. Slim and impossibly beautiful, with a rich mane of long golden hair, Danielle turned heads, both male and female, wherever she went. That she was oblivious to every stare was a testament to the strength of her relationship with Beth, her wife of ten years. Danielle looked stunning—the dress, in swirling shades of grey, clung to every inch of her, and Alex could only be grateful she'd never crushed on her best friend, because if she had, she'd be struggling to breathe right now.

"You look amazing, as always," Alex said, reaching across the table to pour some water into Danielle's empty glass.

"Thank you," Danielle murmured, as usual looking a little taken aback at the compliment. She frowned. "You look tired. How are you? How has the week been?"

Straight to the point, as usual.

Alex straightened in her chair, suddenly on guard. This was her best friend, the woman she should be able to talk to about anything, especially after all this time. But somehow, the magnitude of what she wanted to blurt out made her stomach tighten into complex knots and her natural instinct to avoid the truth rise to the fore. She'd been protecting herself like this for so long it was now second nature. But underneath it all, a part of her knew how much damage it was doing. How much unhappiness it was causing, for herself and indirectly for Terri. She huffed out an extended breath.

Danielle sipped from her water and waited.

Alex met her eyes. "I think... It's been hard. She's trying, I know she is. But..."

"What?"

Alex looked away from Danielle's intense gaze. She knew her friend could see right through her, past the words to the truth behind. Why did she insist on trying to hide? But she knew why. Saying a thing out loud made it real. And she wasn't ready for real. Real would lead to mess and complications and heartache, all things she just didn't have the energy for. Not right now.

"We're struggling with...intimacy," she volunteered. She met Danielle's gaze again. "I still have trouble believing it's me she's seeing when she...touches me."

Danielle nodded, pursing her lips slightly. "I can imagine."

The waitress appeared to take their order. As long-time customers, neither of them had opened the menu, knowing beforehand what they'd want to eat.

"Seared tuna," Alex said, smiling wanly at the waitress if only to be polite, when she felt like doing anything but smiling.

"Caesar salad," Danielle requested. She waited until the waitress had moved on before turning back to Alex. "Is that the only issue between you now?"

Alex shrugged. "Not really. But all the other stuff is being dominated by the lack of...sex." Why she was so hesitant to use the word in front of her friend was beyond her. They'd talked about sex before. Although they'd never talked about it in the context of their partners at the time, so maybe that was colouring her hesitancy. "I mean, if you can't have sex, how can you really communicate and address all the other issues?" Too late, she realised that last statement gave Danielle an opening Alex would rather she didn't take.

Danielle, of course, grabbed it with both hands. "So there are other issues? You are being deliberately vague about this, Alex." She sighed. "You know I won't judge you, yes? You know I will support you in whatever you choose to do?"

Alex nodded and had to swallow hard before she could speak. Danielle's unwavering support all these years had always been Alex's one steadying influence. She'd helped pull Alex through the awful aftermath of two years with Jade, and here she was unflinchingly putting herself forwards as a rock for Alex to anchor to once again.

"I know you will. You always do. And I really appreciate it." Alex reached across the table to briefly clasp Danielle's hand. "I'm…very confused, right now. I really don't know what I want to do." Which was essentially true. She was beginning to accept that she knew what she wanted, but she definitely didn't know what to do about it.

"Perhaps your sudden trip to Montreal is a blessing in disguise," Danielle said quietly. "Perhaps some time apart would help?"

Alex nodded slowly. "Yes, we agreed about that, a couple of days ago. We…argued. She was the one who said this break might do us good."

Danielle tilted her head. "Were you okay with that?"

Alex stared at her. "I was…relieved."

Danielle nodded and her fingers played with her water glass as she seemed to take a moment to work out what she wanted to say next.

"I wonder if a week is long enough." Her voice was quiet, but her words hit Alex square in the chest. When Alex made to respond, Danielle held up one slender hand. "I have always said I will support you, and I have always tried to steer clear of direct interference. I listen, and let you tell me what you need to tell me, but I have strived not to try and lead you one way or another. But on this one, I am sorry, I have to make an exception."

Alex had never heard her friend so serious. "Okay," she said, "tell me what you want to say. I won't hold it against you." She braced herself for whatever Danielle would come up with.

Danielle wrapped her fingers around Alex's wrist, her thumb stroking the soft skin on the inside. "I have never seen you so unhappy as you have been these past few months. Even the bitch—" Danielle refused to call Jade by her name "—did not leave you this…empty. I fear you are clinging on to a relationship that has turned too sour to be rescued. Why you are clinging on only you can probably say, but I can hazard a guess. Terri was your safety net, after that bitch. And I think you are scared to leave that, even though it is no longer actually a place of safety. The trust is gone, Alex, and when that is gone, a relationship is doomed."

Alex's cheeks were wet with tears, and she grabbed her napkin with her free hand, mortified to be crying so openly in public.

"Gosh, I am sorry." Danielle's eyes widened. She squeezed Alex's wrist before letting it go. "I completely forgot where we were. This was not appropriate. Sorry, Alex." Her heartfelt words only increased Alex's pain.

"Excuse me," Alex muttered through a tight throat. She pushed back her chair. "I'll be back soon." She turned and fled to the bathrooms before Danielle could respond.

Once locked in a cubicle, she let it out. Sobbing into the napkin she had inadvertently brought with her to the bathroom, she muffled the sound as best she could with the rich cotton fabric. Danielle, as perceptive as ever, had cut right to the heart of the matter, and her simple words had flayed Alex open. The trust between her and Terri *had* gone. Blown apart the minute Terri had told her of her tryst with Liz. Nausea turned her stomach as memories of that confession flooded her mind.

She and Terri had been so…solid in their first three or so years together. Cracks had started to appear in the year after that. Just little things. Small differences in how they wanted to spend their time and where. More time spent with others in a group, rather than on their own. More silences in the evenings they did spend together, TV providing a welcome excuse not to really talk to each other.

They'd started to have bigger arguments in the few weeks prior to that fateful night; Alex's job had been demanding following her promotion, and she'd been coming home late more often than not. Terri was resentful all of a sudden. But Alex had truly believed the bedrock of their partnership was still firm, even if it was changing. Discovering that Terri had fallen into the arms of another woman, out of the blue, had literally pulled the ground out from underneath Alex. Everything she thought they were built on had crumbled to dust in just two minutes. The two minutes it took for Terri to say haltingly, through her sobs, "I'm sorry, babe, so sorry, but…that night I didn't come home last week, when I said we were out celebrating that deal? I… Oh God, I slept with Liz. I'm so, so sorry. I don't know how it happened…"

Shock was an extraordinary thing, causing a person to do irrational things that afterwards they either couldn't remember or couldn't understand. She'd been reading a book on her Kindle before Terri had asked to speak to her, and she remembered calmly picking it up after Terri's blurted confession, switching it off and slipping it back into its case before she realised some kind of response was required. It was a delayed reaction, she knew now, brought on by hearing something so unbelievable, so awful, that her brain couldn't quite catch up with the words it had been given to work with. But when it did, when it finally sunk in that her partner of five years had just told her that she'd slept with someone else, the pain that had swept through her entire body was like nothing she'd ever felt before.

Shadows of that pain racked her now as she perched on the edge of the toilet, her arms wrapped round herself in a vain attempt to cocoon herself from more agony. It wouldn't go away, she knew that now. She would never be able to look at Terri and not feel some measure of this, on some level. And, for the first time since she'd naively promised Terri she would try to forgive her and work for them to stay together, Alex knew that Danielle's words were probably true. Their relationship was more than likely doomed, because how could it not be when this ache wouldn't leave her?

When she returned to the table, Danielle looked relieved, although concern was etched across her features.

"Alex, are you all right? I am so sorry—"

"No, it's okay. Please don't apologise," Alex said, her voice raspy from crying. "You just hit a nerve, that's all. But…nothing of what you said is untrue." Danielle's frown deepened. "It's up to me now to decide what to do about it."

She was interrupted by their meals arriving, and she glanced down at her plate with no appetite for the beautifully presented food in front of her. She looked back up at Danielle, who was also ignoring her food for the moment.

"I'm going to take the week away to try and be honest with myself about how I'm feeling. Deep down, I think I know we are doomed, as you say. But doing something about that isn't easy. Nor is walking away. Not after five years together."

"I know, Alex. But you have to do what is right for you. No matter what promises you have made each other since then, yes?"

Alex sighed. "I know."

They stared at each other for a few moments.

"Eat here or takeaway?" Danielle gestured at their plates.

Alex smiled. "Rather fancy for a doggy bag, isn't it?"

Danielle smiled.

"No, I should eat here," Alex continued. "I know if I take it back to the office, I'll probably end up throwing it away." She exhaled and looked back at the meal before her. "Come on, let's eat."

They ate in silence, for the most part, commenting only on the high quality of the food—something they'd come to expect from every visit here anyway. Danielle insisted on paying, and Alex couldn't muster the energy to argue with her. She'd get the next one.

"Now," Danielle said, "it has occurred to me that Sonia is in Montreal again at the moment. Do you remember her?"

Alex cocked her head, racking her memory banks. Sonia… "Oh, hang on, yes. Your cousin, the one who lives in New York? I met her at your fortieth, didn't I?"

Danielle beamed. "Yes! You and she got on well, I think?"

Alex nodded. "Yeah, she was a lot of fun."

"Excellent," Danielle said, slipping her credit card back in her purse and dropping some coins onto the table to tip the waitress. "Well, she splits her time between various cities these days—far too much money for her own good, really. Anyway, I am fairly certain she is in Montreal this month, for some charity event she is helping to put together for an AIDS foundation. How about I contact her and see if she would meet up with you, maybe treat you to lunch one day? It might be nice for you to meet a friendly face while you are over there."

"Danielle, I don't know. I'm not exactly the best company right now." Thinking about being sociable with someone, especially someone as bubbly as Sonia, started a tangle of nerves buzzing in her stomach.

Danielle waved a hand lackadaisically in the air in front of her. "Rubbish," she said. "Look, I will simply put you in contact with each other. Whether you meet up with her is entirely up to you, but at least you will have the details of someone you *could* meet with if you were inclined. All right?"

Knowing when she was beaten, Alex shrugged. "Okay, deal."

They said their goodbyes outside the restaurant. Danielle wrapped her long arms around Alex and held her slightly tighter than usual.

"Please take care of yourself," she whispered. "I am very worried about you."

"I know you are," Alex said, squeezing her friend tightly against her. "But like I said, I plan on making the most of this week away from Terri to really sort through my feelings. I promise I'll look after myself in the process."

They pulled apart, and Danielle placed a soft kiss on Alex's cheek.

"Call or e-mail anytime, and we will do dinner as soon as you are back."

Chapter 4

JUSTINE INDULGED IN A LONG sleep in on Saturday morning, finally rousing from her bed around eleven. Another joy she'd rediscovered for herself since the breakup with Nadia. Nadia had been a fitness fanatic and was always out of bed at the break of dawn on the weekends. Justine had shared her interest in cycling and often joined her on the long rides she took out of the city. But the visits to the fitness centre Nadia insisted on fitting in around the cycling were not to Justine's liking at all, so on the mornings when Nadia leapt out of bed early to take part in a Zumba class, or whatever fad was Nadia's flavour of that month, Justine would stay home and play house. Of course, hindsight was a wonderful thing, but she should have perhaps realised that fitness classes didn't really take that many hours in a day.

As she made herself a coffee and heated up a couple of croissants, once again the embarrassment of not realising her partner had been having an affair swept through her body, flushing her skin and increasing her heart rate. How could she have been so stupid? How could she have believed all the lies Nadia told her? When Nadia came home sweaty and in desperate need of a shower, Justine had never thought to check what else she smelt of. If she'd have stepped close enough, she knew now, she would surely have picked up the scent of the sex Nadia was having for hours on end with the instructor she'd seduced six months before Justine had found out.

And finding out had only been a fluke. She had a quiet week and on a day with no meetings scheduled, Justine had excused herself from work and swung by the fitness centre to see if Nadia wanted to grab lunch at the end of the spin class she was taking. Justine still remembered how incredibly painful it was to stand across the street from the entrance to the centre and see Nadia in a passionate clinch with that…that woman. Heather. The tall, impossibly gorgeous and superbly muscled woman who had let Nadia into her bed at the drop of a hat, despite knowing Nadia was in a long-term relationship. Despite having met Justine with Nadia at a social event only a month before they'd started their affair. Heather had known Nadia was unavailable, she knew Justine existed, and yet…

Justine sighed as she settled herself in the window seat with her breakfast. Blaming Heather was deflecting. Nadia was the one who had made all the moves. Nadia was the one who had lied to Justine, had broken her heart. Nadia was the one who had dismissed Justine, and all that they had, with one wave of her hand when Justine confronted her about it that night.

"I'm bored, Justine," she'd said in a tired and uncaring voice. "What we have doesn't do anything for me anymore. I mean, I like you, and we live together really well. But, you have to admit, the sex has really trailed off lately, hasn't it? You're always tired, and you don't seem to want to do half the things I do."

Everything about that statement had hurt. Deeply. Justine had compromised on all her desires and needs to please Nadia, and just like that, Nadia had thrown it all back at her as if none of it mattered. But Justine could now accept that Nadia had done her a favour. In being so cruel and heartless, she had made Justine's decision easy. Within a few hours, Justine had called Christina and Sylvie to ask for their help, packed up all her belongings, and loaded up their car. It had taken two trips, and it had crammed their guest room to the rafters, but they'd done it. Nadia, who had left after the confrontation, had seemed genuinely shocked to return home that evening and find Justine in the last stages of moving out.

"But…why?" she had asked, her eyes wide.

Justine had let rip. To this day she couldn't remember exactly what she'd said, only her parting words.

"You've broken my heart, Nadia. I loved you. So much." Her voice had cracked. "And you've just walked all over that like it meant nothing. Nothing! So yes, I'm moving out. Of course I am. I never want to see you again."

She had walked past a stunned Nadia to the front door and slammed it behind her without looking back.

It had taken a few weeks, but eventually she'd found this apartment, and she was delighted with it. Only one bedroom, but it had a great little balcony that was a gorgeous sun trap in summer. A polished wood floor and big windows framed with rich, dark wood gave it some character, and she'd decorated it with a mismatched assortment of furniture and soft furnishings to give it a distinctly bohemian vibe. A far cry from the sterile, minimalist environment she'd lived in with Nadia.

She gazed out at the quiet street below. The window seat was her favourite place in the whole apartment. The window ledge was wide, and she'd scattered cushions on it to be able to sit and watch the world go by outside. She leaned back against one side of the alcove and propped her feet against the other.

She wouldn't say she was totally happy these days. Not yet. But the progress she'd made in the last eighteen months had been, for the most part, good. The one-night stands had been—usually—a nice distraction from the ache in her wounded heart. Her job was going well, and she had a great place to live and two wonderful friends to spend time with. She was lonely, she could admit that much. But equally, she could admit she was still damaged goods and definitely not ready for something more meaningful. She had time; she was only thirty-eight. Plenty of time to get her heart ready for someone new to steal it away.

Her phone rang on the table across the room. She debated not answering to give herself an entire weekend of freedom, but then gave in and stumbled across the room before the call went to voicemail.

"*Bonjour, Justine. Comment ça va?*" Sylvie's silken voice sounded in her ear.

"Hey, Sylvie. I'm good, how are you?"

"*Bon, merci.* I'm calling because Christina is abandoning me for the week." Justine laughed as she heard a muffled cry in the background. Sylvie giggled. "Okay, perhaps not abandoning. But she has to go away, and I wondered if you and I could perhaps meet at Lèvres on Monday night? It's a long time since I have been. I know it is short notice."

Justine smiled. "Hey, no problem. I'd love to go. I think it's been long enough since the last time I made a fool of myself there that people won't remember."

31

Sylvie laughed. "You did not make a fool of yourself. You just had a good time."

"Um, Sylvie, I drank so much I fell down the stairs and had to be carried out to the car by you and Christina. If that's not making a fool of yourself, I don't know what is." But Justine was laughing too. She'd been embarrassed the next morning, but having stayed away from Lèvres for a few weeks now, she did feel she could walk back in with her head held high. "But anyway, yes, count me in. I would love to go."

They made arrangements for a time to meet, then hung up. Justine set her phone back down on the table, smiling to herself. A night out at the start of the week. It could get messy, but she'd just make sure she was on her best behaviour to avoid that. Although, of course, if there was someone who caught her eye...

She rolled her eyes at herself. Apparently, some habits were going to be hard to break.

Alex zipped up the case and clicked the buckles together on the straps that pulled the lid tight against the base. Packing hadn't taken that long. Business trips were always fairly easy to pack for—a couple of suits with different shirts to mix and match through the week, and two rather more casual outfits for eating by herself in the hotel in the evening. Or meeting up with Sonia.

She was still undecided about that, but Sonia had e-mailed Friday night to say she'd be delighted to spend time with Alex and had suggested brunch on Sunday. That didn't sound so bad. She remembered Sonia being a bit of a party animal, so Alex supposed she should be grateful Sonia hadn't suggested going clubbing until the wee hours of the morning.

Although, the way she was feeling lately, maybe a night out to let off steam would be a good thing. She'd been so focused on her job and her floundering relationship, she was wound as tight as a drum. She'd pushed so hard to get that promotion, the culmination of everything she'd worked for over the years, but now she'd reached that pinnacle, she was a little deflated. If working that hard had contributed to weakening the foundations of her relationship with Terri, had it really been worth it?

Lately she'd been resentful of her job, even as she sank herself further into it to avoid going home.

She exhaled. A week away. A week to think about what to do next and to try to relax. Her schedule wasn't demanding, not compared to what it had been on previous visits. So maybe she had some room in it to attempt some fun. She shook her head. She wasn't sure she could remember what fun was.

Alex glanced around the room, making sure she'd got everything. Her gaze fell on Terri's discarded jeans on the chair in the corner of the room, and her body flushed with mixed reactions—memories of how hot Terri had looked in them the night before, coupled with sadness at how things had been left between them this morning.

"I don't think I'll hang around until you go," Terri had muttered over their morning coffee. "I've got some things I could do with catching up on at the office."

Alex was a little disgruntled, then admonished herself for being unfair. How could she expect Terri to make any effort with her this morning when things had been so tense between them all week? They'd barely spoken to each other after dinner the night before and gone to bed at different times.

Terri left shortly after finishing her coffee, declining Alex's half-hearted offer of breakfast. She gave Alex a perfunctory kiss goodbye before picking up her handbag and walking swiftly down the hallway. The door had slammed shut behind her.

Alex sat on the edge of the bed and pulled on her sneakers, then wrapped a soft scarf around her neck over her long-sleeved shirt. Standing, she checked herself in the mirror one last time. She sighed. Her green eyes looked dull and lifeless. She flicked a few stray strands of her long fringe away from her forehead. Even her hair looked a shade duller than its usual glowing auburn. She leaned closer. Was that what she thought it was? Yep, great—more wrinkles around the corners of her eyes.

She turned slightly to her left and back again; her jeans looked a little loose on her hips. She wouldn't be surprised if she'd lost more weight. It had been gradually coming off these past few months. Stress and the resulting loss of appetite had done her a favour in helping her drop the extra five pounds or so she could never quite shift. But she didn't need to lose any more; already her cheeks were showing a hint of hollowing. She noted her pale skin, her Irish ancestry doing her proud, and sighed again. What she wouldn't give for a couple of weeks in the sun somewhere.

She squared her shoulders. The car service would be here any minute and standing around here feeling sorry for herself wasn't going to achieve anything.

She hauled her case and laptop bag out to the hallway and pulled on her soft ankle boots. Just as she was checking that her passport was in her handbag, the door buzzer rang. She let the driver in and smiled politely when he appeared moments later on the doorstep, reaching for her case before she'd even had a chance to say good morning.

As she swung the door to her home closed behind her, a wave of something indefinable swept over her. She shuddered with it, swamped in sadness, regret, and yes, relief. A week away. God, she hoped to hell she could get her head sorted in that time. Because this really had gone on long enough now.

Heathrow was busy but manageable. And, of course, she was thankful to be flying business class, which meant she was able to use the lounge before boarding. As she eased herself into one of the plush armchairs, a glass of champagne—why not?—in her hand, she gazed out the window at the activity on the tarmac below.

She felt…numb.

Surreal.

As if she were standing on a precipice, precariously balanced, looking down on a blurred landscape where nothing was as defined as it should be, and no clear way through was obvious. The feeling was terrifying, and her heart rate increased at the decisions that faced her.

Step off the ledge, into God knew what, in the hope that she would find some way to be happy again?

Or stay on the ledge, continuing to work with Terri to see what, if anything could be retrieved from their current situation, and hope that eventually she'd be pulled back from the edge somehow?

She was forty-six years old, and the idea of starting out again, on her own, was frightening. And yet, as she'd acknowledged to herself only yesterday, what she and Terri had was pretty much beyond repair, wasn't it? So didn't that really only leave her one choice?

Chapter 5

Yawning, Alex slipped out of the bed and walked across the room to the bathing area of her ridiculously large room at the W Hotel. She flipped the shower on and a few moments later she was sighing in contentment as the hot water streamed over her body.

Once dry, moisturised, and dressed, she reached for her phone. She was feeling refreshed enough that brunch with Sonia sounded appealing.

Hi Sonia, brunch in the Village sounds great. I am jet-lagged and in need of food! See you there at ten

Sonia's response was quick and to the point: *Excellent!*

Glancing at her watch, Alex reluctantly pulled her laptop out of its bag. She'd done a lot of work on the plane but had two or three more e-mails she'd rather get done today. Her eyes still felt tired from the journey, but she forced them to look at her screen, and within minutes she was immersed in her work.

At nine forty-five she took the lift down to reception and strolled towards the front doors.

The doorman greeted her. "*Bonjour, Madame.*"

"*Bonjour.* Could you get me a cab, please?"

"But of course. One moment, please." He shot out of the front door, and she watched, smiling, as he marched out onto the pavement, looking to his left down the one-way street that wrapped around Square Victoria in front of the hotel. The staff here always impressed her with their eagerness to serve. After a couple of minutes, he waved his hand vigorously at something, and moments later, a yellow cab pulled up to the kerb. She left the warmth of the lobby, pulling her jacket tight around her as she stepped outside into the frigid air. Hopping into the back of the cab, she smiled her thanks at the doorman, then gave the driver her destination. If he was surprised to be taking someone from one of Montreal's classiest hotels deep into the heart of the Gay Village, he said nothing. Even Alex had been surprised at Sonia's choice of meeting place, but Sonia had insisted it was the perfect place for them to catch up.

Twenty minutes later Alex walked into a lovely, lazy Sunday morning buzz. The place Sonia had selected was lovely, with couples and groups all meeting to share what looked like a long meal out of the cold. Sonia arrived only moments after Alex, and they swapped kisses on each cheek in greeting.

Alex was taken aback at Sonia's appearance but hoped she hid it well. The last time they'd met, six years ago at Danielle's fortieth birthday party, Sonia had been slightly overweight and going through a deeply femme phase with long hair, lashings of makeup, and tight-fitting dresses. She'd looked fabulous then, but the woman in front of Alex now was much slimmer and stunningly androgynous. Her blonde hair had been cropped short, but she wore beautifully applied eye makeup that made her blue eyes leap out. She must have lost at least twenty pounds, and her newly svelte body shape looked fantastic in pleated trousers and a silk shirt with a loosely tied silk tie hanging halfway down its front. An enticing amount of cleavage was on display in that shirt opening, and Alex had to wrench her gaze away before Sonia caught her ogling. Yes, the new look certainly suited Sonia, and Alex was surprised at her own response to it. Looking at other women that way wasn't something she made a habit of. It was unsettling.

"Alex, it is so lovely to see you again!" Sonia was as exuberant as Alex remembered her, and her French accent just as delicious. Sonia was French Canadian, having been raised in Montreal. Danielle had told Alex she now split her time between her home city and her two favourite cities in the world, Paris and New York.

"Thank you so much for arranging this. I'm sorry if I was a little slow in responding, but it's been a busy week."

Sonia waved a hand and smiled. "Not at all. I understand. So how long are you here for?"

They chatted amiably while they were served fresh filter coffee in large mugs, and huge platters of omelettes, fried potatoes, grilled mushrooms and tomatoes, and heaps of sourdough toast. Sonia shared details of the event she was in Montreal to organise, and Alex told her a little of what had brought her over to Canada this time.

"So you will actually do the training yourself? I would have thought you would have some minion take care of that." Sonia flashed a grin as she spoke.

Alex laughed. "In the UK, yes, I would normally have, as you say, a minion to do that. But while I am here to meet with other execs, it makes sense to double up rather than pay for someone else to make the trip just to do three training sessions. The actual training will only take about six hours of my week. The rest, unfortunately, is all meetings."

"You don't like meetings?"

Alex grimaced. "I hate them! I'd actually much rather be doing something than talking about it, you know? That's why I don't mind getting my hands dirty, so to speak, when it's my turn to deliver training. It's a great break from the tedium of sitting around in meeting rooms all day."

Sonia nodded. "I can see that. I suppose my days are so varied, I never have to worry about that. Especially with an event like this—one day I will be researching venues, caterers, entertainment; the next I will be at a photo shoot and meeting with the marketing team. I love it."

"It sounds it. Good for you."

"So will you be expected to meet these other executives for dinner every night?"

Alex couldn't quite read the gleam in Sonia's eyes. She shook her head. "No, actually. Not this time anyway. I think because my trip was organised so last-minute. The only commitment I have is a lunch on Wednesday. Other than that, I have my evenings to myself, which is good."

Sonia smiled, wickedly, and waggled her eyebrows. "Ah, so that means I can steal you away for an evening, yes?"

Alex's first reaction was to refuse. She would be tired. She had work commitments to meet. Although, as she'd just told Sonia, they weren't that demanding this week. And she had thought the idea of letting off some steam was tempting...

"I guess it would depend on what you had in mind."

Sonia's smile transformed into a lascivious grin, and Alex blushed at the tease. She really shouldn't be responding this way to another woman, but her body wasn't listening.

Sonia laughed and reached across the table to pat Alex's hand.

"Don't worry, Alex. I promise I am only playing. You are a married woman, and so am I." She smiled and sat back in her chair. "I mean only to show you a fun evening out in this lovely city of mine. There is a women-only bar that has a great atmosphere on a Monday night, if you can believe. I have no idea why it is so successful, given that everyone has to work the next day, but it is." She shrugged. "So I know you will be tired, and we don't have to make it a long night, but would you like to meet me there for some drinks, maybe some dancing?"

Alex smiled, totally charmed by this lovely woman. And pleased that, judging from how Sonia had spoken about Alex's relationship, Danielle had apparently not told her cousin anything about Alex's recent problems with Terri. She wouldn't feel comfortable talking about it with someone she barely knew.

"I can't make any promises, because it really does depend on my energy tomorrow, but a drink at least sounds good. The dancing, maybe not. It's been a long time since I went dancing." She smiled as old memories attempted to resurface. She had used to love dancing. "But tell me where and when, and I will meet you there, okay?"

"*Parfait*," Sonia said, beaming.

―――――――⇒∘⊂⇔∘⊂―――――――

Alex flopped onto the bed and kicked off her boots. Although she'd showered that morning, the huge bath looked rather inviting right now. She'd walked back from her brunch with Sonia—the weather had been nose-nippingly cold, but she'd needed the exercise. They'd had a good time catching up, but she'd eaten way too much, and the long walk back had been perfect to work that off.

A quick glance at her watch as she flopped back on the bed told her it was two o'clock, which meant seven in the evening back home. She ought to call Terri. She'd not bothered when she'd arrived the day before—she'd simply fired off a text message saying she'd arrived, knowing it was late and Terri would more than likely be in bed already. Although, she now realised,

Terri hadn't even responded to that message on Sunday morning, when she was surely awake. Guilt snagged at Alex. Had Terri expected her to call and now was upset with her, hence not responding to her text?

She sighed. She didn't even know what they would talk about if she did call, but she ought to, shouldn't she? It would be ridiculous to think she wouldn't talk to her partner the entire week. If she got it over with now, she'd have more of an excuse as the week rolled on, when the five-hour time difference between their waking and working hours would genuinely make talking extremely difficult.

She stood and walked to her handbag, then paused as she replayed her last thoughts. *Got it over with*? What kind of feeling was that to have about talking to your partner of five years?

She took a few deep breaths before dialling Terri's number.

"Hi." Terri's voice was muffled, and Alex thought she could hear music in the background.

"Hi. How are you? Did you get my text last night?"

"Yeah. It was pretty late and I knew you'd be jet-lagged, so I didn't call." Terri sounded distant, as if her attention were elsewhere.

"You okay? Have I caught you at a bad time?"

"No. Sorry." There was the sound of a door opening and closing. "I'm just out for a drink with some friends. Just finding a quieter place to talk."

"Oh." *What friends?* "How's your Sunday been?"

Terri chuckled. "Lazy. I only got off the sofa about half an hour ago."

"Sounds good." Alex knew her answers were sounding flat and stood to pace the room to try to inject some energy into the call.

"You sound tired. Jet lag bad?"

"Yeah, must be. Brunch with Sonia was good, but I am tired now. Although I need to catch up on some work, so I need to wake up a bit."

Terri tutted. "You're allowed Sunday off, aren't you?"

Alex closed her eyes for a moment, willing away the spike of irritation at Terri's snippy tone. "It's my choice." She breathed in and struggled to soften her tone. "Afterwards I'll run myself a hot bath and soak myself to prune status with a book and a glass of wine."

"That sounds good." Terri's tone had softened a tad. "I'm glad you're going to relax too. You worry me, all this working out of hours you do."

"Like your job is much better for that? Weren't you the one who went into the office yesterday? A Saturday?" Alex snapped the retort out before she could think to tamp it down.

Terri hesitated just slightly before responding. "Oh, yeah." She cleared her throat. "Okay, fair point."

Alex took a deep breath. "I didn't mean to snap."

"And I didn't mean to sound like I was having a go." Terri exhaled sharply. "I think we need to talk when you get back. Talk properly, I mean."

Alex's pulse quickened further. She wasn't sure she was ready for this. But then, why not? Surely it would be easier if both of them were finally prepared to face the situation. Instead of forcing it into being something it wasn't. Or hiding from what it really was.

"Yes, I think we do." Simple words, yet they felt monumental in that moment.

Terri let out a long, slow breath. "I think this week it would be best if we have no contact. Let's both do some thinking while we're apart. I'll text you if anything important comes up, but otherwise, I'll see you at home Saturday morning, yes?"

"Yes," Alex said quietly. Her throat was tightening. "Terri?"

"Yes?"

She wanted to thank her, for being the brave one to finally put it out there. But in the moment she went to blurt out the words, they sounded crass. Insensitive. And also a little bit hypocritical, given that she herself had not found that bravery. But then, she never did.

"I-I'll see you on Saturday. Have a good week." She cringed at how bland her alternative words were, but she just couldn't bring herself to give more.

"You too." The hum of the slight background noise on the line disappeared as Terri ended the call.

Alex immersed herself in an hour or two of work, to force her brain to stop thinking about Terri and their disintegrating relationship. The bath she ran afterwards was hot and full of bubbles. She poured herself a large glass of red wine and took a big mouthful of it as she sank into the water. The wet heat felt fantastic on her skin, but her mind was already roiling again from their phone conversation, and the sensuality of the bubbles tickling her breasts and arms did nothing to alleviate that.

She was so torn. A part of her didn't want to walk away from Terri, from all they had shared. But the reasons she didn't want to leave were blurry and getting more so as each day passed. Fear of being on her own again. The loss of what had once been so special between them. Her sense that no matter what Terri said or did, now and in the future, Alex would never fully trust her again.

She closed her eyes and leaned back against the high end of the tub. Being with Terri had been so easy to begin with. Yes, they hadn't exactly had constant fireworks, even from the beginning, but their relationship had been solid, and reliable, and Terri's care for her had soothed her damaged soul. She supposed that was part of how they'd drifted the way they had before Terri slept with Liz. They'd become comfortable. Boring, maybe.

Danielle's words came back to her, about Terri being a safety net that caught her after the pain of extricating herself from Jade. That was true, she could acknowledge that.

But that didn't mean being with Terri had been wrong.

It had never felt wrong, even if it had never felt overwhelmingly right.

Monday passed slowly, meeting following meeting. Finally, at around three, she had a break and escaped to the cubicle they'd set aside for her in a quiet corner on the ninth floor. RCS Incorporated occupied five floors in one of the larger office buildings that edged Square Victoria, directly opposite her hotel. The two-minute commute was a luxury she revelled in whenever she was here. The window behind her cubicle looked out over the busy square, and she took a moment to watch the world go by as she sipped at the remarkably good coffee the machine in the reception area churned out.

Her phone bleeped beside her and she swept it up to see a text message from Sonia.

I know you are probably tired, but come out to play anyway?! Please?

Alex smiled. Yes, she was tired, but her day was not yet over, with more potentially tedious meetings in her calendar, and suddenly the idea of even just one drink out and about, with someone who made her laugh, was immensely appealing.

You've twisted my arm. Tell me where and when

Sonia texted her an address followed by a series of smiley faces that left Alex chuckling. Slipping her phone back into her bag, she huffed out a breath as she sat.

Time to prepare for more meetings.

Ugh.

Chapter 6

ALEX SIGHED AS SHE LOOKED at herself in the full-length mirror. She wasn't sure the top with its abstract glitter motif was really how she was feeling the evening, but it was the dressiest thing she'd packed, so she didn't really have an alternative. Still, it worked with the black jeans and boots, and the diamond stud earrings added another little element of sparkle to the ensemble. She ran her hands through her hair, pushing it first behind her ears, then not, then back again. She laughed. Really, what the hell did it matter what her hair looked like? Pulling it back from behind her ears one last time, she touched the corners of her eyes to make sure her eyeliner hadn't smudged and stepped back to take in the full look one last time.

Passable.

The doorman summoned a cab for her again, and she gave the driver the address from Sonia's message. When he pulled the car up in the Gay Village, she hopped out into the bitterly cold air and walked to the main door of the bar-slash-club Sonia had suggested for their meeting.

Alex pushed through the doors and a pleasant warmth greeted her. The place wasn't huge, but it had an inviting feel. The front area was taken up with loosely arranged sofas and armchairs, which then led into a proper bar area with high stools along the full length of the metal-topped bar itself. Beyond that was a cluster of small tables with bistro-style seating. She glanced around; no sign of Sonia. She smiled to herself—Sonia was fashionably late again.

She walked up to the bar. The place had a total of perhaps thirty women in it. Finding a sizeable gap towards the far end of the bar, Alex inserted herself into the space and quickly caught the eye of the woman serving. Alex ordered a beer and perched on one of the stools while she waited for Sonia.

Warm hands on her waist a couple of minutes later announced Sonia's arrival and Alex turned to smile at her.

"Sorry I am late." Sonia looked contrite as she leaned in for the obligatory two-cheek kiss.

"No worries." Alex held up her glass. "I'm good. I have beer."

Sonia laughed and signalled the bartender over, then ordered a glass of wine for herself. "Shall we get one of the small tables?" She nodded towards the back of the room.

When they'd settled at a table, they clinked glasses.

"So how was your first day?" Sonia asked after she'd taken a couple of sips of her wine.

Alex shrugged. "Tedious. Meetings all day. With some people who were pretty unhappy about how some things have gone."

Sonia lifted her eyebrows.

"Do you remember I told you it was a takeover?" Sonia nodded. "Well, it wasn't hostile, but not exactly welcomed with open arms."

"Ah. People do not like change."

"That is definitely true. From the sound of it, I may have my work cut out for me in the training sessions. The new people are reluctant to learn, apparently. Which, really, is why I'm here, I suppose. If they were okay with it, I wouldn't be needed."

"Well, I am glad you're here, even if they aren't," Sonia said with a wink.

Alex laughed. She knew Sonia wasn't flirting, not for real, but her playfulness was heartwarming. And flattering.

"Sonia!" They both turned at the voice that came from behind them.

"Sylvie!" Sonia leapt out of her chair and practically ran around Alex to greet the petite woman standing behind her. Alex watched as they hugged fiercely, exchanging multiple kisses and laughing.

Out of the corner of her eye, she saw another movement and swivelled slightly in her chair. Standing behind the two hugging women, and presumably Sylvie's company for the evening, was a tall blonde, a laconic smile on her—wow—beautiful face. Alex stared. For the second time in two days, she was physically responding to another woman, something that hadn't happened in years and definitely nothing that had happened while in the relationship with Terri.

She should look away, try to get this unnerving response under control, but she was helpless. The woman in front of her was gorgeous. Her hair fell just past her shoulders in what looked like totally natural twisty curls. Her eyes were a pale blue. She looked to be a couple of inches taller than Alex but had the same slim build. Dressed in low-slung jeans, boots, and a dark green button-down shirt, she was casually sexy, and even more so when she shoved her hands in her pockets and settled her weight on one hip. Alex let her gaze travel back up the body before her, trying extra hard not to stare at the flat stomach and small breasts, and startled as the stranger caught her staring.

Alex looked away, her face ablaze.

"Alex." Sonia grabbed her arm, urging her to stand. Alex was extraordinarily grateful for the interruption of her mortifying moment. "This is Sylvie, a dear friend I haven't seen in about, what, six months?"

"Something like that, *oui*," Sylvie replied, smiling widely. "It's a pleasure to meet you, Alex." She held out her hand and shook Alex's before air-kissing Alex on both cheeks. She was shorter than Alex by a few inches and had to lean up to effect the greeting.

As she let Alex go, she gestured to the stunning woman beside her. "Sonia, Alex, this is my friend, Justine."

Alex swallowed hard before turning to face Justine, who stepped forwards and smiled confidently at her and Sonia as she shook their hands.

"*Enchanté*," she whispered as she kissed Alex's cheeks. Her lips were incredibly soft against Alex's skin. Her hand gripped Alex's a little tighter and lingered a little longer than was normal. Alex swallowed, overwhelmed with a surge of desire that swept up out of nowhere and scorched her body. As soon as Justine let go of her hand, Alex stepped back, only just avoiding clutching at her chest to check her thumping heart. This was…ridiculous.

She watched as Justine greeted Sonia, and noted with a discomforting sense of triumph that Justine's attention to Sonia was significantly muted in comparison to that which she had bestowed on Alex.

"Can they join us?" Sonia asked.

"Of course," Alex replied, inwardly groaning. Her pulse was racing and a warm flush still held court in the hand Justine had held on to for those delicious few moments. She dropped back onto her stool, willing her breathing to settle and her hand not to shake as she reached for her beer. She needed to get on top of this, whatever *this* was, and fast. What the hell was happening to her this week? First Sonia, now Justine?

The two new arrivals pulled up chairs from a table nearby, and Sylvie and Sonia immediately launched into a conversation about the last time they'd seen each other. Alex sipped her beer and listened, smiling politely at the two friends' amusing banter. But she was aware of Justine the entire time. She didn't dare look at her, fearing her flushed cheeks would give away her completely unexpected reaction to the beautiful woman sat beside her. This visceral level of response to another's presence had never happened to her before. It disturbed her greatly, and she wished she could just shake it off.

The sudden and almost desperate need for some breathing space propelled her out of her chair.

"Bathroom," she muttered at Sonia's questioning look, then followed the way Sonia pointed out for her to the washrooms at the back of the bar.

Alex locked herself in a cubicle and perched on the edge of the toilet, breathing deeply. She took her time, rationalising away her response to Justine. She was tired, still jet-lagged, in fact. Emotional after the turmoil of the last few weeks. Justine was beautiful—anyone would have been flustered to be greeted so warmly by someone so visually appealing. Alex was lonely, and having someone pay attention to her like that, even for just a moment, had been flattering. She'd been feeling unattractive, undesirable even, after Terri took her attentions elsewhere, so a kiss and a touch from a beautiful stranger was bound to stir her libido a little.

Wasn't it?

———⌬———

Justine sipped her beer, laughing at the interaction between Sylvie and Sonia, but her mind was elsewhere.

Alex.

God.

She'd promised Christina and Sylvie she'd take a break from sleeping around, but if there was any way she could take Alex home that night, she would do it. She was...gorgeous. Sexy for days, with her auburn hair, stunning green eyes, and slim yet curvy body. Curves Justine's hands itched to travel a path over. And that zap of…something between them when they had shaken hands. *Wow.*

She took another sip of her beer, her eyes flicking towards the back of the bar to see if Alex had returned yet. When she saw Alex pushing through the washroom door, Justine sat up a little straighter in her chair, watching Alex advance towards their table. She felt Sylvie's hand on her thigh and turned to look at her friend.

"Justine…" Sylvie's face was creased by a frown. "You said—"

Justine exhaled swiftly. "I know, I know. But look at her," she whispered, turning her gaze back to Alex, who was now only a few feet away.

Sylvie tugged on her arm, bringing Justine back round to face her.

"Justine, just take a moment," she said, a wry smile on her lips. Sylvie flicked a glance at Alex as she sat back down alongside Sonia and they began chatting. "Remember what you said? Remember how you admitted your life was a little empty these days?"

Reluctantly, Justine nodded.

"So now is your chance to try something new. Why not break out of your pattern and actually get to know this woman? Talk to her. Learn something about her. And go home alone tonight."

Justine sat back, her breathing deep. She knew, deep down, Sylvie was right. Why had her first reaction been to see how quickly she could get Alex back to her place and into her bed? Surely she needed to change things, and soon—this bed-hopping lifestyle really wasn't what she wanted anymore. So, yes, why not start changing things, here and now? She looked at Alex, who was laughing at something Sonia said, her head thrown back, her hair bouncing on her shoulders. It would be difficult; Alex was so attractive. But it was long past time Justine stepped away from her past and made at least some effort towards changing her future.

She turned her gaze back to Sylvie and smiled. *"Merci, mon amie,"* she whispered and pulled Sylvie into a quick hug.

"You mean you'll actually do it? Listen to my advice?" Sylvie looked shocked but there was a twinkle in her eyes.

Justine released her from the hug and tapped her arm playfully. "Oh, very funny," she said. "Please try not to gloat *too* much to Christina."

Sylvie sniggered. "Oh, *chérie,* I am not going to promise that!"

Justine sighed, but she was smiling.

"So Justine," Sonia said, leaning across the table, "how do you know Sylvie?"

"Sylvie stole my best friend," Justine replied, dropping her face into a sad-puppy expression. Sylvie snorted and the other women laughed. Justine smiled at Sylvie. "Sylvie is the woman who makes my best friend, Christina, very happy. Christina and I go way back, to college."

"Ah, I see! Yes, Christina I have met a few times. She is lovely."

"She is," Sylvie said, sighing blissfully, and the others laughed again. "And you, Alex, how do you know Sonia?"

Alex shifted in her seat before answering, and Justine tried not to stare at her as she spoke. Tried not to imagine again what it would feel like to kiss the smooth skin of her cheeks, or her lips, or… *Stop! Just talking, remember? Break the habits. Break the habits.* Justine repeated the mantra to herself as she listened to Alex's response.

"My best friend, Danielle, is Sonia's cousin," Alex said. "I met Sonia at Danielle's fortieth birthday celebration a few years back. When Danielle knew I was coming to Montreal at the same time Sonia was going to be here, she put us in touch with each other." Justine loved Alex's accent, having rarely heard a British accent other than on TV.

"Lovely," Sylvie said. "And what brings you to Montreal?"

"Work. My company has a large office here."

"So how long are you here?" Sylvie asked.

Justine tried to ignore the sinking feeling in her stomach; Alex was only visiting. Should she even bother to get to know her? Maybe she should just try to get her into bed instead and—

Her thought process was derailed by a quick, sharp pinch on her arm. She looked round to discover Sylvie frowning at her and knew that Sylvie knew *exactly* where her thoughts had taken her. It was irritating—and a little scary.

"All week," Alex replied. "I arrived Saturday, and I fly back on the overnight on Friday."

"And what do you do?"

"Oh no, please let us not talk about work!" Sonia broke in. "Alex is only here to attend some very dull meetings."

Alex laughed. "Yeah, that's about right." Justine smiled at the way Alex's face transformed when she laughed. Her eyes sparkled and a little dimple appeared just to the left of her mouth.

"So, what *do* you want to talk about?" Sylvie grinned at Sonia. "If work is not allowed, what is?"

"Art. Food. Life. Sex!" Sonia enthused. "There are so many more interesting subjects than work."

Justine caught the cute way Alex blushed at the mention of sex. Shy? She didn't think so. Something about the way Alex carried herself, a quiet confidence, didn't speak of shyness. What then? Simply a case of the infamous British reserve?

"Shall I get us another drink?" Alex asked suddenly, standing. "Same again?" She gestured around the table at their nearly empty glasses. All three women nodded enthusiastically.

"Would you like some help?" Justine started to rise from her chair.

Alex shook her head, blushing faintly. "Oh, no. I-I'm okay. Really."

Justine smiled and it took all her strength to resist pushing, which was what she would have done if she'd been intent on pursuing Alex as a one-night stand. But with Sylvie's hawk-like eyes staring at her—she could feel them like lasers on her back—she pulled herself back and shrugged lightly.

"Okay, just wave if you change your mind."

Alex smiled and walked quickly towards the bar, and Sonia excused herself to the washroom.

"Well done," Sylvie murmured close to Justine's ear.

Justine turned to face her, her grin rueful. "Have you any idea how hard that was?"

Sylvie laughed lightly. "Oh, yes, Justine, I do. But I am very proud of you."

"Thanks, *Mom*," Justine said, smiling to take the sting out of her sarcastic tone.

Sylvie's expression transformed to serious in an instant. "I know she is only here for a week, but I stand by what I said. You could use this as, um, practice—" Justine snorted "—in how to do this. How to take the time to talk to someone." Sylvie shrugged. "And hey, you may end up with a new friend out of it."

"Damn it, you're right again," Justine said, throwing her arms up in mock disgust. "You can stop now, you know. Enough's enough."

Sylvie guffawed and they chuckled together until Alex returned with a tray of drinks.

"Wow," Justine said, pointing to the tray, "table service. Very impressive."

Alex laughed as she placed the drinks down on the table.

"I think the bartender took pity on the poor, weak Englishwoman. She's got considerably more muscles than I have and must have feared I'd never make it with four glasses." She blushed again, and Justine wished she didn't find it so endearing. Alex sat just as Sonia returned to the table.

Sonia launched immediately into a conversation with Sylvie in French, and Justine took a big breath before leaning slightly forwards onto her elbows to talk to Alex.

"So have you been to Montreal before?"

Alex nodded. "A couple of times, yes. Are you from here?" Her voice wobbled slightly.

"Yes, born and raised." She smiled as Alex's eyebrows pulled together in a cute frown.

"You don't speak French?"

Justine smiled. "I do, but as my second language. I have an English-speaking father and a French-speaking mother. English was the first language at home, but French at school."

"I was hopeless at languages at school. I'm envious."

"If you learn from early enough, it's easy because you don't know any different."

"True. When I was at school, you didn't start until you were ten."

"Oh, that's too late, surely?"

"Well, it certainly was for me." Their gazes locked and Alex smiled broadly. The sight warmed Justine in a way that went beyond physical desire. Something about Alex tugged at her in ways she hadn't felt for a long, long time. She mentally pulled herself up. *Remember, just talking.*

Sonia and Sylvie had switched to English and were in a lively discussion about a fashion show they both hoped to catch the following week.

"Justine, could you come too?" Sylvie asked.

Justine snorted. "Fashion is not my favourite subject, as you well know. Count me out," she said with a grin.

Sylvie shook her head in a display of exaggerated disappointment.

Alex was smiling, her dimple on full display.

"I'm not a huge fan of fashion either," she said conspiratorially. "I like my clothes simple and functional. Quite boring, actually."

"Oh, me too. She loves all that catwalk stuff," Justine replied, pointing at Sylvie and rolling her eyes.

"So if fashion isn't your thing, what is?" Alex's questioning had a hint of shyness, and it was utterly endearing.

"I like to read. History and biographies, mostly. I also like to cook."

"I like cooking too. And I'm a bit of a movie fan. Not that I often find time to go to the cinema these days. It's mostly DVDs or Netflix."

Justine noted that Alex seemed to be relaxing a little now that they were talking. Justine was enjoying it too—it actually felt good just to talk and to not keep working out how to turn on the charm.

"I don't watch much TV. I do like to dance, though. They have two dance floors here, you know. The music will start up soon, actually," she said, glancing at her watch.

"Hm, I haven't danced in years," Alex said with that wonderful smile again. "I'm not sure I'd remember how to."

"I'd be happy to remind you." Justine just caught herself from adding a hint of flirty teasing to her words—that was the sort of comment she would have used to full advantage before. But not tonight.

She breathed out as she sat back and listened to Sonia and Sylvie talking about a movie they'd both seen recently. Alex joined in the discussion, but just before she did, she and Justine shared a moment, a brief smile that held…something. Justine wasn't sure what, but it felt very different from anything she'd had since Nadia.

It felt good. Really good. But also a little…scary.

Chapter 7

CHATTING WITH JUSTINE WAS MAKING Alex feel good in ways she wasn't entirely comfortable with. She admonished herself for responding to it so…hungrily. Justine wasn't giving her any signals that this was anything but a nice, friendly chat between new acquaintances, so she needed to calm down. It was…flattering, in a way. Justine seemed genuinely interested in her as a person, as someone of interest. But Alex couldn't quite relax in her presence and she wasn't sure why.

Huh, you know why.

Yes, she did. Justine was truly gorgeous, and her physical beauty had, for a moment, set off a physical response in Alex that was shocking. Not even Jade, that seductress extraordinaire, had managed to elicit such an intense…craving. Alex had quashed it as soon as she recognised it for what it was, but even so, Justine's closeness was more than a little intoxicating. Hints of a musky perfume tantalised Alex's olfactory system and caused disconcerting pulses of arousal to fizz across her body.

It was ridiculous—Justine wasn't even flirting with her. Alex was the one imbuing the occasion with a deeper meaning. But holding someone's attention that way was confidence boosting. It made her feel like she had something to offer, something that meant she wasn't entirely unattractive, at least not intellectually. And yes, she had caught Justine looking at her a couple of times, but that didn't mean anything. Or did it? Was Justine interested in her that way and Alex was too out of the game to realise it?

She blanched. Shit, maybe she was. Maybe she should just tell Justine she had a partner.

But then, what if Justine wasn't thinking of Alex that way? How embarrassing would it be to make a big deal out of having a partner at home when Justine simply wanted to be friends? She blushed at the thought.

And actually, the last thing she wanted to do with these new acquaintances was talk about Terri. How could she bring the whole evening down talking about the quagmire she'd left behind in London? No one wanted to hear that, and definitely not two women she'd only met an hour ago.

She downed the last dregs of her second beer and noted the warm buzz the alcohol was giving her. Time to slow down. She definitely didn't need to be getting drunk—she had a long day ahead of her tomorrow. And she knew from past experience that too much alcohol loosened her tongue in ways that could end up embarrassing her. That was the last thing she needed now.

"Another?" Sonia asked, gesturing to her empty glass.

Alex shook her head. "Just some water, please."

"Are you okay?"

"Fine. I can't drink much with jet lag. Seems to have twice the effect on me." It wasn't a total lie.

Sonia grinned. "I know, but sometimes that's a good thing." She winked. "Anyway, sorry I have been talking so much to Sylvie. I didn't mean to ignore you."

Alex smiled. "It's fine. I've been chatting to Justine."

Sonia's mouth curled into a wry grin. "I noticed."

Alex's heart faltered in its rhythm. "W-what do you mean?" It came out more defensive than she wanted. *Damn.*

"Hey, nothing. I am only teasing." Sonia frowned. "Are you sure you are okay?"

Alex closed her eyes for a moment. *Stop overreacting.* "I'm sorry, Sonia. I didn't mean to sound so..." She left it unsaid. "It must be the jet lag. Scrambling my brains."

Sonia smiled but didn't look convinced. The noise level in the building increased as thumping music came from both below and above.

Raising her voice, Sonia said, "Great, the music's started! Soon we can dance."

Alex shook her head. "Not me. Haven't danced in years. And I'm too tired."

"Pah!" Sonia said, just as Justine leaned in to their conversation.

"I'm with Sonia," she said, smiling warmly at Alex. "Dancing is exactly what you need."

Alex laughed. "Maybe later." She tried—and failed—to tamp down the arousal that flared again at Justine's proximity. Why couldn't she get a hold on this?

"Well," Sylvie chimed in, "why don't we have another drink first and then see how we feel?"

Alex sipped her water and chatted comfortably with all three women. Justine still gave no indications that this was anything other than a friendly evening, and Alex gradually relaxed, chiding herself for overthinking it earlier.

The bar was filling rapidly, and she noticed many women heading for a set of double doors at the far end.

Justine followed her glance. "They lead to the dance floors. Are you sure you don't want to indulge just yet?"

"Not yet. But…maybe later."

Sonia leaned over the table. "I am pretty sure I remember Danielle telling me you two used to dance all the time, yes?"

Alex's cheeks burned from the flush that swept over them—memories of the wild times she and Danielle had shared always did that to her now. They'd been good times but also just a bit too crazy. They'd got themselves into some dodgy situations in those early days. Thank God they'd both grown up fairly quickly in the following years.

"That was a long time ago," she muttered.

"Oh, is there a shady little past we need to hear about?" Sylvie teased.

"If Danielle is her friend, then yes." Sonia's eyes glinted.

Alex waved her hand in the space between them. "It was a long time ago," she repeated, but her smile was wide as she glanced around at the three expectant faces in front of her. "Oh, all right, then." The women smiled and leaned forwards further in their seats. Alex grinned, unused to being the centre of attention but loving how it made her feel. "Danielle and I met at university, in the LGBT group. We hit it off straight away, and, well, decided to assist each other in our quests to, um, meet women."

Sonia's eyebrows rose the quickest. "Meet?" she said, making air quotes. Everyone laughed.

"Okay. Have sex," Alex blurted out, her blush instantly reappearing. Her audience guffawed.

"And how successful were you in this endeavour?" Justine's eyes had darkened a tad, and Alex lost her train of thought for a moment.

"Um, quite successful."

Sonia giggled. "And you and my cousin, you never…?"

"Ew, no!" Alex shuddered. "I can't think of her like that."

Sonia's laugh was loud. "Okay, okay. I'm sorry I mentioned it."

Alex laughed too. "No, it's okay. It is funny, though. Neither of us ever felt like that about each other, yet everyone at uni assumed we were a couple."

"Did that cramp your style?" Justine asked. Alex glanced at her, then away again. There was something almost magnetic about Justine's eyes— she couldn't look at them for too long without a strange yet not unpleasant warmth spreading through her body.

"Sometimes. It also got us—" She stopped, suddenly aware of what she'd been about to reveal.

"What?" the other three asked in unison.

"Nothing. Doesn't matter." Her face was burning again.

"Oh no," Sonia said firmly. "You've started now, so you must finish. What else did it get you, hm?"

Alex huffed out a breath. "Well, it, um, it got us…offers. You know. For threesomes."

Sonia cackled and Sylvie shrieked. Justine, however, wore a slight frown as she murmured quietly, "And did you take up those offers?"

"No! God, no." Alex grimaced. "Definitely not my thing."

The relief that swept across Justine's face seemed out of proportion to the situation. Had she been burned by something like that in the past? They stared at each other, and Alex's breath hitched in her throat at the sudden intensity of the gaze.

"Well," Sylvie said, unwittingly breaking the spell, "I think we should all hit the dance floor and let you relive some of those earlier times."

Alex laughed. "I don't need to relive them, thank you very much. They are best left forgotten."

"Okay. Then how about creating some new times?"

She smiled, knowing there was no way she was going to get away without dancing tonight. "Okay, you win. Let's dance."

"Yes!" Sonia let loose a mini fist-pump that had Sylvie howling with laughter. The four of them pushed back their chairs, grabbed their drinks, and headed for the double doors.

"The dancing is on two different levels in the building," Sylvie said as they moved away from the table. "The basement is the recent music. It gets very hot and packed down there. And I'm too old to understand how to dance to that." She smirked over her shoulder. "Upstairs is more my era. I prefer that one, if you don't mind?"

Alex laughed. "No, I think old school is definitely where I'd fit in."

"Me too," Sonia chipped in, smiling.

"Justine?" Sylvie gave her a questioning look.

Justine shrugged and grinned. "I'm happy wherever we go."

They climbed up two small flights of steps and pushed through a swing door into a decent-sized room that was mostly dance floor, with a handful of tables at one end. Alex instantly recognised the music and it put a bigger smile on her face than she would have anticipated.

They put their drinks down on one of the tables and sat down. Alex looked over at the dance floor. It was busier than she would have imagined for a Monday night. Many more women must have walked into the bar while she'd been distracted by her thoughts surrounding Justine and their interactions.

"I see what you mean about this being busy on a Monday," she said to Sonia.

"I know, it's crazy, huh? I don't know how it happens, but I love it. It is such a great atmosphere to find so early in the week."

"Perfect for someone like you who doesn't keep regular hours, I guess?"

Sonia smiled. "That is true. Do not worry, I won't keep you out too late. I know you are tired and have a busy day tomorrow."

"I do. But now that we're here, I think I could be tempted out there." She gestured towards the dance floor, realising the absolute truth of her words as she spoke. The music was already making her toes tap under the table, and a hint of chair dancing was happening in her upper body. She felt a strange tingle on the back of her neck and turned to find Justine watching her, wearing an amused expression. Alex blushed but smiled.

"Well, come on, then." Sonia grabbed her hand and pulled her up out of her chair in one smooth action.

"Okay, okay." Alex laughed as Sonia tugged her none too gently towards the dance floor. Something told her Justine was following, and she had no idea where that sixth sense came from. Or what it meant.

Sylvie joined them a moment later and they eased themselves into a space on the floor. Alex tuned in to the rhythm and moved her feet, her hips swaying easily. She smiled, lost in the music and the moment. She didn't know where her head was right now, and she didn't care. It had been years since she had danced, had let herself truly go with the music without a care in the world. Terri didn't like to dance; it was something they'd never indulged in together. Alex hadn't realised until this moment just how much she'd missed it.

She threw her arms up and laughed as she moved her body, her hips, revelling in the euphoria of the moment.

A Whitney Houston track came on and virtually every woman on the floor let out a joyful shout. The atmosphere cranked up a notch and Alex's face ached from the smile that wouldn't leave her face. Sonia danced beside her, bumping her hip and laughing when Sylvie joined in from the other side.

And all the time there was Justine, moving smoothly and—*oh God*—so sexily in front of her. She could admit it, the woman was stunning to look at. If only Alex's body didn't pulse the way it did when Justine looked at her. Justine wasn't even doing anything in particular to cause that reaction—this was all coming from within Alex and she had no idea what to do about it. Other than fight it and not do anything stupid.

A few tracks later, Alex needed a breather. She pushed her way through the throng of dancers back to their table via the bar for some more water, glugging gratefully at it once she'd collapsed in her chair. She was hot and aching a little in muscles she'd forgotten how to use, but it felt wonderful.

Sonia appeared a couple of minutes later with four beer bottles clutched in her hands.

"Dancing is thirsty work!" she said over the music. "And one more won't hurt. Besides, I compromised for our old bodies and bought light." She winked and Alex's protestations died on her lips. Yeah, what the hell? Her first meeting tomorrow wasn't until ten. So what if she didn't go into the office until then? Somewhere inside she wondered just who she was right now. Carefree. Having fun. She really didn't feel like herself. Or, at least, not the person she had been these past couple of years.

She threw back her head and chugged a couple of mouthfuls of the deliciously refreshing beer, which tasted better than she'd imagined a light beer could. She smiled her thanks at Sonia and took a couple more gulps before Sonia hauled her out of her chair again. Grinning, she bounced after Sonia back onto the dance floor. Justine smiled widely as she appeared and reached out a hand to grab her wrist.

"Where were you?" she asked, her mouth close to Alex's ear so she could hear her above the music. The heat of her breath on her ear sent exquisite shivers down Alex's body and she recoiled slightly. This was…wrong.

But, God, it felt so good.

She glanced at Justine and away again; her face, her lips, were just too close for comfort.

"Needed a drink," she shouted, then subtly moved away, launching herself into the next track, fighting the dangerous attraction for Justine that was racing through her body and threatening to overpower her.

Over the next hour or so, she kept herself away from Justine, or at least tried to. She was enjoying dancing again and feeling so free. She knew she might regret it all in the morning and knew she definitely shouldn't drink any more beer. She wrapped herself in the music again, closing her eyes and smiling as she moved. She and Danielle used to do this two or three times a week. Before Terri. Before Jade. Alex knew things changed as you got older, but somewhere along the way, she'd lost so much of herself. Things about herself she'd enjoyed and liked. More so in the last few months. What had happened with Terri had numbed her, made her lose touch with what really made her happy. Right here and now, on this dance floor, some parts of her that she'd forgotten were flooding back, and it was exhilarating.

On another trip back to the table to take a break, Sonia approached and bent her head to Alex's ear. "Are you okay?"

"I'm fine, thank you. Just tired."

Sonia nodded. "I'm not surprised. Well, I don't know how much longer you want to stay, but I need to leave soon anyway. We can share a cab?"

"Sounds good."

Justine appeared, with Sylvie not far behind.

"Phew!" Sylvie plopped into a chair. "Now I remember why I don't do this that often."

Sonia laughed. "Me too! I am going to leave soon. Alex and I will share a cab. Do you guys want to stay or come with us?"

"I'll come with you," Sylvie said.

"I'll leave at the same time," Justine said. "I can walk home from here." She caught Alex's gaze, and Alex's heart jumped a little at the look in Justine's eyes. There was…something…there, something Alex couldn't read. And she didn't dare ask.

"Let me just go to the washroom," Sylvie said.

"Good idea." Sonia grabbed her hand and they wandered off.

Justine shuffled a little, her hands hitched in the pockets of her jeans. "Have you had a good time?"

Alex smiled. "Definitely. This… It's been a long time since I danced."

"You're good at it. You should do it more often."

A blush hit her cheeks again.

"Forgive me mentioning it, but you blush easily, don't you?" Justine said, smiling.

Alex closed her eyes momentarily and laughed. "Yes," she said. "Bloody Irish heritage—I'm all pale skin and red hair as a result."

"Your hair's gorgeous," Justine said, then it was her turn to blush. "Sorry, that—"

"Hey, no worries. That was a…lovely thing to say. Thank you." Alex's heartbeat sped up and she willed it to calm down.

They stared at each other for a few moments, and only Sylvie and Sonia returning from the washroom broke their gaze.

"Everyone ready?" Sylvie asked, glancing between them.

"Sure," Justine said abruptly, moving away to grab her jacket from one of the chairs. Alex was grateful for the break in the moment they'd been sharing and busied herself with gathering up her own coat.

After winding their way down the stairs to the ground floor, they all wrapped up in their coats and stepped out into the cold night.

"This was such a good evening," Sonia enthused as they stood in a small circle, their breath frosting on the air.

"Agreed!" Sylvie said. "Now I just had a thought." She turned to Alex. "I know you may have plans with work this week, but I was going to drag this one out—" she pointed at Justine "—again tomorrow night, just for some food. Would you like to join us?"

Alex opened her mouth to speak, then closed it again. Justine had shot a quick glance at Sylvie, a quick glance that seemed to say "What the fuck?", and Alex had no idea what that exchange meant. Perhaps declining would be best if Justine wasn't that keen on spending more time with her.

"Oh, no, that's fine," Alex said. "I could probably do with a night in, to get some rest."

"You would not be interrupting," Sylvie said, lightly placing a hand on Alex's arm, "if that is what you are thinking. We are just going to our favourite easy spot, Gabrielle's. Nothing fancy, but you are more than welcome to join us. Isn't she, Justine?"

Justine startled at the mention of her name. "Oh, yes. Sure, that would be really nice." While her words were strong, her shoulders had a tense set to them that had Alex confused.

She hesitated. Spending more time with Justine would be lovely. They had laughed and chatted so easily with each other—who wouldn't want another evening of that? But was she really being honest with herself about the situation? Wasn't she just a teensy bit attracted to Justine, and was therefore enjoying her attention a teensy bit more than she should?

She met Justine's gaze, and Justine smiled widely at her. Once again, warmth pervaded Alex.

"Well, okay, then," Alex found herself saying. "Why not?"

Sylvie grinned. "*Parfait*. Okay, so we will see you at Gabrielle's tomorrow. Sonia, could you give Alex directions?" Sonia smiled and nodded. "Okay," Sylvie continued, "we will be there from eight. Join us any time that suits you."

Chapter 8

JUSTINE SHIFTED IN HER SEAT again. It was eight fifteen and there was no sign of Alex. For once Justine had been on time, making an extra effort to ensure Alex wouldn't wander into Gabrielle's and not see a familiar face. A friend would do that, right? But how long should she sit here waiting for Alex? Stupidly, they hadn't swapped phone numbers, relying instead on Sylvie's casual yet forceful invitation to bring them together at the appointed time.

Only Alex wasn't here.

For about the tenth time, Justine scowled at the empty seat beside her. Sylvie had called her two hours ago, apologising profusely as she explained why she wouldn't be joining them this evening.

"My sister is in meltdown," she said, sighing. "Big opening night at the gallery and no babysitter. I cannot let her down, *chérie*."

Justine couldn't argue with that—Sylvie's sister was infamously dramatic at the best of times, so she could only imagine the state she was in, in those circumstances. It was just… Sylvie had arranged all this, without consulting Justine first, and she felt off balance as a result. They had exchanged some heated text messages earlier that morning, with Justine questioning Sylvie's motives over the invite she had extended to Alex.

Are you saying you don't want to carry on getting to know her? Sylvie had messaged eventually, and Justine had had to give in.

No. I do. Thank you. I think.

Sylvie had simply responded with a smiley face and that was that.

So, now, here Justine was, waiting on her own for Alex and still trying to sort through her conflicted thoughts about what was happening between them. On the one hand, she certainly wasn't going to turn down the chance to spend more time with Alex. The evening at Lèvres had ended all too rapidly, just when Alex had seemed to be relaxing completely. But Justine couldn't kid herself—she was very much attracted to Alex, and that physical attraction could derail things if she wasn't careful. She also had no idea if Alex was in any way attracted to her. Sure, there'd been a few looks, and Alex's almost constant blushes, but for once Justine couldn't actually read what those signs meant. It was disconcerting to say the least. Everything she thought she'd learned over the last eighteen months about the signals women could give was failing her dismally when it came to Alex.

The opening door caught her attention, and she sucked in a breath as Alex quickly entered the bar. Justine raised a hand to get her attention and caught the slight falter in Alex's steps as she realised Justine was alone at the table.

Don't worry, I'm just as nervous about that as you are.

"Hey, how are you?" Justine asked, rising as Alex reached the table. "Sylvie sends her apologies. Her sister called with a babysitting emergency."

Alex smiled and her features relaxed the small frown they'd been sporting. "Ah, I see." She placed her coat on the spare chair and sat.

"How was your day?" Justine asked, motioning the waitress over.

"Good. Busy. That's why I'm a little late; I got caught in a meeting. Still, I slept pretty good last night, which helped get me through the day— must have been all that dancing, wearing me out." Alex's voice had a slight croakiness, and she cleared her throat. Was she nervous?

Justine smiled, reining herself in from reaching out to comfort Alex. "Well, that's good."

Alex ordered a glass of wine and sat back as she sipped it. "How about you?" she asked, setting her glass down again. Justine noticed the slight quiver in her hand as she did so. Yep, definitely nervous. But about what?

"Oh, so-so. Nothing major."

"What is it you do? We never did get around to talking about work after Sonia banned it." Alex's smile then was bright and relaxed, and Justine's entire body lost its tension. They could do this.

"I'm a project manager," Justine replied.

"Prince2?"

"Yes, and an MBA too."

"Impressive," Alex said, nodding.

"What about you?"

"I work in HR. I'm the training director for my company."

Justine smiled and tipped her glass in Alex's direction. "Equally impressive."

Alex laughed. "Thank you."

"So do you come to Montreal often?"

"This year I have—this is my fourth trip. Last year only twice, though."

"Do you like travelling?"

"Oh, yeah, I do, actually. Not the flying so much, but landing somewhere new, yes, I really love that."

And just like that, that easily, they were immersed in conversation. Justine couldn't remember the last time she'd been so at ease with someone. Before their food arrived they talked about all the places they'd travelled or would love to visit. As they ate they discussed food and wine and the best meals they'd ever had.

"So what's your secret craving when it comes to food?" Justine asked as the waitress dropped dessert menus in front of them.

Alex blushed that endearing pink again and laughed. "Oh, God, this is embarrassing." She paused. "Er, it's custard."

Justine snorted. "Custard? As in that awful yellow stuff?"

"Hey, don't mock my heritage!" Alex laughed. "It's a throwback to when I was a child. My mum would heat me up some custard and throw some sultanas in it, whenever I was feeling poorly. It was my comfort food, and still is."

Justine smiled. "I get that."

"So? Yours?"

Justine squirmed in her seat. She'd had many women baulk at this notion in the past—how would Alex take it? And why did she suddenly care so much what Alex thought of her? "Er, well, it's..."

"Come on," Alex prompted, smirking, "spit it out!"

"Cold pizza," Justine said, wincing. "For breakfast."

Alex's eyes widened and she looked horrified. "Ew," she said, but she was laughing, "that's gross!"

"Hey, fair's fair." But Justine couldn't help joining Alex's laughter. "Have you ever tried it?"

Alex shook her head. "No, fair point. I haven't. But, ew, the thought of all that cold, congealed cheese and dough that early in the morning. Really doesn't sound like something I'd like."

"Don't knock it until you've tried it, that's all I'm going to say."

"Well, you knocked my custard."

"Yeah, but I have actually tried that and I *know* I don't like it."

They declined dessert and instead ordered a second glass of wine. As they sipped slowly they moved on to books, and movies, and sport. The time passed in a warm, hazy blur that had Justine's nerves tingling in so many delicious ways.

As they finished their drinks, Justine excused herself to go to the washroom. She stared at herself in the mirror as she washed her hands. The evening was going better than she'd dared hope for. Sylvie was definitely right, getting to know someone like this, without putting any pressure on herself to woo them into her bed, was a revelation in enjoyment. Of course, she had to be honest and acknowledge that she thought Alex was wonderful and that she would, under different circumstances, want to see where they could take this. The cynic in her, the old Justine who wouldn't quite lay down and die, reminded her that she could have her cake and eat it—she could have the nice conversation and connection and still take Alex home for a night of what she was sure would be incredible sex before Alex jetted off back to the UK in a couple of days.

The trouble was, the newly emerging Justine, the one who thought she really ought to say goodbye to that wild time she'd lived for the last eighteen months, already liked Alex more than as just a one-night stand.

———⊰⊱———

Alex fidgeted with her empty wine glass and huffed out a breath.

She was in trouble and she had no idea how it had happened. It had just…crept up on her, without her noticing.

Once again, Justine had done nothing overt to suggest she was interested in anything other than friendship. But Alex was dazzled from being under the spotlight of Justine's attention. No one had been this interested in her in years—just her, Alex, not the Alex who was Terri's partner, or the Alex who was a director at RCS. Only Alex. The evening they had shared had, even more than last night, touched her in so many ways. Ways she'd forgotten she knew how to feel.

She blew out her cheeks and exhaled slowly. She'd been of two minds about coming here tonight—saying she'd got caught in a meeting had been a little white lie. Actually, she'd been pacing in her hotel room for twenty minutes, wringing her hands and trying hard to build up either the courage to go to Gabrielle's or get Sylvie's number from Sonia and beg off the evening entirely.

And it was all because of Justine and how she had made Alex feel last night at the club. Eventually her pacing had led her to rationalise that at least Sylvie would be with them at Gabrielle's, so ignoring the buzz she got from being around Justine would be far easier. Then, of course, she'd arrived to find Sylvie couldn't make it and she had a whole evening alone with Justine.

It was...intoxicating, and she'd loved every minute of it, but as much as she didn't want to walk away from Justine, she knew she should. Twice already she'd had to stop herself from reaching out to touch Justine when she had said something funny or adorable.

You have a partner, you are in a relationship. Yes, it might be a doomed one, but why are you even thinking about Justine this way?

The answer came swiftly: *Because she makes me feel special. Interesting. Funny. Smart.*

She shook her head. No, it didn't matter. She knew she was at risk of saying or doing something really stupid that would only embarrass her in front of this new friend. The better policy, the safer one, was simply to put on her coat and leave. Walk away from temptation and all the confusion it was bringing her.

She tensed her shoulders, then relaxed them again. Yes. She had to.

Standing, she pulled her coat from the spare chair and pushed her arms quickly into the sleeves. Just as she was pulling some notes from her wallet, Justine returned from the washroom.

The look of hurt that washed over her face, before she could mask it, made Alex's stomach drop.

"You're going?" Justine asked as she reached the table, her voice soft but with a slight tremble to it.

Alex couldn't meet her eyes. "I really should," she said. "I've got more of those dull meetings to deal with tomorrow, after all." She wrapped her scarf around her neck and finally braved a glance at Justine.

Justine smiled, but it barely lifted the corners of her mouth. Her eyes narrowed and she shook her head slightly. "But…I thought…well, I thought we were having a nice time."

"We were. Are," Alex said quickly. "I just really think I should go."

Justine glanced at her watch. "It's, well, it's only nine thirty. Are you tired?"

Just lie, tell her that's what it is.

"No, it's not that. It's…" She looked anywhere but at Justine. Despite that, she was aware of Justine walking around the table, of Justine standing just a little too close to her.

"Alex, I have really enjoyed spending time with you. I'm not ready for that to end, and I don't think you are either. We can spend some more time together, can't we? Just a little more time, please."

Alex dared to look at her, and it was her undoing. Justine's expression was open, and warm, and…there it was again, that unidentifiable something that tugged at Alex and wouldn't let her go.

Justine leaned towards Alex. "Stay," she said, and she reached out to touch Alex's hand.

The touch electrified Alex in ways it really shouldn't.

She should go.

"There's a great little bar a bit further down the street that plays really cheesy music from the eighties. It's such a fun place. I'd really like you to see it." Justine waggled her eyebrows. "And we could dance again." Her smile lit up her face and another piece of Alex melted.

She should walk away from this situation because she knew she couldn't handle it. Because she knew how tempting it would be to stay and continue feeling the way Justine made her feel, even if for just another hour or so. But hell, what would be wrong with that, actually? That didn't mean she'd do anything about it—Justine clearly wasn't interested in her that way. Although how she was looking at Alex right now, her gaze intent and a soft smile parting her lips, cast a smidge of doubt in Alex's mind.

Tell her about Terri. Tell her.

Justine's eyes widened slightly, and in shock Alex realised she had grabbed on to Justine's hand. When had she done that? She made to pull away, but Justine stopped her and held Alex's hand tightly. Alex could feel the warmth of Justine's fingers as they meshed with her own.

Tell her about Terri. Or at least tell her you have to leave.

That gaze. That…something.

Oh God.

"Okay. I can stay a bit longer."

———⋖⋗———

A thrill ran through Justine at Alex's words. She had no idea what had possessed her to reach out and touch Alex and to lay on the persuasion in the way she had. All she knew was she didn't want this evening to end, didn't want to say goodbye to Alex. Not yet. This whole experience had lightened her, somehow, and who wouldn't want to keep feeling that way?

She held the door open for Alex as they departed Gabrielle's and was rewarded with a gentle smile that made her heart lurch. She couldn't help it. Alex was intelligent, funny, and had something indefinable that drew Justine to her in a way that made her feel strangely disorientated, as if the ground wasn't quite steady beneath her. She just hoped she was hiding it well—there was no point complicating things by trying to act on all that she was feeling. *Just practice, remember what Sylvie said.* If she took the time to learn from this evening, exactly as Sylvie had advised, then when she was ready, someone like Alex, just like Alex, would come along to try to fill her heart and soul, and maybe, by then, she would let them.

The bar they moved to next was only three blocks away, but the night was cold enough for the walk to rosy up their cheeks by the time they arrived. They spoke little on the way, hands tucked deep in their pockets as they strode along, faces hunkered down in their scarves. She risked a glance at Alex as they walked up the steps and into the bar, wondering if she would see doubt and hesitation.

What she saw in Alex's expression stilled her own doubts and started a warm glow deep in her belly. Alex's mouth was parted in a gentle smile, and her eyes were wide and filled with thrilling excitement.

"What is this place?" she asked, her tone full of wonder as she gazed around the large room. The bright pink walls were speckled with the glint from a dozen mirror balls that dotted the ceiling, and "Mamma Mia" by ABBA blared out of the sound system. A surprisingly large number of bodies grooved and gyrated on the dance floor at the centre of the room, and almost the same amount lined the two bars that framed the floor.

Justine smiled and her stomach did a little flop at the happiness on Alex's face. She'd put that there and that felt very good indeed. "It's one of Montreal's oldest institutions. Part drag bar, part disco, part who knows what. Okay for you?"

"Oh my God," Alex said, laughing, "I bloody love it!"

Justine grinned and gestured Alex towards the coat check. "We can leave all of our stuff there, okay?"

Alex nodded, and before long they wove their way to the bar, both free of any encumbrances save some cash in their jeans pockets.

Water bottles in hand, they leaned against the bar, facing the dance floor.

Justine watched Alex watching the crowd. Alex's head bobbed to the music, and she wore a blazing smile. She looked relaxed, and comfortable, and happy. The sight made Justine break out into her own wide smile.

After only a couple of minutes, Alex turned to her.

"Dance?" she said, gesturing with her head towards the throng.

Justine grinned and Alex laughed, the sound sweeter than any of the music playing behind them. "Lead the way," Justine said, gesturing for Alex to walk ahead of her.

She let her gaze wander down the back of Alex's body as she followed her onto the dance floor. She couldn't help it; it really was a glorious view. Alex's top clung to her torso, highlighting her trim waist before it tucked into her jeans. The jeans themselves moulded perfectly to her ass and thighs, and her walk contained just enough of a hip swing to get Justine's temperature rising in ways she was supposed to be suppressing. But this sudden heat she couldn't fight.

She wanted Alex in the fiercest way possible. There, she'd admitted it. And it wasn't just physical—everything they'd shared the last two evenings had thrilled Justine in ways that had her shaking her head in disbelief. But now, watching Alex move into the centre of the floor, her body flexing as she insinuated herself into the midst of the dancers already there, Justine's mind went numb and her body took over.

Alex dancing set every nerve tingling in Justine's skin as she fantasised about Alex's body moving beneath hers. The sway of her hips alone made Justine's breath catch multiple times. She forced herself to look away and tried, in vain, to tamp down her arousal.

Alex turned and reached out a hand tentatively to Justine, which she took without thinking, enfolding Alex's palm in her own. Alex's expression was one Justine couldn't read. Nervous? Excited? Possibly both. And something else entirely, the nuances of which were lost on Justine right now. The warmth of Alex's hand in her own was completely distracting her, and when Alex tugged on her hand to move them further into the crowd, Justine happily followed.

As soon as they reached the space Alex had clearly set her sights on, she extricated her hand from Justine's and moved to the music, her gaze averted from Justine's for a minute or two. It was as if she needed to immerse herself into her own space before she could acknowledge Justine's presence in it. Justine respected that and began her own movements, picking up the fast rhythm and revelling in the freedom she always felt when she was in the middle of a dance floor.

Chapter 9

ALEX TRIED TO FOCUS PURELY on the music and the adrenalin rush that dancing was giving her. It was extraordinarily tricky with the gorgeous distraction of Justine so close by and the quite different kind of rush her proximity gave Alex. She was still reeling from her relatively easy acceptance of Justine's request not to say goodnight too early.

She felt as if she were two people.

Sensible Alex admonished her for potentially leading Justine on—although Alex still thought she was flattering herself with that notion—and for not telling her about Terri, for putting herself in a situation that may turn out to be awkward to get out of, to say the least.

Excited Alex was glorying in how fantastic she felt right in this moment. Dancing again, completely free of inhibitions or cares. Having fun. Something she had most definitely forgotten how to do for quite some time now.

She laughed as she swung her arms above her head and banished Sensible Alex to a faraway place in a corner of her mind.

Justine danced up to her and bent her head to Alex's ear.

"Would you like something other than water to drink?" Justine asked, her lips so close to Alex's ear she was practically kissing it. Alex shivered.

"No, I'll stick to water, please," Alex said, placing her own mouth close to Justine's ear and unable to keep herself from breathing in the subtle hint of Justine's perfume as it wafted close to her nose. She was acting in ways she simply didn't recognise in herself.

Justine raised her head to meet Alex's gaze. "No problem." She smiled, then she was gone.

Alex turned around and launched herself into the next track, something by The Black-Eyed Peas, if she wasn't mistaken. Hands landing on her waist from behind startled Alex for a moment, but then she smiled. Justine had returned quickly and decided to get playful. She didn't mind, even though Sensible Alex tried to have her say. She allowed the contact for a few moments, indulging herself despite her circumstances, and inched round slowly to face her.

Whoa.

Not Justine.

The woman in front of her now was much taller, with cropped, bleached-blonde hair. She was just as stunning to look at as Justine, but Alex realised immediately that this woman did nothing for her. Whatever it was Justine had, this woman couldn't get close to it.

Easing herself back out of the woman's hold, Alex smiled and shook her head. The stranger smiled forlornly but then shrugged and walked away. Breathing an inward sigh of relief, Alex turned away—and locked gazes with Justine on the edge of the dance floor.

She had a look on her face that stopped Alex in her tracks. She recognised it instantly, as if it had been shouted across the space between them, and her heart thumped in response. The look was pure desire, mixed with jealousy, mixed with a…possessiveness that almost rocked Alex back on her heels. It was potent, and arousing, and stirred something more than physical in Alex that she immediately shied away from as fast as she could. She didn't know what the hell had changed between them, but she couldn't pull her gaze away from the heat in Justine's blue eyes.

Sensible Alex was trying to be heard above the clamour of Alex's body but getting nowhere.

Justine walked slowly towards her, and Alex swore the air literally sizzled between them.

"You okay?" The edge to Justine's tone hinted at her displeasure at what she'd just witnessed, but Alex knew it wasn't aimed at her. The blonde should consider herself lucky she'd stepped far away from Justine's firing line. Alex was amused; she'd never had anyone get so riled up on her behalf.

"Perfectly fine," she said, grinning. "She was a pussycat."

Justine guffawed, her shoulders shaking. "I'd like to see you call her that to her face."

Alex grinned again and was thankful the mood had lightened. The intensity had been unnerving, and she needed some breathing space.

The DJ switched to Madonna and the place erupted. Alex laughed and threw herself back into her dancing, surrounding herself with hot bodies in the steamy atmosphere. There she could ignore the other kind of heat that threatened to engulf her, but her respite didn't last long. Every time she turned around, Justine was there. Not invading her space but just…there. Watching Justine move, her hips grinding out each beat with a sizzling sensuality, robbed Alex of breath. Her gaze, which locked with Alex's frequently, made Alex shiver with its intensity. Justine was now focused only on Alex, her gaze unwavering, her eyes telling Alex loud and clear that the heat of the moment they'd shared earlier had not diminished, not as far as Justine was concerned. This level of attention was something Alex had never experienced before, and it left her breathless; it was like being drip-fed an erotic drug.

Like an addict, she could feel her resistance to whatever the hell this was, crumbling.

Just tell her about Terri. Tell her and put a stop to this.

But she didn't.

After months of questioning her attractiveness, despite how much Terri tried to convince her otherwise, here was someone gorgeous validating that element of her again. And Justine was being very open about it now, her gaze making it abundantly clear that she wanted Alex with an untarnished desirability that felt too good to ignore. She didn't know how they'd got here, and a sudden fear of being deep into something she didn't understand made her turn away. She sucked in lungfuls of hot air and tried to calm her racing heart.

After a couple of minutes, she felt back in control and turned around to face Justine, whose half-smile was quizzical.

"It's hot!" Alex said, fanning herself, feeling a little guilty at the not-quite-truth she used to explain her change of mood.

Justine nodded, and a lazy and definitely flirtatious smile crossed her lips.

They danced on, and Alex began to think she'd imagined it all—Justine had suddenly seemed to back off and was now simply dancing alongside

Alex, only occasionally looking her way. Alex almost laughed at the disappointment she felt at no longer being under such intense observation.

Just as she thought she'd fully relaxed and shrugged off that intense phase from earlier, the music dropped in tempo to a seductively slow R&B track.

Justine turned to Alex and her expression had shifted again. Alex wondered if Justine had any idea how clearly she communicated with just her face and eyes. Right now, a sultry hunger played out across her features, and Alex had absolutely nothing in her to resist when Justine stepped into her space and placed her arms lightly around Alex's waist.

Oh God, what was she doing?

"Can we?" Justine asked, her mouth close to Alex's ear once more.

No.

This was way too dangerous. Dancing up close like this, touching…

She shouldn't be doing this. She should just stop and—

Alex shuddered, and melted, and gave in to everything wrong about this moment that felt so bloody right. "Yes, but if I step on your feet, be nice."

Justine's smile was soft, and her face full of longing, and Alex was captivated by her beauty.

Justine started moving, eyes closed, her hands roaming slowly in small circles on the sides of Alex's body. Alex watched her, saw her face relax and the hint of a smile cross her mouth. Justine's hands were nowhere near any erogenous zones, but even so, the heat from her fingers seared through Alex's top and left goose bumps in its wake. Her own eyes shut at the sensation, and she became super-aware of every tingle. When she felt Justine move behind her, and place her hands on her hips, Alex shocked herself by moving without hesitation. She pushed back against Justine, who bent her knees slightly, bringing Alex's ass into contact with Justine's groin. With their thighs touching front to back, their rhythm matching in perfect synchrony, they ground their hips slowly from one side to the other.

Justine clutched tighter at Alex's hips and worked the deliciously slow beat with her. Alex pressed into her even further, tipping her head back so it rested on Justine's shoulder, bringing Justine's mouth into the vicinity of her neck. Justine's breath was hot on her collarbone; the shiver it sent down her body nearly made her lose her footing. Then Justine's lips lightly touched her neck, and the thrill of it sent bolts of desire shooting through her from head to toe. That small voice of alarm clamouring to be heard was far too easily pushed away. She was consumed with this moment, the intensity of it making her heart pound. So when Justine's mouth pressed more firmly against her skin, and Justine's hands tugged harder at her hips, Alex didn't stop her.

Justine pulled Alex round in front of her, and her desire was blatant, exposed on her face like bright sunshine. Alex knew her own face reflected exactly what Justine was feeling. That feeling was flowing through her now like warm honey; sensuous, dangerous, and deliriously exhilarating.

When Justine dipped her head and gazed at Alex as their mouths drew nearer to each other, Alex reached out, oblivious to anything except the two of them and this electrically charged moment. She wound her hands into Justine's soft hair. In the next moment their lips met and Alex couldn't stop the moan that came from somewhere deep in her chest, or the flood of desire that crashed over her body at just that simple touch.

Justine pulled Alex against her and crushed her mouth with her own. Alex's mouth was already opening, her tongue already reaching for Justine's. They devoured each other, pressed close as if they were one body. Alex's hands tightened further in Justine's hair, and Justine's hips moved subtly against Alex.

The power of the kiss seemed to stun them both; they pulled apart suddenly, breathing heavily, staring at each other.

Alex knew this was the moment.

Now, panting in Justine's arms, she had a choice.

Step back from something she knew she wanted more than anything she'd wanted in a long, long time and in doing so, save her conscience.

Or go with it, let herself be swept up in whatever this turned out to be, just so she could feel like this again, feel truly desired.

Justine looked at her quizzically and made as if to speak, but Alex shook her head, smiling, her decision made from somewhere deep inside, somewhere she didn't know she possessed. Hunger and need outweighed everything she thought she knew about herself.

She reached up to place her lips on Justine's, tasting them properly this time, letting the tip of her tongue explore the shape of them. Justine shuddered in her arms. She pulled Alex even closer, thrusting her tongue into Alex's mouth, pressing their breasts, hips, and thighs together.

Alex was drowning in sensation.

This passion, this need, had never played a part in her relationship with Terri. Something like it had formed the basis of what she'd had with Jade, but it had been soiled with Jade's need to control and hurt. But this, with Justine, was something else again. Alex ached with a desire she never thought she'd feel, and it was scary and exhilarating all at once. She returned Justine's kisses with a fervour she couldn't temper, loving the feel of Justine's hot, wet mouth on her own, running her fingers through Justine's curly hair again, amazed at how the texture of it made her hands tingle.

How long they stayed there neither of them could have said, but when eventually Justine lifted her head and pressed her lips close to Alex's ear, Alex knew what Justine was going to say, and knew what her answer would be.

"Come home with me," Justine whispered hoarsely, her voice thick with desire. "I want you so much."

Alex didn't hesitate, didn't stop for even one moment to consider her next move. She simply nodded and let Justine take her hand and lead her to the coat check.

They retrieved their warm outdoor clothing and handbags, but for Alex this activity passed by in a blur that later she wouldn't remember. Nor would she remember much of their silent walk to Justine's apartment. Only a block and a half from the club, it was accessed via a steep staircase on the outside of the building. The evening was cold, with a clear sky. For a moment, standing on the top step, waiting for Justine to unlock the front door, the cold nearly seeped into Alex's brain enough to wake her from the haze of out-of-control desire that had descended on her back in the club.

Nearly, but not quite.

Finally the door swung open in front of Justine and she pulled Alex into the warm apartment. Pushing the door shut, she pressed Alex up against it, her hands firm as they removed Alex's coat, scarf, and gloves, her mouth embarking on a delicious quest over Alex's neck and jaw. The wet open-mouthed kisses made Alex shiver and squirm, and Justine's hands cupping Alex's breasts had her aching in ways that left her breathless.

Justine stepped back for a minute to rip her own outerwear off and she was back before Alex could begin to gather herself. Justine's mouth plundered Alex's, her tongue delving deep and instantly drawing a flood of wetness from between Alex's legs. When was the last time anyone had kissed her like this? Like she was water and they had been drought-stricken for days? Justine consumed her, enflamed her like wildfire.

She burned even brighter as Justine's hands flicked open the button on her jeans and yanked down the zipper. Moments later her jeans and underwear were down around her knees, and Justine's hot hand stroked through her swollen pussy in ways that made her dizzy. Alex wrapped her arms around Justine's shoulders and clung on, panting into Justine's mouth, then emitting a wrenching groan as Justine pushed two fingers slowly inside her.

Justine being inside her was possibly the most exquisite experience she'd ever had. It was perfect. And yet...

"Oh, God, you feel incredible," Justine whispered against Alex's lips. She flicked her thumb over Alex's clit as her fingers plunged even deeper, and Alex's brain, which for a moment had begun to awaken, switched off. She gave herself fully to the incredible sensations Justine was creating in her body. "I want to hear you come," Justine said, her voice strained. "Please. Come for me."

Shockingly, unbelievably, it was all Alex needed. She'd never come so fast or so hard. Her hips arched upwards as her spine curved, her head thumping back against the door as a wholly unrecognisable guttural sound leaked from her throat.

Justine held her up, her mouth covering Alex's, swallowing her moans while gradually her fingers slowed their movement inside Alex.

"Oh, my God," Justine murmured, lifting her head a little to be able to meet Alex's eyes. "You...that..."

Alex nodded, dumbly, a searing ache in her chest.

She couldn't hide from it anymore. Something was stirring, somewhere in the deep recesses of her mind. Something that was bringing discomfort, and dread, and pain.

Justine smiled and reached for Alex's hand, bringing it to the button fly on her jeans. "Hurry," she whispered, still smiling. "I can't wait for you to touch me."

Alex's hand froze, and her heart started pounding in fear.

There was a darkness, coming at Alex from all angles, threatening to engulf her, to strip away that unfettered and unburdened freedom the last two hours had bestowed.

What had she done?

Oh God, what the hell had she just done?

"What?" Justine asked in a whisper, raising a hand to stroke Alex's cheek. Alex pulled away from her touch and moved sideways—awkwardly with her jeans around her knees—out of Justine's embrace. "What's wrong?"

Alex shifted again, shuffling her feet until there was enough distance between them that she could reach down for her underwear and jeans and pull them up. She was numb, yet at the same time she was close to imploding. She couldn't meet Justine's eyes as she fastened her clothing back together.

"I...I have to go." She stooped to pick up her coat, and wrapped her scarf haphazardly around her neck. "I'm sorry. I..."

"What do you mean? Why are you leaving? I thought—" Justine's eyes were wide. "I'm sorry. Did I hurt you? Was it too rough? I just got carried away, I think."

Alex held up a hand. She just wanted—needed—to leave. Every defence was crumbling and the tears were only moments away. Her throat was too tight to talk.

She reached for the door handle and yanked open the door.

"Alex, wait! Please!" Justine called as Alex trotted swiftly down the steps.

Alex didn't respond, didn't even turn round. There was nothing she could say.

She walked up the dark street with no idea where she was heading but hoping in the one corner of her mind that was still functioning that she'd be able to flag down a cab.

After a few minutes she saw one and managed to squeak out the name of her hotel to the driver.

The tears started and she couldn't stop them. She ignored the concerned looks the cab driver sent her in the rear-view mirror and scrabbled in her bag for tissues. Blowing her nose loudly on one, she used another to wipe ineffectually at the steady streams pouring from both eyes.

She hung her head back against the seat. Her mind was in free fall while, in a bizarre twist, the remnants of the incredible pleasure she'd experienced only minutes before still tugged at her clit and breasts.

She'd cheated on Terri.

They were the only clear words her brain could latch on to. Everything else was a blur.

She'd cheated on Terri.

Yes, their relationship was in a heck of a bad place these days, but what she'd just done with Justine made her no better, surely? How could she look Terri in the eyes? How could she dare to aim any more recriminations in Terri's direction?

Oh God, she hadn't done it so they'd be even, had she? Had some twisted part of her subconscious thought fucking another woman was somehow okay if Terri had done it first?

She shook her head and stared out at the dark streets passing by.

No, it hadn't been that. It had been pure, unadulterated attraction, and need, and…fire. A desire so fierce she'd never known anything like it.

It hadn't been revenge or because she was drunk. It was all about Justine. A woman she'd only known for a little over twenty-four hours. A woman who had quite literally taken Alex's breath away with one kiss.

And what had followed had been all about them. Together. Nothing and no one else had mattered from the moment they first kissed.

The irony hit her next and it turned to acid deep in her gut. Having found that fire, that connection with someone who made her feel like she could fly, she'd never see Justine again.

Waves of self-pity churned her insides and caused a desperate sob to escape her throat.

Chapter 10

HER EYES LOOKED DREADFUL. ALEX glared at herself in the mirror, poking with disgust at the puffiness underneath them. She grabbed her concealer stick and went to work. The combination of too many tears and insufficient sleep had her looking like a dog's breakfast on another day when she had to stand up in front of fifteen people and breezily convince them of the merits of the new timesheet system they were required to use. Like that was going to go well with the way she was feeling.

She smoothed the concealer over the dark patches of skin and sighed. Her emotions were all over the place, but she didn't dare latch on to any one thought in case the tears started again. It took all her effort, but she was just about succeeding in pushing all those emotions into little boxes throughout her mind, locking them tight and hoping she'd lose the keys. She was walking a tightrope of despair between her situation and revulsion at herself.

It was a toxic mix.

She ate her breakfast on autopilot, the croissants and juice seeming tasteless to her dulled senses. She'd just drained the last of the juice when her phone bleeped from across the room. After picking it up she closed her eyes briefly when she saw the notification of a text message from Sonia.

Hey, how was Gabrielle's last night? Hope you had a good time x

She paused for a few moments, pondering how to respond. There was no way on God's green earth she was going to tell Sonia what had transpired. At that thought, images of Justine assaulted her, causing her heart to lurch unpleasantly. The feel of Justine wrapped around Alex from behind on the dance floor, and the heat of her body scorching through Alex's clothes. The taste of her mouth, and the incredible sensations her tongue had engendered when it dipped slowly and seductively into Alex's mouth. And oh God, the way Justine felt inside her—

She clutched the phone tighter and willed her breathing to slow from the ragged panting that had overtaken her.

Had a lovely time, nice meal, good laugh. She tapped out her response slowly, feeling only a twinge of remorse for the lie.

Great. Call me later for a chat, if you want?

Alex exhaled slowly, relieved. Bullet dodged. From what little she knew of Sonia, even if she had told her the truth, a grilling probably wouldn't have been forthcoming, but best not the take the chance. Alex was feeling miserable enough without having someone she barely knew berating her.

She glanced at her watch.

Time to face the day.

She tried, in vain, to ignore the fear that rippled through her at the thought. It would take every ounce of energy she had to keep it together for the next ten hours or so.

<hr />

Justine slumped over the breakfast bar and stirred her coffee half-heartedly. She watched the swirls of cream as the blackness slowly subsumed them.

She knew how they felt.

She hadn't meant to pounce on Alex as soon as the door was shut. God, she hadn't meant to pounce on her at all, but her resistance to her own feelings had shattered on that dance floor. Alex's movements, her smile, her gorgeous body—all of it had just worn down what little self-control Justine had left after two evenings in the company of this amazing woman. The kiss on the dance floor had short-circuited her brain, and all she could think of was getting Alex home.

On the walk to the apartment, she'd had visions of them maybe starting on the couch with a heavy make-out session before transferring to the bedroom. But her hunger for Alex had just taken over the minute Justine got her inside the apartment. Even then, she hadn't meant to fuck her up against the door—just kiss and caress and warm things up before moving elsewhere. But she'd lost all sense of place and rational thought the moment they were kissing, and suddenly all she wanted, more than anything, was to be inside that incredible woman.

Then Alex had left.

Not since Nadia had Justine felt so low. Her sleep had been fitful; when she was awake, all her brain would allow was the same loop of questions with no answers, mingled with searing images of Alex's body, her skin, her mouth. When she slept, her dreams were confusing and downright weird.

She sipped at the now-lukewarm liquid in her mug. The main question she couldn't shake careened around her head yet again.

Why had Alex left so suddenly?

She was temporarily saved from her torture when her phone bleeped beside her.

So how did your evening go? Sorry again that I had to cancel

Sylvie.

Justine groaned and hung her head.

She had no idea what to tell her. Sylvie would presumably be livid at her for repeating her old behaviour. And while she was beyond confused at how things had turned out, she was also a little embarrassed. Usually she was the one making the fast exit from her trysts. Having it done to her, and in such spectacular fashion, caused an uncomfortable heat to spread across her face if she thought too long about it.

So maybe she would just ignore Sylvie's message until much later in the day.

Or, even better, tomorrow.

She stood and walked over to the sink to throw away the dregs of her cold coffee. As she rinsed out the mug, she couldn't stop the images and memories of Alex sliding into her mind for the hundredth time. The way she'd kissed Justine, with a hunger that had both excited Justine and, if she were honest, scared her just a little. No one had ever needed her quite like that. What scared her the most about it was that for a moment, just a moment, she'd let her own need run loose, and the depth of it shocked her. Their encounter had been so much more than the one-night stands she'd enjoyed, despite being one of the briefest and only one-sided.

81

God, if only she could see Alex again. Even if it was just to get an explanation for last night, because the not knowing was driving her mad. She'd thought they were on the same page, that the desire was completely mutual. Especially after they'd got on so well over the course of two evenings. So why the hell had Alex run out on her? Sure, she wasn't in Montreal long, but they could still have had last night, and maybe tonight, and…

As she glanced at her phone again, feeling a twinge of guilt at ignoring Sylvie, an idea poked its way into her brain. She smiled to herself as she picked up the phone and began typing.

Long story. Will tell you later. Any chance you could get me Alex's number from Sonia? Please??? xxx

———————

Alex plugged her laptop into the port that allowed her to display her presentation on the huge TV screen that filled most of the end wall of the conference room. A few keystrokes and her opening slide filled the screen. Technology-wise, she was ready. Energy-wise, not so much.

As she stretched her neck, her upper vertebrae made some alarmingly loud creaking sounds. After pouring some water into a glass, she perched on the edge of the table at the front of the room. In the silence she took her time breathing in and out as slowly as she could. She needed to focus on the next hour and leave behind all the stress the last twelve hours had wrought.

Her trainees began arriving a couple of minutes later, and she mustered all her professionalism to smile warmly at each one. They began to fill the seats around the large table in the centre of the room. As usual, no one took the seats at the front to begin with—the later arrivals found themselves forced to sit near "teacher", and Alex allowed herself a small internal smile at this often-seen pattern of human behaviour.

She didn't have a list of names to tick off, but she did know that fifteen people had accepted the appointment. When she had thirteen bodies in the room, she decided to get started—she'd learned long ago never to wait for stragglers who then usually didn't arrive.

"Good afternoon, everyone. My name is Alex Saunders, and I'm based in our London office, where I head up the team responsible for HR-related training. Thank you for coming to this session today." It was her standard intro, already honed after the two sessions she'd held yesterday. Thank God she could pretty much recite it with her eyes shut.

A few attendees smiled, but she noted with some trepidation the distinct lack of enthusiasm from most people in the room. Same as in the other sessions. She squared her shoulders and stood up.

"Okay, so today I'm going to be explaining to you the timesheet system we use here at RCS. This system has been in use for over three years now, and is therefore a tried and tested solution for our—"

The door opened to admit her two stragglers, a tall man with the broadest shoulders she'd ever seen, and what she thought was probably a woman, although she couldn't really tell as the man was standing in front of the other person.

"Sorry we're late." The man looked genuinely apologetic. Alex flashed him a warm smile and gestured towards the empty seats at the front of the room.

Then she feared her heart had stopped as he stepped toward the seat, revealing the person he'd partially hidden.

Justine.

No.

No, no, no, no, *no*!

How could this be possible? How could the universe be so...unfair?

And if she thought Justine had looked sexy in her casual outfits over the last two evenings, she looked breath-taking in a business suit. Alex allowed herself just a moment to take in the visual. The dark blue trouser suit hugged Justine's lithe body in all the right places. The vibrant blue shirt underneath would probably set her eyes off spectacularly, but Alex didn't dare look to seek confirmation of that theory. One look in those eyes and she knew she'd fall to pieces. She stopped herself from lingering in her admiration, especially when she realised Justine hadn't actually looked in her direction yet. She'd look soon, because she'd have to, and Alex waited, counting down until...three, two, one.

Yep, there it was, Justine's moment of recognition.

Comical, if it wasn't so awful. Justine's face was a picture of stunned shock. In the next moment the look transformed into one of hurt confusion that cut through Alex like a knife. At that, her professionalism kicked back in and she swiftly looked away back to the centre of the room. Out of the corner of her eye, she saw Justine and the broad-shouldered man take their seats to her right. She was acutely aware that Justine was now only about eight feet away from her.

She was also acutely aware that Justine was staring at her.

Alex cleared her throat and picked up where she'd left off, her heart thudding too fast.

"As I was saying, the system is our tried and tested solution for recording all the time we spend on the work we do for both our clients and for any internal projects." She was inordinately pleased when her voice didn't waver.

She moved on with her spiel, and to her immense relief, the process gradually allowed her to forget—almost—the stunning woman who sat to her right.

The next forty minutes passed in a smooth blur. She got a couple of awkward questions at the end, from people clearly not happy with having to use the system at all, but she used all the charm she'd nurtured from years of similar presentations to tell them that, essentially, they had no choice but to just suck it up. She sugar-coated it, of course, but the message was clear.

Soon people were standing and dispersing, and her heart beat even louder because she knew exactly what was coming next, and she couldn't possibly avoid it. Her stomach churned and she wished she could be anywhere else, anywhere in the world, right now.

Right on cue, Justine stood and walked slowly over to where Alex was unplugging her laptop. To Justine's credit, she waited until everyone else was well out of earshot before she spoke, and Alex had to silently thank her for that.

"Hey," Justine said.

Alex exhaled slowly and looked up. Even meeting Justine's gaze was hard; she didn't want to see what she thought she would find there, so she directed her view to somewhere near the vicinity of Justine's right ear.

"Hello."

Justine let out a half-chuckle, half-sigh. "This is…unexpected, isn't it?"

Alex couldn't help herself—the snorted laugh flew out of her lips. "Just a little. Yes," she bit out.

Justine recoiled slightly. "I would really like to talk to you. But I know that here and now is inappropriate."

Thank God for that—at least she's as professional as I am.

But further conversation between them was just not going to be possible. There was no point. Alex had made an awful mistake, something she should never have done and would probably regret for a long time. And no matter how much Justine had stirred in her the night before—or now, standing in front of her in all her gorgeous glory—in the cold light of day, Alex had to walk way.

Had to.

"I don't think—"

"Please." Justine's whisper was laced with tortured emotion that cut Alex to the quick. She dared to meet Justine's eyes and it was her undoing. Everything flooded back—the heat, the need, the connection that had blown her apart.

Then she was nodding and Justine was smiling in relief.

"Can we meet after work? Maybe grab dinner?"

Alex sighed. What the hell was she doing? She seemed to have no resistance to this woman.

None at all.

"I…I don't know about dinner. But yes, we can meet." She closed her eyes for a moment. Something told her she would regret this even more than last night, but the way Justine was looking at her and the warmth of her presence close by demolished all of the flimsy walls Alex had erected since leaving Justine last night. "I'll be finished by six."

"Thank you." Justine reached out a hand, then stopped herself as Alex flinched. "There's a bar two blocks down from here, on Rue McGill. Hugo's."

Alex nodded and had to look away. Whether Justine was aware of it or not, the need in her expression had an intensity that burned. It was ripping Alex to shreds. She'd spent her whole life doing this—sacrificing her own feelings to keep everyone else happy. Why, now, couldn't she stop doing that when it mattered the most?

One drink. Just one drink, then walk away.

———————⟿◦⟾———————

Justine strode back into her office and shut the door behind her. She flopped down in her chair and huffed out an extended breath.

Seriously? They worked for the same company? The universe was a fucking comedian.

She leaned back in the chair and her head dropped back, sending her gaze to the ceiling.

This was both ridiculous and fortuitous. Although how fortuitous would depend on how she handled their conversation later. Judging from Alex's reaction to seeing Justine in that conference room, Justine would not have very long later to try to understand firstly, what had happened the night before, and secondly, if anything more could happen in the future.

She puffed out her cheeks. Why was she even thinking about a future? Alex lived in London. She didn't live in Montreal. Why think there could be anything more than last night?

Because... Because last night had been the most intense interaction she'd ever had with a woman, and something that good should not be written off so quickly, surely. Because there might be a way. Because there might be a chance. Even if just for the rest of this week. To feel that fire again, even just one more time. Because, holy shit, why wouldn't she want to feel that way again? Yes, Alex had left her...hanging, and her own pleasure had not found release. But even so, touching Alex had been just as satisfying, just as exciting.

She sat up straight and brought her laptop to life. She opened the appointment in her calendar for the training session that had just taken place, noting Alex's full name as the organiser. Alexandra Saunders. Switching to the company directory, she found Alex's entry. Director of HR training systems, based in the London office. Worked for RCS for eight years, always in Human Resources. Responsible for a team of six directly, fifteen altogether indirectly, so it wasn't one of those empty directorships— Alex had significant responsibility, much like Justine herself, even if Alex was at least two pay grades above her.

The photo was a standard corporate pose in half-profile with an overly bright background. But still... Justine drank in the sight of her. Alex's hair was pushed back behind her ears, and her face seemed slightly fuller than Justine remembered. The green of her eyes was enhanced by the lighting used in the photo, and her mouth was parted in a soft smile. Justine shivered as she remembered that mouth on hers.

A knock at her door pulled her from the heat-inducing memories and she shut down the directory.

At five thirty she slapped the lid of her laptop closed with a satisfying thunk. Her latest project plan was complete and e-mailed out to all relevant parties. She stood and stretched, then glanced at the clock on the wall. Her stomach performed a flip that brought a nervous laugh from her lips. Thirty minutes before her arranged time to meet Alex.

Assuming Alex showed, of course.

Justine sighed and again mentally ran through what she wanted to say to Alex. She'd taken a break from her project plan an hour or so previously to try to put her thoughts in some sort of order, as they'd been spinning like planets in erratic orbits since she'd got back to her office. She didn't want to go into tonight's meeting with a script as such, but at the same time she had a couple of key things she wanted to talk about and knew she'd need to word them carefully to get Alex to open up.

At ten before the hour, she packed up her bag and slipped out of her office. The walk to the bar took only a few minutes, but it chilled her— they'd had more light flurries of snow during the day, and the cold air fogged her breath as she walked down Rue McGill. Weaving in and out of rush-hour commuters, she reached the bar and yanked open the heavy wooden door. A blast of warm air hit her and she rushed into the room to let it envelope her.

She took a quick look round but didn't see Alex yet. She spotted a small empty table halfway along the room and swiftly unwrapped her layers as her body temperature climbed in the cosy heat of the dim bar. A waitress appeared and took her order for a glass of Pinot Noir—her go-to warming drink on a cold evening—and Justine sat in the chair facing the door, willing her feet to still their tapping and her hands to cease their trembling. Her actions and reactions in the past forty-eight hours were a mixture of mystery and revelation. She'd worked so hard to convince herself these past few months that she was perfectly fine being a single lesbian, hopping from one bed to the next, never bothering with last names or phone numbers. But a combination of Sylvie's words and her own response, both physically and emotionally, to Alex, had her defences down and some hard truths forcing their way through.

She was lonely. And, to some degree, still bitter. She knew now she didn't want to be that person, not anymore.

Alex wasn't the answer to that. Justine knew that too, deep down.

But...

The door to the bar opened and Justine's breath stalled in her throat. She was here. She'd actually turned up.

Justine rose from her seat to catch Alex's attention. She noted Alex's nervous glance around the bar and her hesitation before she moved in Justine's direction.

"Hi," Justine said, sitting again, knowing Alex would not appreciate an attempt at a kiss in greeting, even though Justine ached to do so. Alex looked adorable with her cheeks flushed from the cold.

Alex smiled wanly and peeled off her coat and scarf, draping them over the back of her chair before sitting in it. Justine took a moment to re-admire the way Alex wore a pants suit. It had blown her mind in the training session, and the repeat performance now had no less impact. The material clung *everywhere* and emphasised everything in the best of ways. She tore her gaze away as Alex looked up—being caught in full lust mode would probably not be conducive to coercing Alex into talking.

"Would you like a drink?" She motioned for the waitress before Alex could respond but snapped her hand back down to the table when she noticed it shaking.

Alex motioned to Justine's glass with her head. "What are you drinking?" she asked quietly. She wouldn't meet Justine's gaze.

"A Pinot Noir. Very smooth."

Alex nodded. "Sounds good."

The waitress smiled and within a couple of minutes was back with a glass of the ruby liquid, placing it in front of Alex.

"Thank you for coming," Justine offered after the waitress had walked away and they'd each taken a sip.

Alex put her glass down and clenched her hands together on the edge of the polished wood of the tabletop.

"I...I'm still not really sure this a good idea," she said, finally meeting Justine's gaze. She cleared her throat. "What happened last night was—"

"Fantastic. Incredible," Justine interrupted, impatient and already concerned Alex would run off before she got to say her piece.

She could see Alex's blush even in the subdued lighting of the bar. "Yes, but..." Alex closed her eyes briefly before continuing. "But it was a mistake. I'm so sorry. I don't mean to—"

"Wait. Please." Justine held up a hand. "Before you write it off, can I please just say some things?"

Alex slouched back in her chair and dropped her hands to her lap. When she didn't say anything, Justine took that as her opening.

She took a deep breath. She was hyperaware of Alex's distance right now and knew she was probably fighting a losing battle. But she had to know.

"You... Last night, we had an amazing connection. Actually, over both nights. At least, I thought so." She waited for some acknowledgement from Alex, but none came. Alex simply stared at Justine, her face an emotionless mask.

All of Justine's prepared words went out the window.

"Why did you run off? I just don't understand." It came out sounding more hurt than she'd been prepared to reveal. Alex's eyes widened slightly, but still she said nothing. A muscle twitched in her jaw.

Justine leaned forwards. "Last night was wonderful, Alex, and I don't just mean what happened at my apartment. I know you felt it too. I know it." She stared at Alex intently, as if by willpower alone she could get Alex's armour to crack.

That muscle in Alex's jaw twitched again, and Justine pushed on. "You don't live in Montreal. I get it. But you're here for the rest of the week. We could have a very lovely time while you are."

Alex's eyebrows rose and she straightened up in her chair. Ouch, that had probably been the wrong tack to take. Alex stared at her and shifted forwards in her chair, her gaze landing anywhere but on Justine. Understanding dawned and Justine's insides squirmed even as she laughed ruefully.

"Oh, wait. I get it. I think I'm being beaten at my own game."

She exhaled sharply and slumped back in her chair. Her embarrassment was back in full force, and her cheeks were blazing. Oh, how ironic was this? Christina and Sylvie would have a riot with this one. Maybe she wouldn't tell them. "God, I'm an idiot. You only do one-night stands."

"No!" Alex cried and ducked her head in embarrassment when heads turned from nearby tables. "No. It's not that."

Alex closed her eyes and let out a slow breath. When she opened her eyes again, Justine leaned forwards, holding out a hand. Alex recoiled and pushed her chair back.

"I have to go," she said sharply. "I'll give you some money for the wine."

"Fuck the wine. What is going on? Why won't you stay and talk to me at least?" Oh God, could she get any more pathetic? Why not just let her go? Alex didn't want anything to do with her; she'd made that crystal clear. But there was something there, something she couldn't give up on until she knew for sure just what the hell had happened.

"Justine, please. Leave me alone." Alex was pulling on her coat and scarf, her fingers fumbling in her haste.

Anger spiked in Justine's belly. "Okay, fine. You know, last night I really didn't see this side to you. The bitchy side. Guess I'm lucky you're walking away again."

Alex whirled to face her, her eyes blazing. "I'm not a bitch, for fuck's sake," she snapped. "I have... It's complicated. That's all. I should never have gone home with you last night."

"So you keep saying." Justine couldn't stop. Something about how much this was surprisingly hurting her kept her arguing when she should just get back to her wine and watch Alex walk away. "I guess I didn't realise just how awful it was for you when you came so fast over my fingers."

Alex looked like she'd been slapped, then her jaw set once more. She took a step forwards, and through gritted teeth she said, "You know very well none of that is true. Please don't make it like this." Her hand flew to her mouth as a sob escaped her lips. "Justine, please. I'm sorry. So sorry, but I can't do this. No matter how good last night was."

Her eyes widened as if she'd only just realised what she'd said. Justine leapt at her chance and stood. She rounded the table to stand almost toe to toe with Alex. She held back from reaching out for Alex, but she could see her proximity was unsettling Alex enormously.

"So if it was so fucking good, why the hell are you walking away again?"

"Because I have a partner!" Alex hissed, and recoiled as if she'd been shot. She took first one, then two steps backwards. "I-I'm in a relationship. It's—"

"Oh my God," Justine interjected, her heart racing and her body flushing with a mix of horror and anger. "You...you used me to *cheat* on her?"

How could this be true? Alex was another Nadia?

"It's not—"

"No!" Justine stepped away, agony ripping through her. "No, I can't believe this."

"Justine, please. Let me explain."

Justine held up a hand, her face burning with fury. "Trust me, there's nothing to explain. Get out. Go on, go."

Alex stared at her for a moment, then turned and walked away.

Chapter 11

Alex strode along the empty street, the cold air chilling her face and hands. Thank God she only had one more block to go before she was back at the hotel.

This trip was a disaster, and she'd only been here a few days. Christ, it wasn't even just the trip that was a disaster. Her whole life was one enormous mess right now, and she couldn't see a way past any of it to a happier place.

For the umpteenth time she admonished herself for giving in so easily the night before. Going home with Justine had been an error of judgement so monumental in its stupidity she felt sick just thinking about it.

If only it hadn't felt so good spending time with her. Being held by her, touched and kissed by her.

If only she could find the courage to walk away from the remnants of her relationship with Terri.

If only she could win a million fucking pounds on the lottery and move to a deserted island so she'd never have to deal with anything like this again.

The warmth of the hotel lobby greeted her like an old friend, and she hurried into its embrace. She needed a drink. A large one. She'd barely touched her wine in the bar, and now the oblivion a few glasses of something strong would bring was the only thing she could focus on.

She walked to the lifts, and minutes later she was throwing off her coat, scarf, and boots and striding across the carpet to the minibar. She needed the burn of a whisky and poured out a measure into a tumbler she found by the bed. The large mouthful made her wince as it worked its way down her throat. It hurt, but in a good way.

Sitting on the end of the bed, she stretched her legs out before her. She ought to change out of her suit, but right now she couldn't muster the energy. She couldn't even be bothered to take off the jacket. Another mouthful of whisky, and this one burned less but glowed more.

It was working.

She poured another measure. Probably stupid, but she yearned for oblivion. Three more mouthfuls and she placed the near-empty glass on the side table and lay back on the bed. Her empty stomach gave the whisky free rein through her bloodstream, and it was just what she needed.

She stared up at the ceiling. Annoyingly, despite the wonders of the whisky, her brain wasn't shutting down like she wanted it to. Instead, it insisted on revisiting images from the aborted evening. Justine's horror at Alex's confession. Alex's own distress at being looked at like...like she was something *less*. Something dishonourable and dishonest. Never in her life had she been that kind of person.

But now she was.

The tears came out of the blue. They tracked down into her hair and her ears, but she made no move to wipe them away this time. She didn't deserve not to cry, and she didn't deserve to be comfortable. By going home with Justine last night, she'd lost all right to consider herself a victim or somehow morally better than Terri. Now they were on the same level.

Cheaters, both of them.

At the agony that label caused her, Alex's stomach rebelled. She only just made it to the toilet.

Hours later, woken again from tormented dreams, she got out of bed and poured a glass of water. As she sipped it she pulled the curtains open and gazed out at the dark street below.

Having shaken off the remnants of the disturbing dream, she was now, for once, devoid of all but one thought.

She needed help. She had to talk to someone, purge herself of all that had happened and somehow find a way forwards. Although forwards to what, she didn't know. Right here and now, the future was as about as inviting as jumping off a cliff into a mile-deep chasm.

Finishing her water, she picked up her phone and tapped out a text to Danielle.

If you're around at about midday your time, can you call me?

By the time she slipped back under the covers, there was still no response, but she felt marginally better just for sending the message. Confessing to Danielle would not be easy, but she had to talk to her. The guilt was eating her up. If she didn't get at least some of her thoughts out of her head, she'd go mad.

⸺◦◦⊂⊗⊃◦◦⸺

Justine slammed the door behind her and threw off her coat. Her bag and shoes landed in a heap across the hallway where she flung them.

Stomping into the kitchen, she reached for the bottle of red she'd opened on Sunday. She sloshed the liquid into a glass and took a big swig, not even bothering to sit. After she'd watched Alex leave the bar, she'd finished her own glass of wine as well as Alex's, so this was her third of the evening on an empty stomach. Her head was already spinning, and a tiny part of her brain suggested food might be a good idea. She found a can of soup in the cupboard and heated it. She sat in the window seat as she ate and stared vacantly at the street below as each mouthful was consumed without any awareness of its flavour.

All her brain could focus on was Alex and her stunning confession, even though that was the last thing she wanted to think about.

She just didn't understand. She hadn't known Alex that long, of course, but she never would have thought Alex was like…*that*.

Dishonest.

A cheater.

She flinched. It seemed so incongruous with the woman who'd shyly responded to Justine's friendliness at Lèvres. The woman who'd seemed to be torn between staying out a little later and being the sensible professional who should get back to her hotel. The woman she'd talked with for nearly two hours at Gabrielle's about anything and everything. Unless that was Alex's big game. Play the innocent, tempt someone like Justine, take what she wanted, and split.

But…

Tonight, Alex had seemed genuinely distraught at what had happened between them, despite how much she admitted she'd enjoyed it. Genuinely upset at Justine even thinking she was into one-night stands.

None of it added up, and Justine was going crazy turning it over and over.

Her phone bleeped from where it was nestled in her abandoned bag. Getting up to retrieve it, Justine swayed slightly. Okay, no more wine after this glass.

Sorry, I'm not comfortable doing that. Call me?

She stared at the message, bewildered. What was Sylvie talking about? Then she scrolled up to see the chain she was responding to, and an acidic flicker disturbed her stomach. Oh yes, she'd asked Sylvie to see if she could get Alex's number from Sonia. Yeah, so *that* wasn't necessary now.

Sorry to have asked. Will call you tomorrow.

She couldn't possibly talk to Sylvie now. While it might be good to confide in someone, she was still reeling from the course of events. She would take some time to calm down a little, think it all through herself before she had to listen to Sylvie's disappointment in how Justine had fallen so quickly back into her old ways. She definitely didn't need to hear that tonight.

She padded across the room back to the window seat, where she'd left her wine.

―――――――○○○○―――――――

"Everything okay?" Danielle's voice was tinged with concern.

It was a little past seven. Alex had been awake for a while now, so Danielle's call hadn't woken her. Even so, having requested it, she now wasn't remotely ready to tell Danielle what had transpired. Just the thought of having to say the words twisted her stomach into knots.

"Alex?"

She exhaled loudly. "Sorry. I'm here."

"Are you okay? You're worrying me."

"I-I had sex with someone." Blurting it out hadn't been her intention at all. But there it was, out there.

Danielle inhaled sharply. "You...what?" Danielle's voice was barely above a whisper.

Alex closed her eyes and fought against yet more tears. She had to swallow a couple of times before she could continue.

"Shit, Danielle. I'm in a mess."

"Please tell me what the hell is going on."

Haltingly, and with numerous pauses, Alex did. Danielle, to her credit, said nothing at all while Alex related her sorry tale.

"I've never had anyone look at me the way she did, Danielle. Like I was...scum. The worst of the worst. And I knew how she felt because that's exactly what I was feeling about myself. I am such a hypocrite. I've cheated on Terri. Oh, *God*." She broke off as a sob threatened to break free.

Danielle waited a moment before speaking. "While I do not condone what you have done, I have to say I totally sympathise with how events unfolded and how you found yourself in that situation. It sounds like Justine was very charismatic. And with everything you have been going through these past few months, I can actually understand how her attentions would have made you feel." She paused for a moment, before saying, "And I know I am your best friend and you might expect me to side with you in this, but I am completely averse to cheating, as you well know. So you have presented me with somewhat of a moral dilemma here. I will always support you, because I love you. But Alex, this is just so not like you, and goes against everything you have stood for. What the hell is going on with you?"

Alex expelled a short burst of laughter, but it was an empty sound. "God, if I knew the answer to that, I wouldn't be in the mess I am now." She sat up and clutched at her hair with her free hand. "The only thing I can say in my defence, and I realise how weak it is, is that it was like I was another person. Remnants of the person I was when we were younger, when we danced and partied and didn't give a shit about the next day. Mixed in with the responsible person I am now, who seems to be going through some kind of midlife crisis. It was a nightmare combination."

"Between them, Jade and Terri have managed to make you forget that fun-loving woman I went to university with, haven't they?"

"Hm, kind of. I mean, it's easy to blame them, especially Jade. But partly it's just because I've aged."

Danielle snorted. "You are only forty-six, Alex. You make it sound like you are in your nineties already."

"You know what I mean. I'm in a responsible position at work, my clubbing days are behind me—"

"Well, that does not sound true, from what you have told me about how much you enjoyed that club on Monday night. Never mind what happened with Justine, it sounds to me like you were more alive that night than you have been in a long time. Perhaps it is more that the woman you thought you had lost is not so lost after all?"

Alex sighed as the truth in her friend's words hit home. "Yes," she whispered. "I had such a good time on Monday night. And Tuesday too. Dancing like that again, not caring about the next day. It was like the biggest rush I've felt in years."

"So, I repeat, it is easy to see why you got caught up in that, and did what you did with Justine. Even though I am still struggling to see how you let go of your…principles…quite that much."

"I couldn't resist her," Alex said, her voice hoarse. "I literally couldn't. Danielle, she was…amazing to be with. We just…connected."

"Wait a moment, are you saying you had feelings for her? That it was not just about the sex?"

Alex groaned. "Oh God, I don't know. Yes. Maybe. Shit…"

Danielle huffed out a breath. "And now you know she works for RCS too."

"Oh fuck, don't remind me. I swear I needed a defibrillator in that training session. I've never been so shocked in my life." Alex tried to laugh at the craziness of the situation, but it came out strangled as the awfulness of how she and Justine had left things the night before swamped her.

"And where does this leave Terri?" Danielle spoke the question quietly, but the power of it thumped Alex square in the middle of her chest.

Alex hesitated, her mind churning along with her stomach.

"Alex? Gut answer. Do not think about it. Just tell me what your heart says."

Alex sobbed as the words left her mouth. "Leave her. Leave her and start over."

⊸•◖❀◗•⊷

Justine left her office and made her way up to the ninth floor. The meeting she was supposed to be in had started five minutes ago. She braced herself for the disgruntled looks she would get from the team that had called the meeting, but she was past caring. If they'd had the week she'd had, they'd cut her some slack.

Today had been torturously slow. Waking up hungover from the wine, and tired from lack of sleep despite the wine, she had lurched from one meeting to the next all morning in a depressed daze. After drinking that third glass she'd spent the rest of the evening lying on the couch, staring into space while she tried to figure out what the hell she was going to do. She'd been tempted to pour another glass at about eleven but dismissed the idea almost instantly. Alcohol was not the answer. Still, when finally she'd dragged herself to bed, long past midnight, and slept so badly, she'd wondered if more wine would have helped after all.

She shuffled her laptop under her arm as she swiped her pass over the panel to gain admittance to the ninth floor. She pushed through the door and turned left towards the suite of meeting rooms.

She stopped dead in her tracks when she saw who was bent over the water fountain a little further along the corridor.

Alex spotted Justine as she stood. They stared at each other for a few moments.

Justine hated herself as she gazed at Alex. Despite everything she'd learnt last night, she still felt the pull. The connection. It was palpable between them, and the confusion it engendered was giving Justine a headache.

"Justine," Alex said quietly, taking one step forwards.

Justine held up her hand. "No." She tempered her tone, keeping the anger out of it in respect of where they were. "I can't." No matter that she was still brimming with questions, she had to get to that meeting.

Alex halted her movement, and her head dropped. "I understand," she murmured, and abruptly turned and walked away.

Justine watched her go, admiring the swing of her hips and the slight bounce of her auburn hair across the tops of her shoulders. She remembered pushing her hands through that hair on the dance floor, pulling Alex's mouth closer to her own, deepening the kiss—

She shook her head, trying to still the throbbing between her legs.

Stop.

Meeting.

She strode off down the corridor.

Alex picked half-heartedly at the salad bowl in front of her, then shoved it away. She slumped back in her chair and swivelled round to look out the window.

Seeing Justine that morning had thrown her. Of course they were bound to bump into each other at some point today; the odds were too great for that not to happen. Even so, the shock of it still resonated. Shock at how her body, and mind, had reacted to seeing her. Shock at seeing all of those same reactions reflected back at her in Justine's face.

She sighed. Justine was stunning, she couldn't deny that. She was drawn to her like she'd never been drawn to anyone before.

And Justine clearly felt the same way, despite what she knew of Alex and the pain that knowledge had caused her.

Alex had needed every ounce of professionalism she could muster to stop herself from marching down the corridor and pulling Justine into an empty meeting room so she could explain. She wanted Justine to understand. Desperately. The thought that Justine had her labelled as someone not worth knowing based on one evening of madness was eating away at her.

The irony in understanding that was how Terri must think about her own…indiscretion was not lost on her.

She gazed up at the wintry sky, shivering even though she was in the temperature-controlled environment of the office. The bleak weather mirrored her mood perfectly. This week was rapidly becoming one of the worst of her life. So much for taking some time to think about what she wanted to do, using the space to get some clarity.

Although I guess that is what I've done, in a way. Not how I would have imagined, but still…

She managed to get through the rest of her day on autopilot, hopping from one meeting to another before delivering her final training presentation late in the afternoon. For once she had a receptive group, and that minor element of positivity helped lift her mood more than she would have realised.

She left the office just after six and wrapped her coat tightly around her for the short walk across the square to the hotel. She waited at a crossing for the lights to change and gasped as a hand took hold of her elbow. Justine stood beside her.

"Sorry," Justine said, holding up her free hand. "I thought you heard me calling your name."

As her heart gradually slowed its panic-induced thumping, Alex shook her head. "No. I...I must have been miles away."

"Can we talk?" Justine asked. "Maybe get a drink somewhere?" Her tone was flat, her eyes darting to Alex's and away again.

The lights changed and people pushed past them as they remained rooted to the sidewalk.

Alex took a deep breath. "Sure. I'm in the W. How about there?"

Justine nodded and without another word they waited for the lights to change once more.

Chapter 12

THE BAR WAS BUSY BUT they found seats on a small sofa in the far corner. They didn't speak until after the waiter had taken their order for a glass of wine each.

"Thank you for agreeing to do this," Justine began. Her jaw was tight and her hands kept clenching and unclenching where they lay on her thighs.

Alex braced herself, not sure at all that she was ready for this, now that it was here.

"I'm actually glad you suggested it," she said carefully. "I really do want to explain—"

"My partner was cheating on me for six months before I knew anything about it. I don't actually know how long it would have gone on if I hadn't stumbled across them."

Justine's words were icy, sharp like needles, and every one of them stabbed at Alex's conscience. Justine wasn't looking at her, and Alex was grateful, as she wasn't sure she could handle seeing the pain Justine clearly still felt.

"Oh my God," she whispered. No wonder Justine had been so furious when Alex had told her that she was in a relationship.

Justine reached for her wine, her fingers trembling. Alex's heart thudded.

"So it's a very sore point for me. I can't tell you how to live your life, but I'm…disgusted that you used me in that way."

Alex tried to jump in, but Justine was on a roll.

"But the thing I don't get is that you just didn't seem like that kind of person. At all." Justine was virtually spitting her words out now. "So I'm wondering if you are just a great actress, good at faking God knows what. Or if you really are as callous as Tuesday night makes you look."

Alex reeled as if she'd been struck. The words hurt, enormously, and nausea grabbed hold of her insides.

Finally, Justine looked at her, and Alex wavered under the angry stare.

"I'm actually neither of those things," she said, overwhelmed with sadness. She shook her head. "Not at all."

"Then why—"

Justine's tone was angry and unforgiving, and Alex's temper rose. "Because my life is a fucking mess! Because my partner cheated on me, three months ago, and I've felt completely and utterly worthless ever since. Because this week you've made me feel, just for a few hours, that I was still someone that another woman would want." Her voice broke and she fumbled for the tissues in her handbag.

Justine stared at her.

"So it was all about revenge?" Justine's tone was still sharp, but her eyes had softened just slightly.

"No, of course not," Alex snapped. "God, I am not a bad person! I'm just...I'm just in a very bad place and you got dragged into that." She took a deep breath and dared to meet Justine's eyes again. "For what it's worth, I'm sorry about that. Very, very sorry."

Justine sat back and exhaled loudly.

Alex reached for her wine and downed a large mouthful. She stood. There was nothing more to say. She had hoped they could have a civil conversation tonight; it was the only reason she had agreed to the drink. It hadn't gone that way at all, but in essence she'd said what she needed to say. Either Justine would accept it or not. There was no point elaborating or daring to tell Justine how she made Alex feel, how their connection over the two evenings had been one of the best things to ever happen to her.

"I'll charge the wine to my room," she said, passing a hand over her face as her shoulders slumped. "I probably won't see you before I leave tomorrow, so I...I wish you well, Justine. And again, I'm sorry."

Justine gaped at her as she grabbed her bag and coat.

"Wait," Justine said, half rising from her seat.

"Goodbye, Justine."

Minutes later she was in her room, undressed, and wrapped up in the oversized robe the hotel provided. She flopped on the bed and lay back, her eyes gazing unseeing at the ceiling.

What a mess the week had been. She took in a deep, shuddering breath. Well, she couldn't do anything else about what had happened with Justine, and she was leaving tomorrow anyway. But at least she could do something about Terri when she got home. Her stomach clenched at the thought, but she knew it was time.

Yeah, definitely time.

Justine ate the last mouthful of noodles from the takeout container on her lap and washed it down with a gulp of water. She was wedged into her window seat, her eyes unseeing as her brain repeated, on a loop, the words Alex had spoken.

Because my partner cheated on me, three months ago, and I've felt completely and utterly worthless ever since.

Because this week you've made me feel, just for a few hours, that I was still someone that another woman would want.

When she'd seen Alex leaving the office ahead of her, she'd acted on instinct. Her need for answers had temporarily overridden her anger, and catching up with Alex at the crossing had seemed like a great idea.

But then, when they'd got to the bar and her body and soul had betrayed her yet again with their desire and…need for Alex, she'd got angry all over again.

She closed her eyes. God, she regretted snapping so coldly at Alex, but she hadn't been able to help it. Just remembering Nadia's deceit had stirred it all up again. The pain, the embarrassment, the rage. It had rushed through her, directing her tone, her questions—until Alex had blurted out what she'd been going through, and Justine's anger had deflated almost instantly.

Alex had been cheated on too. She'd been through the same pain and agony Justine had. But unlike Justine, she hadn't left her partner when it happened. Was she crazy? How could Alex stay with her after she'd done that to her? How could she forgive her? Clearly she hadn't, if she said her life was a mess.

Unbidden, images of Alex pressed up against the front door on Tuesday night rampaged through her brain. The desperate way she'd clung to Justine, and the haunted look in her eyes, all made perfect sense now. The hunger in her kisses too.

She groaned. Shit, life just wasn't fair sometimes. Why did it all have to be so complicated? How could she meet someone, finally, who triggered far more in her than simple physical desire, only to discover she not only lived on the other side of the ocean, but she was caught up in a messy relationship?

Universe, you suck sometimes.

"Thanks again for coming over at such short notice." The VP of operations was a sweet man, and Alex smiled and shook his hand.

"No problem. I think it went well in the end."

He nodded vigorously. "Definitely. I've had some great feedback already. I think we'll manage to get this month's billing out on time after all, thanks to you."

Alex basked in the praise. She had been a director for a year, but having her work lauded so highly still felt good. "Remember, call me anytime if you have any questions or concerns. I've got a good team working for me, and we'll be able to sort out any issues you have."

"Great," he said, enthusiastically pumping her hand again.

She smiled as she extracted her complaining hand from his tight grip.

"You okay to get a cab outside?" he asked.

"Sure, no problem. I need to pop back over to the W to get my suitcase first anyway."

He waved her off at the lift, and within minutes she was out on the street marching across the square to the hotel. She retrieved her case and had the doorman flag her a cab. As she waited for it on the snowy sidewalk, something—she wasn't sure what—made her glance up.

Standing on the opposite sidewalk, with a large takeout coffee in her gloved hand, was Justine.

They stared at each other across the cold street. Alex didn't know what Justine was thinking or feeling, but if it was anything like the myriad of emotions coursing through her own mind and body, Justine would be as confused as she was. Desire, sadness, pain, and a deep yearning for something she couldn't have, no matter how much she craved it.

The connection between them was broken moments later by the yellow cab that swept alongside the kerb in front of her. As she stepped forwards to pass her case to the driver, she glanced down to be sure of her footing.

When she looked up again, Justine was gone.

Sighing, she climbed into the warmth of the cab.

The business-class lounge at Montreal was relatively quiet. She found herself a small table and tucked into the pasta dish before her. Somehow, despite how upset the previous evening had left her, a calmness seemed to have enfolded her since waking this morning. Along with that, her appetite had finally returned, and she wolfed down her late lunch in a distinctly unladylike fashion. She mused on her current state as she sipped at a glass of orange juice. Something about at least being able to explain to Justine, in simple terms, what had happened for her on Tuesday night had relieved some of the tension she'd been carrying. Her words hadn't particularly resolved anything—for either of them, she suspected—but it had been a form of release, however small.

Her phone bleeped.

Are you at the airport now? Can I call?

It was Danielle, and Alex closed her eyes against the sudden upwelling of love and gratitude she had for her friend. Danielle couldn't have known Alex really needed to talk to her right now, but her contact was welcome nonetheless.

She texted back and a few moments later her phone rang.

"Hi, Alex, how are you?"

"Hey. Your timing is impeccable. I was just thinking some things and wondering if I could talk to you."

Danielle chuckled. "Well, I am here. Talk to me."

"I love you, you know that?" They weren't her intended first words, but they had to be said.

"I know," Danielle said, a slight catch in her voice. "I love you too."

Alex sighed. "Justine caught me on the way out of the office last night, and we went for a drink."

"Oh." Danielle's voice was laced with surprised shock. "How did that go?"

Alex filled her in on the short conversation.

"Gosh, no wonder she was so hurt by what happened between you. And how did it make you feel, learning that, and telling her what it all meant for you?"

"Upset, at first. But, this morning, something feels like it's…shifted. Like I feel just slightly better for being able to say what I said. I think because, as I left, she didn't seem like she completely hated me anymore. And that felt good."

"I know this week has not proceeded at all to plan," Danielle said and Alex snorted, which made Danielle chuckle again. "But actually I think it has helped you. I think some things are beginning to come through for you, yes?"

Alex shut her eyes briefly as the fear of what she needed to do when she got home twisted itself around her belly. "They are. I'm scared of what I know I have to do next. But I think I know now that I *have* to do it."

"When will you talk to her?"

Alex swallowed. "Sunday. Tomorrow I will be too tired and I will need a bit of time to think about just what I want to say, and how."

"And will it be final? Are you ready to leave her?"

"Danielle, I don't know if *ready* is the right word. I haven't even thought about the practicalities of it—which one of us keeps the flat, for example. I guess Terri would—she always wanted it more than me anyway. But where I will go if I'm the one that moves out—"

"In the short-term you will come to us, obviously," Danielle cut in, her tone brooking no argument.

"Thank you," Alex whispered, turning her gaze to the window to avoid other passengers seeing her glistening eyes. "But," she continued, her voice stronger with her conviction, "it is the right thing to do. I know that much now."

It seemed surreal, to be saying it, to be planning to announce to Terri on Sunday that they were over. But they couldn't go on like they had been, that much was certain.

"I am with you, all the way," Danielle said. "Always."

Alex gripped the phone tighter, as if somehow that would pull Danielle nearer to her. She would give anything for a big hug from her friend right now.

"Thanks, Danielle, that means the world to me."

Chapter 13

THE FOUR HOURS OF SLEEP Alex had managed on the plane were nowhere near enough. Her eyelids refused to fully open and her brain was functioning just enough to meet the driver from the car service, but not for much more. She dozed in the back of the car as he returned her to the flat in Wimbledon. When they pulled up in front of the mansion block she and Terri called home, the nerves and fear returned in full force.

She was equal parts surprised, annoyed, and relieved when she walked into the flat to find it empty. It was only eight thirty in the morning—where on earth could Terri be? Still, at least she didn't have to face her just yet. She wasn't entirely comfortable with how happy that thought made her.

Feeling guilty at the knowledge she had more time on her own, finally Alex summoned the energy to unpack and put some washing on. As she sat at the breakfast bar sipping a hot tea, she was at a loss as to what to do next with the day. Not knowing when Terri would be back was awkward and knotted her stomach with tension.

She took her drink into the living room and flopped onto the sofa. Closing her eyes, she tipped her head back and tried to analyse where her feelings were.

She was scared, yet, at the same time, more determined than she could ever remember being. She'd never been good at doing what was right for herself above all others, but she'd been even worse at it these past few years. She hated to rock the boat, and she detested confrontation. All that meek behaviour had simply led to her being deeply unhappy when she let everyone else get what they wanted to the detriment of her own needs. She gazed around the room—the flat was a case in point. She'd wanted to live somewhere modern, freshly built, where they would have less cause for concern over maintenance and major work. Terri wanted character and a project to work on, and Alex, as ever making sure to keep Terri happy, had demurred. The two years they had spent renovating this place had been incredibly hard work, and the money they'd spent on it still gave her shivers of horror if she added it all up. But Terri was happy, and for a long time that had seemed enough for Alex.

Not anymore.

She knew that wasn't even because of what had happened with Justine. It was everything that had evolved this past year. The promotion had given her a professional validation that was about as high as she'd ever hoped to get. The resentment that change in her working life had elicited from Terri was a shock, and an eye-opener into a part of Terri's personality that she'd not seen before. Then, of course, there was the growing distance between them as both their jobs demanded more of their attention, along with Terri's gravitation towards her night with Liz. All of it had gradually chipped away at Alex's ingrained need to…settle. To put up with things even when, in the deepest recesses of her psyche, she knew they weren't what she wanted.

She sat up suddenly as the front door opened. Reassembling her face into calm composure took significant effort, but she had managed it by the time Terri rushed into the room.

"God, sorry! I ran out to get you a nice breakfast, but it looks like I misjudged when you'd be home." Terri's words tumbled over themselves, and Alex stared at her. Terri was flushed, her hair—normally so perfectly tousled—now looked just…messy. Terri flapped her hands around her head. "Didn't even bother showering, just got right out of bed and up to the baker's. Here," she said, thrusting a large bag in Alex's direction. "Freshly baked croissants and pain au chocolat. Your favourite."

Alex reached slowly for the bag, her jet-lagged mind trying to deal with the whirlwind Terri's entrance had resembled.

"Thanks," she said, her insides churning as a wave of fresh guilt swept over her. *Perfect. I've cheated on her and want to end our relationship and she brings me pastries.* "That's really…nice."

Terri smiled, but her gaze wouldn't quite meet Alex's, and Alex couldn't begin to fathom why, even as she acknowledged to herself how much more comfortable it made her.

"I'm just going to grab a quick shower," Terri said, backing towards the kitchen door, "and then I'll put some fresh tea on, yes?"

The smell of coffee woke her. She opened her eyes as the scent wafted strongly past her nostrils. In the next moment, the bed dipped beside her and she turned to see Terri perched on the edge of it.

"Hey," Terri said, a hesitant smile on her lips. "Didn't think I should let you sleep too much longer."

"What time is it?" Alex asked, her voice croaky from sleep.

"Just after one. You've had about three hours."

"Great." She rubbed at her eyes. Breakfast had been awkward, only made easier by Alex recounting stories of what Montreal was like in the snow, and the meetings and training sessions she'd shared. After they'd eaten, Alex had made her excuses and climbed into bed; she definitely needed more sleep if she was going to survive the day.

Terri smiled again, but there was a twitchiness to her body, her gaze again darting to Alex and away, as it had earlier.

Pushing herself upright to lean against the headboard, Alex reached for the coffee Terri had placed on the bedside table. "Thanks," she said, raising the mug to her mouth.

"You're welcome." Terri rubbed absently at the back of her neck.

"So how was your week? You haven't said much about it."

"Oh, it was good. Yeah. Really good." Terri stood suddenly and opened the wardrobe. "Did you get out much in the evenings in Montreal?"

Alex was beyond glad Terri had her back to her at that moment, but she still willed herself not to flush. "Not much. Wasn't that sort of trip."

Was this how Terri had felt, in that week after she first slept with Liz, before telling Alex? The gnawing dread in her insides at the lies she was already having to tell to cover her tracks? The fear that something in her eyes, or a blush across her cheeks, would give her away? Alex was horrified at the level of anxiety already coursing through her body. How would she keep this up until she felt able to sit down and talk properly with Terri? Given how awful keeping this secret was making her feel, she'd barely make it to the end of the day.

She sighed. They were like strangers, making polite small talk, not being able to look at each other. It was almost amusing, yet unbearably sad.

"You hungry?" Terri asked into the awkward silence, turning to face Alex again.

"I could eat."

"Want to go out for lunch? Those croissants were okay, but I could do with something substantial. I wondered about that new Mexican place up in the Village."

Alex nodded. "Sounds great." Being out of the flat might help—having other people around, things to observe and talk about, given that they didn't seem to know what to converse about otherwise.

They walked up to the Village. It was a good stretch of the legs that Alex needed. The extra sleep had helped, but her head was still woolly from jet lag. It was a typical November day in London—grey clouds scudded across the sky, the breeze fresh but nowhere near as cold as in Montreal. They talked about inconsequential things—the weather, football, what food they hoped to eat shortly. It was a tad more comfortable than they'd been in the flat, but not by much, and Alex was panicking that lunch would be a stumbling fiasco of long pauses and stilted words. At the same time, she was grateful for the distraction of their surroundings because she definitely wasn't awake enough to have "the talk" with Terri today.

The Mexican restaurant was busy, but they were seated quickly, not too far from the front window, and were soon perusing menus.

"Great, they do the enchiladas I was craving," Terri said.

Alex smiled. "And the chimichanga that I like too. I'm too jet-lagged to have worked out what else to eat if that wasn't on the menu."

Terri smiled, and it was the easiest they'd been with each other since the day started.

The waitress appeared and they ordered their food. Just as she walked off, Terri's phone rang.

"Sorry," she said, glancing at the display. "I need to get this." She stood and walked out of the restaurant, talking animatedly. Alex watched her go, wondering who was calling her at lunchtime on a Saturday. Presumably work. Terri had looked tired when she'd brought the coffee to Alex, her eyes sporting hints of dark circles beneath them. Maybe she'd thrown herself into her work during the week as a distraction from all that was wrong between them.

She glanced out of the window and her heart rate picked up a notch. Terri was gesticulating wildly with her free hand, the other keeping her mobile pressed closed to her ear. Alex wasn't an expert at lip-reading, but the words *not now* were easy to pick up before Terri turned away from Alex's view and took a couple of paces away from the restaurant. Alex sipped her lemonade, her mind swirling but her tiredness preventing her from latching on to any particular conclusion about what she'd just witnessed.

Two minutes later Terri was back at the table.

"Sorry, work again."

Alex frowned. "Even you don't work Saturdays that often. What's going on?"

Terri flushed. "Well, since Liz moved teams—" she flushed even more "—we've been down a person on the contracts side. Now this big deal's cropped up and there aren't enough of us to do everything."

Alex had flinched only slightly at the mention of Liz's name, immediately dismissing any jealousy she might feel given the new circumstances they faced.

"It must be some deal," she commented, moving them past the awkward moment.

Terri launched rapidly into a narrative of what she was working on, and Alex breathed an inward sigh of relief as their lunch date settled into something entirely impersonal.

Justine listened to the voicemail with a frown. Christina this time. Sylvie had called last night. Justine was avoiding them, and they knew it. She hadn't spoken to either of them since Sylvie had told her that she couldn't make it to Gabrielle's on Tuesday.

Right before Justine took Alex home and her week got shot to hell.

The message from Christina was much blunter than Sylvie's had been, her tone short.

"If you don't call us we're going to kick your door down. Stop hiding and talk to us."

A reluctant smile spread across her face. Knowing Christina, she really would kick the door down, probably wearing those big motorcycle boots she lived in throughout the winter.

Justine huffed out a breath and sat back on the bed. She'd only just woken and it was already noon; her Friday night had passed by in a blur of one too many beers, a large pizza, a couple of movies she'd found on Netflix, and finished with a few chapters of a book until the small hours of the morning. She'd tried everything she could to fill her mind with anything except images of Alex. Seeing her that afternoon as she waited for her cab to the airport had only intensified Justine's confusing maelstrom of thoughts about the woman. Even across three lanes of busy road, the connection between them had been ridiculously intense. Alex's words from Thursday continued to rattle through her brain; she struggled to remember to be angry at Alex for what she'd done.

She stared at her phone. She ought to talk to her friends, if for no other reason than to tell them she was okay. But telling them everything that happened this week was overdue too; she knew that.

She breathed out slowly, then typed a text to Christina.

How about a late lunch today? My place?

They arrived just after two, both wearing concerned looks as Justine opened the door.

"Hey, I'm okay. Really," Justine said, guilt eating at her as they stared at her. She ushered them in. "It's been a crazy week," she said as they peeled off their coats and she hung them up.

Sylvie pulled her into a hug, and Justine clung on harder than she would have imagined. Christina was next, although she backed up her hug with the words "Don't shut us out again. We're your friends" whispered sharply in her ear.

Justine smiled as she pulled away. "Yes, ma'am."

They walked through to the kitchen, and her guests leaned against the small breakfast bar while she busied herself opening the wine they'd brought. When they each had a glass in hand, the questions started.

"Where have you been all week?"

"Are you sure you're okay?"

"Whoa, guys. Give me a chance to answer!"

Christina gave Justine a stern look while Sylvie looked sheepish. Justine gestured towards the living room and they all settled on the couch.

She exhaled a long, slow breath. "On Tuesday, at Gabrielle's, Alex and I talked a lot over dinner, and through a couple of glasses of wine. It was... really good." She blinked. "We had a lot in common, and we made each other laugh. It felt...wonderful, to be making that kind of connection with someone again, just like you said." She glanced at Sylvie, who gave her a small smile. "Then, suddenly, she got up to leave. I didn't think I'd done or said anything to scare her off—" Christina snorted softly "—but she seemed really keen to get out of there. I asked her why, and she said she was tired, but she wouldn't meet my eyes." Justine dared a glance at Sylvie, whose face was a mask of serenity, even as her eyes narrowed. "I...I didn't want to say goodnight. I was having such a good time. I persuaded her to stay out a little longer, and took her dancing at the drag bar."

Sylvie shifted slightly but her face remained masklike. Christina raised her eyebrows.

"And?" she said.

"And...we danced some more, and somehow, I don't know how really, something just...shifted between us."

Sylvie shook her head slightly and frowned.

"Look, before you go jumping on me," Justine said, her hackles rising, "I honestly don't know how it happened, okay? I didn't push it. I didn't once lay on the charm. I just... God, she was there, and she looked so good, and I felt so...new and happy, being with her. The next thing I know, we're grinding out a slow number together and I just..." She looked up at the ceiling. "I kissed her. It was incredible."

"Oh, *chérie*," Sylvie whispered.

"Then it just seemed like the best idea in the world to take her home. And she agreed, without any hesitation. Only, when we got back here, I couldn't, um, well, I couldn't really wait." She blushed slightly. "I kind of had her up against the front door."

This time Christina snorted loudly, and both she and Sylvie looked over to the front door, as if expecting to see evidence of the passion that had scorched it only a few days ago.

"Okay, okay, so she spent the night. Now what?" Christina asked.

Justine shook her head. "That's the thing, she didn't."

"Didn't what?" Sylvie asked, her face scrunched up adorably in a confused look.

"She didn't stay the night. She left. Right after she came." Justine's blush deepened. It was mortifying to admit.

She was beyond grateful that neither of her friends laughed.

"She...what?" Christina said, her eyes wide.

"She left. Like, at lightning speed. It turns out she has a partner back home. Admittedly it's on the rocks, but still..." She trailed off as Alex's words repeated in her brain. She'd looked so distraught, and it tugged at Justine still.

"She told you that as she left?" Christina looked confused.

"Oh, no. I forgot you didn't know this bit." Justine exhaled loudly. "I saw her at work the next day—she works at RCS. She led a training session I had to attend."

"Holy. Crap." Christina's eyes were now so wide, Justine almost laughed. Sylvie was opening and closing her mouth but not making any sound, clearly at a complete loss for words.

Justine pushed her hands through her hair and sighed. "So I persuaded her to go for a drink that night. I really wanted to understand why she'd sprinted away from me when I thought what we'd started was so good. And that's when she told me she's in a relationship." Bile rose as she spoke the words—no matter how much Alex had tried to explain on Thursday evening, Justine still had that reaction.

"Oh, shit," Sylvie murmured. "Oh, Justine, I am *so* sorry."

Justine shrugged, feigning an indifference she really didn't feel. "Not your fault."

"I cannot help thinking it is. If I hadn't cancelled that night, then—"

Justine held up a hand. "Wait. I am not twelve and in need of adult supervision. This is all on me."

She leaned forwards to retrieve her wine glass and took a hearty mouthful. "So there you have it. I finally attempted to do the right thing and it backfired spectacularly." She tried—and failed—to keep the bitterness out of her tone. "The thing is, the thing I just don't get, is that I would never in a million years have said Alex was the cheating kind. I know I only spent two evenings with her, but..." She looked at both of them in turn. "She just seemed too nice for that. She told me her partner had cheated on

113

her, quite recently, and it's all a bit of mess. She also said she's never done this before, but I just don't know what to believe. I do know it hurts like hell," she confessed in a small voice.

Sylvie touched her arm, tugging her into a gentle hug. "Justine, I don't know where to start. What a week you have had." She shook her head. "I feel the same as you about Alex. She did not strike me as someone who would play around. I only spent a couple of hours with her, so I don't really know what I am basing that on, but I cannot help thinking that what she said was true. That she is not that kind of person normally."

Justine sighed. "I know. But you know how I feel about cheating."

Christina snorted again, and Justine and Sylvie looked at her. Christina held up her hands. "Hey, look, you're my best friend and I love you. But, God, sometimes you can be such an idiot."

Justine's mouth fell open. "Gee, thanks, *buddy*," she said, hurt at both the words and their blunt delivery.

"Sorry, that came out harder than I planned." Christine patted Justine's knee. "I just...look, I hate to burst your bubble, but I think you're deluding yourself if you think Alex is the first woman you've slept with these past eighteen months who was cheating on someone with you."

Justine rocked back in her seat and her insides turned to ice. "I... What?"

Christina stared at her. "Seriously? You really believe every woman of the plenty you've had since Nadia were all unattached?"

"I...I guess I assumed..."

"Yeah, you *assumed*. But chances are that more than a few were having some fun on the side. I don't condone it, at all, from any of them. But I don't think it's fair to paint Alex as this terrible person in comparison to everyone else you've had. Actually, I find myself applauding her honesty, even if it was after the fact. But at least she told you. She didn't string you along for the week, making you think something more might be possible."

Justine sipped more of her wine, her mind reeling. She thought back over all the women she'd been intimate with since Nadia. Some she couldn't remember, but a lot she could. If she thought hard enough, she could separate the ones who'd insisted they go back to Justine's apartment rather than their place. The ones who said they couldn't spend the night and left soon after orgasms had been exchanged. Were those the ones playing around? How had this never occurred to her?

She'd been so wrapped up in her own misery, she'd never thought it through.

All she'd sought, every time, was just a few hours where she could forget and simply feel. She hadn't cared enough about the women in her bed to bother wondering what their stories were. She'd just made sure they both had a good time, then said their goodbyes.

"Are you okay?" Sylvie murmured, and Justine shook herself out of her reverie.

"Yeah," she said, shaking her head. "Just realising I have been, as Christina so succinctly put it, an idiot. I...I never cared who the other women were, what their stories were. I guess in that respect we're even—I used them just as much as they used me." It was an uncomfortable truth to swallow.

"But Alex doesn't seem to fit that mould, does she?" Sylvie's voice was gentle but her gaze was probing. "There's something different about her, isn't there?"

Justine sighed and put down her glass. She ran her hands through her hair, pushing it back off her face.

"Yes. There was something between us, way more than just sexual. It was...amazing."

"So what do you want to do about that?" Christina asked.

"I have no idea. I mean, now I know we work for the same company, I could contact her, but no matter how incredible that connection was between us, what's the use?" She ticked off the points on her fingers. "She's in a relationship, however bad that is for her right now. She cheated on her partner with me, which makes me question a lot of things about her. She's three thousand miles away." She looked up at them. "Why am I even having this conversation with you?" She laughed, but it held no mirth.

Sylvie leaned forwards. "Because every time you say her name, something lights up in your face. And it is a long, long time since we saw that happen to you, *chérie*."

"I know," Justine whispered, swallowing the lump that had formed in her throat.

"Okay, so it doesn't have to be her, given all the negatives you just listed," Christina chimed in. "But isn't it good to know you can feel that way again about a woman, after all this time? Does it make you want to try and find that now, with someone more accessible?"

Justine sighed. "God, maybe. I don't know. I think…I think maybe I need a little time to get over this week, to start with. But, yeah, maybe it's time to start looking for something more than the hookups."

As she said the words, the truth of them sank in to her soul.

Yes, if there was one thing her experience with Alex had given her, it was the desire to find that certain someone. A woman who made her feel all the things Alex had.

First, though, she needed to forget about Alex. And that wouldn't be easy.

Chapter 14

"Tea?" Terri asked as they kicked off their boots.

"Yes, that would be great."

Alex watched Terri saunter off to the kitchen. It had been one of the strangest lunches they'd ever had. They had skirted around each other and a multitude of inconsequential topics of conversation, as if they were merely friendly acquaintances, rather than partners who had been together for five years.

She walked into the bedroom to change into her pyjamas. It was still only four in the afternoon, but she had absolutely no intention of doing anything else on this dreary Saturday than sit in front of the TV. The food at lunch had been good and she was feeling more than a little sleepy again. However, she needed to try to stay awake as long as possible now, so some football, then an action movie should do the trick.

She'd just got settled on the sofa when Terri returned with their tea.

"You're in your pyjamas already?" Terri looked quizzically at Alex, her frown deep.

"Well, yeah. Not going anywhere now, so thought I would get comfy."

"Oh."

"What?"

Terri slumped down next to her on the sofa. "Nothing. I...I guess I thought we would go out for that drink later. You know, at Denise's."

"Denise?"

"From the tennis club." Terri exhaled sharply and stared at Alex. "It was her birthday last week, probably a big one, but she didn't want to make a huge deal about it. She invited a bunch of us over for drinks and nibbles. I told you about it ages ago." Her tone held irritation, and it set Alex's teeth on edge.

She tried to moderate her own tone when she finally did think she could speak. "No, Terri, you didn't mention this at all. Ever. And I'm sorry, but surely you understand I just don't have the energy to go out again. Not after flying back this morning." Even as she spoke she was questioning herself. Had Terri mentioned the party? Alex was pretty sure she hadn't. Although, these past couple of weeks they'd not really talked to each other, just exchanged odd sentences here and there. It was highly possible Terri had told her and she'd just not listened. Forgetting something like that was just not like her, though. They had so few social engagements together, surely if Terri had told her about it, she'd have popped it in the calendar on her phone, and she'd only looked at that yesterday and not seen anything...

"I could have sworn I told you." There was a whine to Terri's voice that Alex found nauseatingly unappealing.

"Well, you didn't." Alex tried hard not to snap but didn't succeed.

They sat in silence for a few moments; Terri's fingers worried at a loose thread on her jeans, and her foot tapped in a distinctly annoying manner.

Alex's fight left her in a rush of tiredness and apathy. "You should go anyway. I mean, you're closer to the tennis club people than I am."

"You wouldn't mind?"

Alex sighed. Terri sounded almost as relieved as Alex was at the prospect of more time apart. What a farce this was. Tomorrow, she would definitely find the courage to start the conversation they really needed to share.

"Not at all," she said, injecting a false cheeriness into her tone. "I'm going to sit here and watch loud action movies to keep me awake."

Terri laughed. "Sounds like a great plan. Cool. I'll head out about seven, try and get back before the last Tube." She looked delighted at the plans they'd just made, and Alex tried hard not to feel insulted. She could hardly complain; the idea of the evening on her own was blissful. She only just held back a sad laugh at what they had become.

She waved a hand. "Whatever time you like, no worries. Just promise me, if you find me asleep on the sofa when you get in, wake me up and put me to bed, okay?"

Terri grinned. "Deal."

Alex shuddered as Justine's hands swept over her naked torso. Her hands were strong but her touch was light. Her fingertips feathered over Alex's hard nipples, and her lips swiftly followed, sucking and licking until Alex was writhing and begging for more. Justine smiled and flicked her hair away from her face as she descended to Alex's mouth and kissed her fiercely, the heat of it exploding all over Alex's body. The gunfire that followed was loud and continuous, then Linda Hamilton was yelling and leaping through the door with her gun clutched in her hands and—

Alex awoke with a start. *Terminator* was still playing on the TV. She had a wrench in her neck where she'd slouched to one side and drifted off. Remnants of the dream lingered, part fantasy and part memories of actual touches and kisses that had set her on fire less than a week ago.

She swallowed, aware of the throbbing between her legs, the intense ache that needed to be answered. She slid a hand down inside her pyjamas and wasn't surprised to discover how wet she was. Torturing herself with remembrances of Justine's mouth and hands, she slipped her fingers over her swollen outer lips, arching up into the touch as a shiver ran through her. Placing a finger on each side of her already engorged clit, she stroked firmly and rapidly, Justine's face filling her mind as she got closer and closer. When it hit, her orgasm was a rolling wave of heat that covered her from head to toe. It pulsed through her fingers, but her exhalations of pleasure were tinged with shame. Dreams and fantasies of Justine were forbidden territory, yet she had travelled there so easily.

Far too easily.

She pulled her hand from between her legs and stumbled to the bathroom to clean up. As she washed her hands, she gazed at her flushed face in the mirror with detachment. Her body still tingled with the aftermath of the pleasure she had just bestowed on it, but her mind swirled with the mix of emotions thinking about Justine had stirred in her again. A deep, inexplicable longing mixed with hopelessness.

After drying her hands she pushed her hair back from her tired-looking face. Her eyes were puffy again, and she wanted nothing more than to collapse in bed, but it was still too early, only just past nine. She needed to make it to at least ten before she gave in. Her stomach rumbled, and she padded down the hall to the kitchen. After making tea and toast, she returned to the movie, forcing herself to sit ramrod straight on the sofa so she wouldn't drift off again. And trying oh so hard to push back the fantasy of Justine sitting beside her, her hands reaching for Alex, her mouth nuzzling Alex's neck…

The next time she woke, Terri was attempting to get her upright.

"Come on, sleepyhead." Terri's voice was amused, and Alex grunted as she allowed herself to be pulled to her feet.

"What time is it?" she asked, rubbing her eyes.

"Midnight. Come on, get to bed."

Alex shuffled out of the room with Terri following, switching off lights. "Did you have a nice time?"

"I did. Do you know how long you were asleep on the sofa?"

"No idea." Alex yawned. "I've been drifting off all evening. I'll probably wake really early tomorrow now."

Terri frowned. "Maybe. If you do, don't wake me."

Alex slipped under the duvet. "I'll try not to," she said, yawning again and immediately rolling over onto her side, snuggling down into the warmth of the bed.

A few minutes later Terri was beside her, but she didn't reach for Alex as she said goodnight.

Alex fell asleep with relief coursing through her.

———

Christina and Sylvie left a little after ten. They both lingered in their goodbye hugs, and Justine let them. She wasn't ashamed to admit she needed the comfort of their affection. They'd talked on and off about Alex through the afternoon, as they slowly munched their way through the risotto Justine had prepared. Her friends were trying to understand just what about Alex had affected Justine so, in order to compile a profile of the kind of woman they could set Justine up with next.

"I told you guys, I need a little while yet before I think about dating again." Justine was firm, pointing a finger at them to emphasise her point.

"We know," Sylvie said. "We aren't pushing you, I promise. But we just want to know what we should be looking for."

"We both know a lot of women, you know that," Christina said, smiling as Justine raised her eyebrows and sniggered. "You know what I mean. We can help. We don't have to, of course, if that's what you'd rather."

Justine shrugged. "No idea. Give me some time and I'll let you know. But thank you for your support. It means a lot to me."

Sylvie leaned across the table to plant a soft kiss on Justine's cheek. "We love you, *chérie*. We will always be here for you."

Justine had shed a few tears then, and all talk of Alex, and dating, and relationships was dropped for the rest of the evening.

After they left, Justine wasn't ready to sleep. Her mind churned. Talking about Alex so much through the day had left her in a deep funk she couldn't seem to shake. She really needed to start forgetting about her, but she had no idea where to start. Images of Alex ran through her brain like one of those old, jerky home movies. How she had looked losing herself in the music on the dance floor. The openness she had displayed as they talked. The dry humour she'd often revealed. The wild disarray of her hair when she'd been pressed between Justine's body and the front door. The feel of her breasts in Justine's hands, the soft mounds a perfect fit for her cupped fingers.

She groaned and strode around the apartment, her hands in her hair. Why did she keep torturing herself like this? There was no point, none at all. If she didn't stop soon, she'd have no chance of moving on, of trying to look at other women without comparing them to Alex.

She switched off all the lights, cleaned her teeth, and climbed into bed. The cool cotton sheets were deliciously sensuous against her skin, and her nipples hardened in response. She moaned. Alex's face was in front of her again, her mouth inviting a kiss. Justine ran her hands up her body to her breasts and moaned louder as she cupped herself, pulling at her nipples as she envisioned Alex doing exactly that to her. She closed her eyes tight.

She was hopeless.

Okay, just this once. One more fantasy, and tomorrow, she would move on.

She pinched her nipples once more, then, leaving one hand to alternate between each breast, she moved her other hand slowly down over her abdomen, imagining it was Alex's mouth marking a trail down to the apex of her thighs. As she parted her trimmed curls with her middle finger and slipped into the abundant wetness waiting for her, she arched her hips off the bed. Imagining Alex positioning herself between her legs, she stroked slowly, gently, dipping just inside her entrance and back out again, over and over. Alex's tongue would be this gentle, at first, tasting and exploring, teasing Justine until she gasped out her need. As she fantasised about Alex's tongue thrusting inside her, she plunged one finger in, then rapidly added another. She pressed the heel of her hand firmly against her clit, squeezed a nipple with her other hand, and rocked on the fingers buried deep within. With images of Alex in her head, and Alex's name whispering from her lips, it didn't take long. She cried out as she came, her hips twisting wildly as she rode out every last moment of her orgasm.

She flopped back on the bed, her fingers still enclosed inside herself, her free hand drifting lazily up and down her torso, her mind allowing her a few last images and fantasies of Alex. She would smile from between Justine's legs before slowly crawling back up Justine's body to kiss her...

Justine smiled at the image, but the smile slid off her face as other thoughts and pictures invaded. Alex's faceless partner, completely oblivious to Alex's deception. Alex's own pain at what she said her partner had done to her. Justine thought it probably was true, but given that Alex had cheated on her partner with Justine, who knew what was truth or fact and what were words merely said to smooth things over. At the end of the day, that was always going to be what held her back from pursuing this crazy dream of Alex and her together somehow. Alex had cheated on her partner with Justine. No matter how much Alex tried to explain that away, Justine didn't think she'd ever be able to trust her.

Suddenly cold after the heat of her orgasm, she pulled the covers over herself and lay on her side, willing sleep to come soon and give her a respite from her emotions.

Chapter 15

THE CLOCK ON THE DVD player told Alex it was just after six thirty when she crumpled up the sheet of notepaper and added it to the pile in front of her. Five attempts at working out what to say, and none of them seemed remotely right.

Alex reached for her mug and grimaced as she swallowed tea that was now cold. She stood, grabbing the pile of discarded notes, and quietly walked along the hall to the kitchen. Terri was still dead to the world, and Alex was more than happy to let her sleep on. As she boiled the kettle, she slumped against the worktop. Perhaps trying to plan what to say wasn't one of her best ideas.

The problem was she'd never actually broken up with anyone like this before, as a sort of preemptive strike. She'd finally dumped Jade in a furious phone call, when one particularly painful emotional ploy from Jade had pushed the very last of Alex's buttons. Before that, her two previous long-term relationships with women had both been ended by the other party, not Alex.

This one was different in so many ways. Terri was someone she'd thought she'd be with, well, forever. Despite all the small things that had increased her unhappiness over the last year, culminating in Terri's ultimate betrayal, the comfort and security their relationship had initially given her was tough to leave behind. Now, of course, her own shame over the events in Montreal made it a no-brainer. They were over, no doubt about it. But planning on sitting down and just calmly saying it was giving her indigestion. She had no idea how to do it—hence the notepaper and her stumbling efforts to find the right words.

She had to do it today. Yesterday had been so awkward; they couldn't go on any longer. Surely Terri felt it too. It couldn't really come as a surprise. The biggest issue Alex now faced was just how honest to be.

Did she tell Terri about Justine?

Hanging her head in her hands, she shivered with nauseous fear. She could only imagine Terri's anger and hurt if she did. The accusations she'd throw Alex's way. Words like *hypocrite. Double standards.*

Cheater.

She sucked in a breath. Terri had told her about Liz. In good conscience she couldn't avoid telling Terri about Justine. She'd just have to start the conversation and somehow find the words.

And she'd just have to face the consequences when she did. She knew she would hurt Terri, but she hoped they'd be able to rescue something out of the ruins of their relationship, and she couldn't do that unless she was completely honest with Terri.

By the time Terri surfaced at ten, Alex felt physically sick. She'd taken to pacing the living room, words flitting around her mind and forming themselves into ridiculously jumbled sentences.

She stopped in the middle of the room, her shins bumping the coffee table, when Terri appeared in the doorway looking rumpled and sleepy.

"What are you doing?" Terri's face shrank into a frown. "You woke me up."

Alex swallowed hard. "We need to talk," she blurted.

Terri waved a hand dismissively. "Not until I've had coffee." She marched out of the room before Alex could speak again.

Jesus, this was hard enough without that kind of attitude from Terri. Anger formed, low and hot in Alex's belly. She stomped out of the living room and down the hallway to the kitchen.

"No," she said as she entered the room, then stopped in her tracks as Terri hurriedly set her mobile phone down on the counter. What was that about?

"No what?" Terri said, her tone as tight as her frowning face.

Alex pulled her gaze away from Terri's phone. "No, it can't wait. We need to talk. Now." Alex shifted from one foot to the other. "You know we do," she said, her tone softening.

Terri stirred her coffee. "I take it you've done some thinking while you've been away. I think I can guess what your conclusion is."

"We can't go on like this, Terri."

There, it was out there. A start, at least.

"And whose fault is that?" The harsh words, and Terri's icy tone, did nothing to quell the anger roiling inside Alex. Quite the opposite, in fact.

"Seriously? You want to blame *me* for this?" Being so blunt, so confrontational wasn't like Alex. But then, a lot of things she'd done lately weren't like her.

Terri folded her arms across her chest. "I've apologised until I'm blue in the face. I've done everything I can to get us back on track. None of it has been good enough for you. You refuse to give us a chance."

Alex shook her head slowly. How could this be happening? How could they have such vastly different views on the situation? Well, at least she had her answer—they were definitely over if this was how far apart they were.

Pointing a trembling finger at Terri, Alex said, "Don't you dare. Don't you fucking *dare* try and make this all my fault." The heat of her anger flushed her chest, her neck. "A lot of women—" she thought of Justine, then immediately swept the thought away "—would have left you on the spot. A lot of women would never have given you a second chance. *I* did. I gave you that chance. And what did you do? Keep cancelling sessions with Gloria. Keep working all hours and getting home at crazy times. Keep accusing me of not moving on quicker from the pain of you shagging that...that woman." She was shaking all over now, and reached out to steady herself against the door frame. "Don't you fucking *dare* pin this on me."

Terri glared at her, her eyes narrowed and her body rigid. "Oh, right, Miss Holier-than-thou. Because you're completely blameless in this, aren't you? Alex never does anything wrong. Alex is Little Miss fucking Perfect."

"What the hell?" Alex took a step forwards, throwing her hands in the air. "I've never claimed to be any of those things."

Terri snorted. "Not out loud, maybe. But it's in everything you do and say, and you expected me to be the same. You treated me like some knight in shining armour, rescuing you from that bitch, Jade. Have you any idea how fucking hard it was to live up to that all the time? How I always felt like I had to be so perfect, constantly, so that I never let you down?"

Alex stared at her, at Terri's livid expression, at Terri's mouth curled up in an ugly snarl. "I...I never expected that from you. And you never told me any of that." Alex's voice broke. "Why didn't you tell me?"

Terri uncrossed her arms and took a few steps away from Alex, leaning against the fridge and huffing out an extended breath. "Because you were never here. You were working so bloody hard on trying to get that directorship." She looked away for a few moments. When she looked back, her mouth was set in a grim line. "I guess I gave up. It was easier." She shrugged. "So, yeah, I shagged Liz. She wanted me. You didn't."

It wasn't the words themselves that felt like a punch to the gut, but the way they were delivered, as if Terri really didn't care how much they would hurt. Alex never thought she'd experience this callousness from the woman she'd spent five years of her life with.

The tears that pricked at her eyes annoyed her, and she swiped them away. Of all the ways she'd thought this conversation would go, she hadn't planned for this scenario at all. There was no way she was going to mention what happened in Montreal now; it would only seem as if she were trying to get some revenge, and she refused to stoop that low. No matter how much more hurt Terri had piled on her during the last ten minutes. She was staggered by how quickly, relatively, everything had unravelled between them. Four months ago they were still a couple in every sense of the word— struggling a little, yes, but not beyond redemption, she'd thought.

Now, here in their kitchen, they were strangers who simply happened to be breathing the same air.

Gathering every last bit of strength she could muster, she inhaled deeply and straightened her spine. Enough.

"I don't think there's anything more we have to say to each other. I'm going to shower, then I'm going to pack." It was such an easy decision to make, requiring very little thought. Moving out was the only option; there was absolutely no way she wanted to stay under the same roof as Terri now the bitter truth was out.

"Pack?" Terri's confused look was almost amusing.

"I'm leaving," Alex pronounced, proud of how strong her voice sounded. "I'll take enough now to move in with Danielle and arrange something with you later to get the rest." She locked her gaze on Terri. "And you need to think about what you want to do with the flat. I don't want it." Her laugh was hollow. "I never really did, actually. So you either buy me out of my share, or we sell up."

"But...but I can't afford to buy you out. And I love this flat!"

"Tough," Alex said.

———————————⊶∘⊷∘⊷———————————

"She said *what*?" Danielle sounded outraged, but Alex was too weary to take that on.

"I know, but can we maybe talk through that later? Right now I just need to get sorted out. I think it will take me about an hour to figure out what I need for the next couple of weeks at least."

"We will be there as soon as we can. Is she still there?"

Alex snorted. "Nope. Ran out of here the minute I'd finished in the shower. She looked genuinely shocked at my decision to leave. Barely said two words to me as she went out the door."

"Well, at least that makes it easier. Unless she comes back..."

"I don't think she will." She sighed. "I think she knows it's best if she stays out of the way while I do this."

"Alex, I hate to ask this, but... Do you trust her not to do anything stupid with what you leave behind? I mean, are you sure you wouldn't want to take all of it now? I am sure we could obtain a van at short notice."

"No, it's okay. I think it'll be fine. And I still need to have that discussion with her anyway, about who gets what. As bad as this morning was, I don't think she's anything except hurt and angry, not crazy."

"Hurt!" Danielle snorted. "How dare—"

"I know," Alex said; she needed to focus on packing, not dissecting.

"Sorry."

"It's okay. I'm feeling the same way, but I just need my energy for other things right now, okay? We can thrash it all out later over a large glass of wine, yes?"

Danielle exhaled. "Of course. Although more than one, I suspect."

Alex smiled. "Thank you."

After hanging up, she sat for a moment on the bed. Danielle and Beth were coming through for her again; she really couldn't ask for better friends. This was one of the hardest days she'd ever had to deal with, yet love still

127

infused it. She lay back on top of the duvet, taking a few minutes just to breathe. Then she slapped her hands on her thighs.

"Come on," she muttered. "Just get this done."

Within an hour she had one suitcase packed and a pile of clothes waiting on the bed to go into a second case. She folded methodically, her brain thankfully restful in the mundanity of tucking in sleeves and doing up buttons. With the lid pressed down tightly on the second case, her work in the bedroom was done. She moved both cases out to the hallway, then returned to the bedroom to pull a small backpack from the bottom of the wardrobe before heading to the bathroom.

Danielle and Beth arrived a few minutes after she'd packed up her makeup and toiletries, and her friends embraced her warmly as she let them into the flat.

"How are you?" Danielle asked, her hands on Alex's shoulders, fingers squeezing.

Alex shrugged beneath the warmth of Danielle's hands. "I'm okay. A bit numb, really."

"Much more to do?" Danielle looked around the hallway at the small collection of goods Alex had accumulated.

"Just want to grab a few pieces from the living room, and then I'm done. Want a drink?"

Beth shook her head after a quick glance at her wife. "No, I think we're good. I think we just want to get you out of here, actually."

Alex smiled wanly. "Yeah, okay. Probably best." She took a deep breath. "Give me a few minutes."

She walked into the living room. The large bookcase held photos and mementoes that spanned the five years she and Terri had been together. Her eyes misted over as she slowly scanned each shelf. How much of this did she really want? Would looking at stuff like this hurt? Or one day would she look back and regret not taking at least some of it?

Her gaze fell on a larger photo on the middle shelf. She and Terri on Lesbos, four years ago. The photo had been taken by a woman they'd met one day in a café. Alex and Terri had been lounging on one of the outdoor sofas, snuggled up into each other, eyes only for each other and not for the beautiful scenery that surrounded them. The woman had snapped the photo without either of them noticing, and it captured that first year together perfectly—the closeness Alex remembered, the joy she had felt at being cherished by someone as loving as Terri. She sighed. Had that all been an illusion?

Bile rose in her throat. Suddenly she couldn't bear to look at any of it. She turned away; she'd make her decisions on all of that later. Much later.

"Okay," she said, returning to the hallway, where Danielle and Beth were talking quietly. "I'm done. Let's get out of here."

As well as the two cases and the backpack, she had a box of books and files, her gym bag, and a large plastic bag she'd crammed full with all her shoes and boots. Between the three of them, they ferried it all downstairs to Beth's car in one trip.

As Alex closed the front door behind her, her stomach plummeted. The reality hit her like a body blow—she'd just left her partner, her relationship, of five years. That she had no real choice in the matter was irrelevant; it was still excruciating.

"Okay?" Danielle asked when Alex turned away from the door to follow them down the stairs.

"No," she said, swallowing. "But I guess one day I will be."

Chapter 16

THE MORNING'S MEETINGS HAD DRAGGED on. Christmas was only a week away, and Justine couldn't wait for the holiday ease down to start in earnest. Her team was lethargic and disinterested, and she couldn't blame them. For her, these past few weeks had been interminable. She needed a break and smiled as she thought ahead to her plans to spend Christmas with Christina and Sylvie. For once she wouldn't be going home to her parents' place; they'd treated themselves to a ski holiday. Her brother was staying home with his wife and children, and although he'd invited Justine over for Christmas Day, she'd politely declined. Being with her friends, who would understand why she might be a little quiet, would be better than trying to put on a big front with her brother.

She still hadn't lifted herself up from the week Alex had blown into— and out of—her life. She'd spent a lot more time at home since Alex left four weeks ago; her desire to be out at the bars and clubs had disappeared almost overnight. Instead, she'd indulged herself in her love of cooking, often inviting Christina, Sylvie, or both round for a meal after work. She wasn't putting in so much overtime anymore either; her boss had noticed but hadn't given her a hard time over it, as the work was still being done. And that was because Justine was throwing herself into it more, immersing herself in the details to keep her brain from dwelling on thoughts of a woman with luxurious auburn hair and sparkling green eyes.

Opening her laptop as she sat down, she entered her password and dived into her inbox. As usual, one morning taken up with meetings had left her over twenty e-mails to deal with when she returned. She skimmed through them from oldest to newest, deleting the ones she knew she didn't need to read. As she neared the top of the list, a flag on one of them caught her eye. It was marked *Private*, and her brain took a moment to register the sender's name.

Alexandra Saunders.

She pushed away from her desk as if she'd been bitten. *What the—*

Why would Alex be e-mailing her? She was scared to open it.

Scared and curious.

After a few tortured moments, curious won. She clicked it open and read, forcing herself not to skim and actually concentrate on Alex's words.

Dear Justine,

I apologise for e-mailing you at work, but obviously I have no other way of contacting you. I appreciate it's not very professional, but I have at least tagged the message as private to keep other eyes away.

I just wanted to explain some things to you. It's up to you if you feel you want to respond, but that's not why I'm doing it. I just need you to understand what happened and why I'm so sorry for upsetting you.

Back in August, my partner of five years, Terri, cheated on me. A drunken one-night stand with a woman she works with. While we hadn't been doing brilliantly in the year leading up to that, her cheating was the last thing I would have expected from her. She seemed very remorseful, and so we tried to rescue what was left. We went to couples' counselling, but it became rapidly obvious that things were very wrong, and beyond saving. I had just about come to that conclusion when I was asked at short notice to fly to Montreal. The night you and I met for dinner at Gabrielle's, I was so confused and scared about where my life was going. That doesn't necessarily justify what I did that night, but I have to be honest with you about what that night meant for me. Because it wasn't about getting revenge on Terri, or using you to make me feel better somehow. Actually, doing what we did made me feel worse, that I was just as bad as Terri. And I know it upset you hugely given what your ex did to you—finding out you'd been a party to yet another cheater must have been awful for you, and I can only apologise for putting you in that position.

However, what happened between you and me was nothing to do with me and Terri. You talked about the connection we had, and I didn't dare confirm it. But you were right. It was there, and what happened between us was just about us. I wanted you to know that. I hated that you thought you'd been used or that I didn't actually want to be with you and was merely treating you as a symbol of something. It was just you, Justine. And that's also what you gave me that night—you made me feel like someone could find me attractive again. Someone wanted me, as I was, knowing nothing about me or my awful year or any of the things that made me doubt myself.

So I wanted to thank you for that. You may not want to hear that, but as I have now left Terri, and I'm working through all the things I need to get my life moving again, writing to you and saying that to you was high on my list.

I wish you well, Justine, and again, I am sorry for the way I treated you. I hope you can believe it wasn't you; it was just about all the crap happening in my life, and you unfortunately got caught in the middle.

Alex

Justine locked her screen and walked along the corridor to the break room. She made herself a drink and returned to her desk. As she drank her coffee, she slowly reread the e-mail. Three times.

When she'd finished, she sat back in her chair, trying to sift through her reactions to the words. Alex's explanation definitely brought her a little relief from her anger and hurt. Without aiming for the sympathy vote, Alex had shown Justine just what a terrible few months she'd had, and Justine could empathise with that. Even after Alex had blurted out in Hugo's that her partner had cheated on her, somehow Justine still hadn't realised what that must have meant for Alex and how tormented she must have been. Justine sighed. She'd been too busy feeling like the one who'd been crapped on and unable to take Alex's feelings into account.

Alex's e-mail also made her sad. For Alex, and for herself. Because Alex had acknowledged the connection they had, and they couldn't do anything about it. Even if Alex wanted to, which her words didn't suggest.

Justine clasped her hands behind her neck and rocked slightly in her chair. Out of all her conflicting emotions, frustration was the strongest. The universe had conspired to bring them together but in circumstances that made doing anything about it impossible.

What a waste.

———————◦◦◦———————

It was probably the worst Christmas Alex had ever endured, but as she'd assumed before it even started that it was bound to be, somehow she got through it. Danielle and Beth had spent Christmas Day with her at their house, then she had the place to herself as they did family visits on Boxing Day. Alex's mother had offered her a place to stay for the whole week, but she couldn't face it. She'd told her mum before Christmas about splitting up with Terri and she'd been less than understanding.

"I just think, at your age, you need to be thinking about the long-term. Who's going to look after you when you're older if you're single?" Her mum had practically tutted down the phone line. "I know you're upset about what happened, but she said she was sorry and she loves you. Surely you can work it out?"

Alex had huffed a breath. So typical of her mother, who had settled for her lot in life from an early age and turned a blind eye to every affair Alex's father had in the forty years they were married. When he died of a heart attack a few years ago, she claimed she'd lost her soulmate and wore black for two years afterwards. Well, Alex wasn't going to become that. Just because it was good enough for her mother didn't mean she had to put up with it. Good enough wasn't good enough, not for Alex. Not anymore. She might never find it, but she wanted to feel like the woman she was with only had eyes for her, that Alex fulfilled her in every way she needed, and vice versa. But she would take her time looking again. The last few months had taught her that she wasn't being true to herself. She needed some time to find out who the real Alex was before she let anyone else in.

She travelled into the office on the days between Christmas and New Year's, just to have something to do. On New Year's Eve she spent the morning filing and sorting out her office. Over the year, various papers, handbooks, and conference materials had stacked up haphazardly on the shelves, and it felt like the right day to take on the big clean-up. Start the new year with a clean office and no clutter. A metaphor for her entire life.

E-mail traffic had been light all week, as she would have expected, but she took a break from her housekeeping to sit down with a cup of tea around noon and check her inbox. Her gaze narrowed in on an e-mail that had literally just arrived.

From Justine.

She held her breath as she opened it. She'd meant what she said to Justine in her own e-mail before Christmas—and she hadn't written it to get a response. Her message had purely been about purging her own soul of what she felt was unfinished business from that fateful week.

But now she had an e-mail back.

Hi, Alex,

Thank you for writing to me. I needed some time to think through things before I replied. I know you said I didn't have to write back, but I wanted to.

Thank you for your explanation of what that week meant to you. It did help me. I am sorry to hear you and Terri have parted, but at the same time it does sound like it was completely the right thing to do, at least for you. I hope you're okay. As someone who has been in your position, I can guess how you are feeling right now. I hope you have some good support from friends and family. I was lucky to have Christina and Sylvie to help me through my situation.

I am sorry if I hurt you that week with some of the things I said. But I think you know where they came from, and now I have your story I do understand how we happened. Thank you for acknowledging that it was about us, and that connection.

I hope the coming year allows you to move on and do whatever you need to next in your life. My new motto is to always look forwards. I hope you can do the same.

Justine

Alex placed a hand on her chest and closed her eyes. The absolution Justine had just bestowed brought her relief of the highest order. Her immediate reaction was to fire off a thank you in reply, but she paused. Was she deluding herself? If she got into e-mail exchanges with Justine, wasn't that playing dangerously? They'd both spoken in their e-mails of that connection they'd shared. That pull they had towards each other was simmering just under the surface. If they started conversing regularly, wouldn't they be at risk of trying to make something happen out of pretty much impossible circumstances? Alex didn't need that. She needed time to work out who she was, what she wanted, and what she needed. Even if what a large part of her wanted was a gorgeous Canadian woman with blonde, curly hair and pale blue eyes.

With some reluctance Alex closed the e-mail and returned to her tidying.

———— ⋄∘❦∘⋄ ————

"Did it make you feel better, to send her that e-mail?" Christina asked, dipping her bread into the last of her soup.

Justine waggled her hand. "Yes and no."

"Explain."

Standing, Justine reached for Christina's empty bowl and stacked it with her own. She was playing for time and Christina would call her on it soon. The contrasting styles of her friends' support had actually worked well for her over the last few weeks. Sylvie was gentle and nurturing, teasing answers out of Justine in a cautious way. Christina was bolder, more demanding, pushing Justine whenever she appeared to be wriggling out of the hard conversations. It had been a cathartic time—coming to terms with the fact her needs were changing had caused a significant shift in the way she looked at life now.

She took the dirty bowls into the kitchen and stacked them in the dishwasher.

"More wine?" she called out in the direction of the couch where they'd been eating.

"No, I'm fine. Get back in here."

Laughing, she re-joined her friend on the couch. "Okay, I'm here."

"So explain already."

"It did make me feel better, to thank her for the effort she'd made in contacting me. But..." She sighed. "I can't stop thinking about her, and so contacting her just brought her to the forefront of my mind. And I need to get her out of there because I need to move on."

"Yes, you do. I take it she didn't write back."

"No, and that's probably a good thing too." She'd sent her e-mail about a week ago. When no reply came back instantly, she'd been a little hurt, then admonished herself. She really did need to get Alex out of her mind, so no more contact was a good thing. She just wished she could lose the ache that seemed to have taken up residence in her chest since she'd got Alex's e-mail.

"How would you feel about meeting someone? Is it too soon still?"

She stared at Christina. "You've got someone lined up already?"

"Maybe. Only if you really want to. If you need more time, that's totally okay."

She definitely needed more time; she knew that. But at the same time, she wondered how she was ever going to get rid of this crazy yearning for Alex unless she did just get back out there.

"What's she like?" she asked, and smiled as Christina grinned.

———— ◦◦◦ ————

"Toast?"

"Please." Alex smiled at Danielle, then giggled as a sleepy-looking Beth appeared in the kitchen.

"Morning," she mumbled, hauling a chair away from the oak table and plonking herself down in it.

Danielle crossed the room and kissed the top of her wife's head. "Coffee and toast, my love?"

"Mm-hm," Beth replied, tilting her head back for a kiss on the lips.

Alex watched them with a mixture of affection and envy. What they had seemed so…perfect. She aspired to it for herself, but had no idea how to go about finding it.

They ate their first round of toast in record time, and Danielle laughed as Beth and Alex handed her their two empty plates with alacrity. She busied herself putting a second round on and topping up their coffee cups.

"How you doing?" Beth looked at Alex, a warm smile on her face.

"Okay, I guess." Alex shrugged. "I swing so much from sad and confused, to calm, and something that borders on happy, it has my head spinning sometimes."

Danielle placed another plate of toast in front of Alex and wrapped her arms around her from behind.

"You can talk to us anytime, you know? You do not have to keep so much of it to yourself."

"I know, and thanks. But a lot of it is just me working through stuff in my head. I've spoken to a counsellor a couple of times too."

"You have?" Danielle looked startled.

"Yes, through work. We have a contract with an employee assistance programme. It's been helpful. Just on days where I've felt like there was no way forwards and I couldn't even string a coherent thought together."

"Things you cannot share with me?" Danielle's tone was loaded with hurt, but before Alex could respond she held up a hand. "Sorry, that sounded rather petulant and childish. Of course you should talk with whomever you feel can help you best."

Alex grasped Danielle's hand and held on tight. "Sometimes a stranger is just better, somehow. Please don't be offended. I still value your judgement and support. Hugely."

"I know. Please ignore me," Danielle said, winking.

"I'll be glad to see the back of January, I'll tell you that much. It's been non-stop at work."

A month of meetings, of updating training schedules for the forthcoming months. A month of staring at the e-mail from Justine from New Year's Eve that she had retained in her inbox. She didn't know why she hadn't deleted it. Actually, that wasn't entirely true. Somehow, for all sorts of crazy reasons, she still wanted some link to Justine. Something that connected them. She'd never answered it but had been tempted many, many times, despite her vow to follow Justine's motto and look forwards, not backwards.

And thinking of moving forwards made her recall the tense phone call she'd had the day before with Terri, who had made a decision about the flat finally. She'd tried to work out financing to be able to buy Alex out but had failed and had begrudgingly admitted they'd have to sell.

"The good thing is the market's pretty buoyant right now," Terri said, her clipped tone making her displeasure at the situation abundantly clear. "At least it's gone up in value since we bought it."

"Okay. So we came into it with fifty-fifty money, so we'll just split the proceeds down the middle, agreed?"

"Yes, of course. And we'll share the fees too."

"That's fine. Let's just do everything even. I'm okay with that."

Terri huffed out a breath. "I suppose I'll need to do all the estate agent work, be here for viewings, et cetera? I can't imagine you'd be able to do it, given you're living in Crouch End now."

"Yes, unfortunately that's true. I would offer to help, but it makes more sense for you to do it."

"I suppose most viewings can take place without me here at all," Terri mused, and Alex heard the resignation in her voice. "I'll get the flat tidied up and then get it on the market as soon as I can."

"Thank you," Alex said quietly.

"So when do you want to get the last of your stuff?"

"I'll try to do that at the weekend, then it's much less clutter for you to tidy away before they take the photos. I'll let you know when I'll be over. I assume my keys will still work?"

Terri tutted. "Of course they will. I'm not that much of a bitch."

"I didn't mean—"

"And furniture? Anything you particularly want?"

Alex sighed. It was so hard to work with Terri's bitterness. Especially when Alex thought it was completely unwarranted. "I think the only things I want are that chest we used as a coffee table, and the pair of paintings in the bedroom. That okay with you?"

"Fine."

They had ended the call rather abruptly after that, and Alex had spent the rest of the afternoon tucked away in her room, swamped with sadness and reluctant to inflict it on anyone else.

"And how are you feeling about the weekend, about getting the last of your things?" Danielle asked, unwittingly tapping into the very thing Alex was thinking about.

"I think it will upset me. I'm prepared for that. Even though I've known for a while now that this is the right thing, it will make it very final, you know?"

Her friends nodded. "Endings are always painful, whatever form they take," Danielle said. "But I am so proud of you for doing this, and for handling it the way you are. All of it—leaving Terri, not pursuing that woman in Montreal. A clean slate is exactly what you need to move on."

Alex thought guiltily of the e-mail in her inbox. Danielle delivered her next question in a tone dripping with suspicion.

"What is that look for? That frown that crossed your face when I mentioned Montreal?"

Swallowing hard, Alex said quietly, "I still think about her. I…I kept her e-mail. I can't quite seem to delete it."

Beth frowned and Danielle sighed and slumped back in her chair. "Alex, my darling friend. What are you doing? It is bad enough you slept with her while you were still technically with Terri. But the fact that you are still thinking of contacting her is madness. To what end?"

Alex stood up suddenly and began pacing. "I don't know," she said, frustrated both at the line of questioning and her own stupid reluctance to let this go. "I know it's crazy, I do. And I know I have to move on. I just wish—" She'd nearly blurted out her most secret desire, something she'd not dared to voice to anyone, and had barely acknowledged to herself.

"Wish what?" Danielle stared at her.

"Nothing. It's nothing." Alex turned away, unable to maintain eye contact under Danielle's withering glare.

Danielle took hold of Alex's arm and tugged her round to face her. "Tell me, please. I want to help you, if I can."

Alex sighed. "I know what I did in Montreal was something you are not comfortable with. And I hate that I may have gone down in your estimation as a result. But," she ploughed on before Danielle could interrupt, "you have to understand, or at least accept, something important about that. As crazy as it might seem, Justine and I had something so special that week. Something I yearn to have again. And yes, I know it would be impossible

139

with her, and I will let go of this eventually. But she is just…there—" she tapped her head "—all the time. Crazy," she finished, her mind throwing her an image of Justine on the dance floor, her eyes sparkling as she reached out to pull Alex close. Justine, who lived three thousand miles away and whose e-mail made it abundantly clear there was no way forwards for them regardless of that physical distance.

"I don't think I realised quite what an impact she had on you. I made some assumptions about what was involved between you, that it was something superficial and meaningless. I am sorry, Alex, if I did not take it seriously. I let my own feelings about infidelity get in the way."

"It's okay. I understand." Alex shook her head. "I didn't ever really explain me and Justine to you, not completely."

Danielle squeezed her hand. "At the end of the day, Alex, I just want you to be happy. I suppose I doubt whether pursuing Justine would lead to that, to be brutally honest."

Alex smiled wanly. "You're not the only one."

Chapter 17

THE RESTAURANT WAS BUSIER THAN she'd anticipated, given the weather, but its warmth was welcome as Justine shrugged out of her coat and handed it to the hostess.

"Do you have a reservation?"

"I'm here to meet someone; the reservation is in her name. Michelle Audet?"

"*Oui*, right this way."

Sucking in a breath she hoped would calm her nerves, Justine followed the hostess through the throng of diners to a small table about two thirds of the way down the room. The woman who sat waiting for her was beautiful, of that there was no doubt. Dark hair cut in a sleek bob that touched her jawline, and an oval face that hinted at an Asian heritage. Although, she wore too much makeup. The lipstick was too bright, and the eye shadow too garish—

Justine closed her eyes briefly. She was already doing it. Finding fault with her date before she'd even sat down. Christina's words rang in her mind.

"I know this isn't easy, going through the whole proper-dating thing again, especially after we encouraged you with Alex and that all went to shit. But will you please just give them a chance? I still can't believe you didn't even go into the restaurant for the last one just because she was wearing a fur coat. You actually need to talk to these women, get to know them a little, before you make a decision. It's as if you're deliberately looking for the minutest fault to be able to escape the date."

Unfortunately, Christina's theory was true. Despite continuing to let her friends set her up on a steady stream of dates—this one would be the sixth since the new year started—Justine just couldn't get into the swing of it. Something was always wrong. Not smart enough. Not funny enough. Not pretty enough.

Not…Alex.

That was the crux. Not one of the women she'd met so far had given her anything like the spark Alex possessed.

Bracing herself and plastering what she hoped was a warm smile on her face, she took the chair the hostess pulled out for her and sat.

"Hi, you must be Justine." Michelle's voice was soft and an octave lower than Justine would have anticipated for such a delicately featured woman.

"Nice to meet you, Michelle."

"I ordered us champagne to start. I was in the mood."

Justine bristled at Michelle's presumptuousness—what if she hadn't wanted champagne? She chastised herself. Champagne was a classic. And not cheap. Michelle was making an effort to impress. *Give her some credit.*

"Lovely," Justine said, reaching for the glass the waiter placed on the table.

"I just love champagne," Michelle gushed, picking up her own glass and tapping it against Justine's, maintaining eye contact the entire time. Justine squirmed. The glint in Michelle's eyes made her feel as if she were prey being sized up by a stealthy predator.

"So," Michelle said, after taking a couple of sips of her drink, "Christina tells me you're a project manager. What does that entail exactly?"

Over the next five minutes or so, Justine explained her current job to the intense woman across the table. Michelle's gaze was intimidating, and a few times Justine was convinced Michelle wasn't really listening to her. Instead, her eyes often roamed away from Justine's—and usually down to the hint of cleavage visible in the V of the deep blue dress she'd chosen to wear for her date at what was a fairly prestigious restaurant. The venue had been Michelle's choosing, and Justine soon realised why she'd picked somewhere so upmarket. As Justine finished talking about herself and gave Michelle an opening to do the same, Michelle grabbed it with both hands. Twenty minutes later, as their starters arrived, Justine knew she would not be seeing this woman again.

Michelle was completely self-absorbed. She owned a small chain of boutiques catering to the women of Montreal's upper echelons and dropped names like confetti into the conversation continuously. It was nauseating.

Why on earth had Christina thought they'd be a good match? Yes, they were both professional, and Justine had insisted upon that. She needed to be with someone who understood the demands of her job; that plans might need to be rescheduled at the last moment if something urgent came up. Michelle would undoubtedly get that, but their similarities ended there. Yes, Michelle was attractive and had what looked like an amazing body. But she was way too pretentious and somewhat shallow, and Justine bit the inside of her cheeks on numerous occasions to avoid responding too honestly to something Michelle had said.

Declining dessert, Justine dusted off her faithful old tactic for escaping a situation she didn't want to continue.

"Michelle, I'm very sorry to do this, but I have a migraine starting. I'm afraid I'm going to have to get my half of the check and leave."

Michelle's face fell comically. "Really? But we were having a wonderful time." She pouted, but if she thought it looked cute, it was anything but—her lipstick had bled slightly as she'd eaten, so now her mouth looked clown-like.

"I know. I can only assume it was the wine." It was a cheap shot, but Justine had been more than irritated at Michelle's insistence on ordering the overly rich Merlot with their meal. Something about Michelle's arrogance had hindered Justine's normal ability to stand up for herself, and that disturbed her. She'd acquiesced far too easily, and the embarrassment of that only aided her desire to escape. Right now.

She waved the waiter over and asked for the check.

"Can I drive you home?" Michelle asked as they settled up.

"No, that's fine, my car is just round the corner," Justine lied.

They retrieved their coats from the hostess and stepped out into the frigid air. Gentle snow fell, adding to the deep coating the city had been sent in the last few days.

"At least let me walk you to your car, make sure you get there safely."

Shit.

"No, that's fine. It is literally just one block over. Thank you so much for the evening."

"Will we do it again?" Michelle's voice dropped further, to a tone Justine had to admit was seductive. It was just a shame the rest of her didn't match.

Suddenly sick of the lies and discomfort the evening had offered up, Justine opted for honesty.

"I don't think so, Michelle. I think we've got more differences than we have similarities."

Michelle's eyes narrowed. "Sometimes that can be a good thing."

Justine smiled wanly. "Not for me. Goodnight, Michelle." Without waiting for a response, she turned and walked up the block. Turning at the first corner she came to, she marched to the next block and flagged down a cab. She couldn't wait to get home. And call Christina so she could rant at her friend's highly questionable taste in suitable dates.

"I thought you'd enjoy the challenge." Christina's protest was coupled with a host of chuckles.

"Seriously? What challenge?" Justine huffed.

"Michelle needs someone to take her down a peg—she's a sweetheart when she's not doing the whole 'look at me, couturier to the rich and famous' thing. I suppose I thought you'd see through that and be keen on what was underneath."

"I saw no evidence of anything underneath that…gloss. Ugh, she set my teeth on edge."

Christina was silent for a moment. "I'm sorry, *mon amie*. I genuinely wanted you to experience someone a little different. Believe it or not, we have tried very hard to set you up with women who we thought would excite you or challenge you in different ways."

"I know you have." Justine let out a long sigh and leaned forwards on her free elbow, the phone clutched to her ear. "And I do appreciate what you are both doing. I do. It's just…"

"What?" Christina's voice was soft.

"I don't know what I'm looking for. And I don't know how to relax around these women. When I was only interested in a woman for one thing, I didn't have to try so hard."

Christina sniggered. "I'm sure you didn't. Hey, it's early days. Don't beat yourself up. Let me have a think, and a talk with Sylvie, and we'll try much harder with the next one. I promise."

"Okay. But there's no rush. I might need a little break after this one."

"Sure. No problem. Still on for dinner next week?"

"Definitely. Sylvie's lasagne is calling me."

They hung up after a quick goodbye and Justine made her way over to the window seat. It was only ten o'clock; she'd cut short the date at just after nine. She sipped at the herbal tea she'd made once home—she needed something to calm her after the evening's adventures.

As she drank she pondered what she hadn't told Christina. She wondered if her friend had guessed, and therefore how long it would be before she called Justine out on it. That every woman she'd dated since the new year Justine automatically compared to Alex, and always, *always* came up wanting.

"A bit higher at your end, if you can," Alex puffed, and was grateful when Beth obliged. The chest that doubled as a coffee table was bulky and heavy, and manoeuvring it down the two flights of stairs from the flat to the ground floor was awkward, to say the least. However, it was the worst part of the move, so the fact they were getting it out of the way first was a relief. "Nearly there," she called in encouragement.

"Thank God," Beth exclaimed. "I think my arms are about to drop off."

Alex merely grunted and relief washed over her as she descended the final step. Two minutes later they'd shoved the chest into the back of the small van she'd hired for the day.

"I am so glad *that's* over," she said, bending over at the waist and breathing deeply, her breath fogging in the cold January air. "I'm getting too old for this shit."

Beth snorted, also bent over double. "I knew I should have given up smoking for my New Year's resolution."

"You know my feelings on that one." Alex stood and mock glared at her friend.

Beth held up her hands in a placating gesture. "I know, I know. You and Danielle both. Soon, I promise."

They marched back up the stairs and each picked up a box of books. As they descended a second time, Alex stopped suddenly. Terri was on her way up the stairs, head down. Right behind her, a step lower, was a woman Alex didn't recognise. She was slightly taller than Terri, with blonde hair pulled back in a ponytail, her face coldly beautiful. Neither of them had noticed Alex just yet.

"Terri?" Alex hadn't been sure her voice would work; her brain was struggling to compute all the things wrong with this moment.

Terri and the mystery woman lifted their heads sharply, and both stopped climbing the stairs.

Terri eyes were wide, her mouth open in shock.

The blonde, however, was smirking, and Alex had the distinct feeling the woman knew exactly who Alex was.

"What are you doing here?" Alex's anger was sharp and instant, fuelled by the smug look on the blonde's face, and the guilty expression that had painted itself all over Terri's.

Carefully putting the box down at her feet, and vaguely aware of Beth doing the same beside her, Alex said, "You told me you would stay away while I did this. And who's that?" She pointed at the woman, who still wore the oily smirk.

Rather than answering Alex, Terri turned to the woman behind her.

"You told me the text message said they'd be finished by eleven." Terri's voice was tight and her hands clenched at her sides.

"Did I? I could have sworn I said twelve." The woman smiled at Terri but it held no warmth. "Darling, you were rather occupied with…something—" she raised her eyebrows "—when you asked me to read the message for you. Perhaps you misheard." Without waiting for Terri's response, she turned to Alex. "Hi," she said, her smirk widening into a vicious grin. "I'm Liz."

Terri tipped her head back and exhaled loudly. Liz's grin did not diminish.

Alex's heart thumped. This was *Liz*. She and Terri were standing here together in front of Alex. Which meant…*what*? Her mind reeled and she feared she was actually going to pass out. Were Terri and Liz *together*? Had they been together all this time?

"You fucking bitch," Beth said quietly, stepping forwards. Terri flinched.

Alex, on autopilot, clasped Beth's shoulder. "No, don't," she said, her voice sounding strange even to her own ears. She turned to look at Terri as her stomach churned. "What…what is this?"

Terri swallowed and made to speak, but no sound appeared.

146

"You?" Alex said. "And her?" She pointed at Liz, who still wore the smirk that Alex had an almost overwhelming urge to slap off her face.

"Alex, I'm sorry. I—" Terri croaked.

"No," Alex said, and it came out loud and as packed with anger as she was feeling. "Sorry doesn't cut it. Not if this is what I think it is. Just tell me one thing." She glared at Terri, her entire body shaking. "All this time? Since the first time?"

Terri swallowed again. "On and off, yes," she said quietly.

Alex thought she'd experienced worse pain in her life right until that moment. Then she knew she'd never felt pain at all. Not compared to what she felt now. She was numb with it, yet at the same time, scorching agony rolled through every cell in her body.

"Go," she said, the word small but containing enough power to threaten the glass in the windows alongside them.

Terri hesitated.

"Go!" Alex screamed. "Get out! Get the fuck out of my sight!"

Terri stumbled backwards, crashing into Liz, who yelped. Beth slipped an arm around Alex's waist, and Alex was thankful as she didn't think her legs would hold her up for much longer. She watched, dazed, as Terri and Liz trotted down the stairs and out of the building.

She turned to Beth. "I... I can't..." Her heart was pounding out a fearful rhythm and she tried to take a deep, calming breath.

Beth squeezed her. "Come and sit down for a moment." She tugged and Alex followed, grateful she didn't need to think. Beth led her back into the flat to the sofa in the living room and pressed her down into it.

"Back in a tick," Beth said, and walked out of the room. When she returned—Alex had no idea how long she'd been gone—she pushed a small tumbler into Alex's hands. Alex looked down and saw what was probably whisky in the glass. She lifted it to her lips and slugged it back all in one go. It burned, but in burning it brought her back to herself.

"I can't believe it," she choked out. She wondered why she wasn't crying because she felt like screaming the building down. "I feel like everything she's done since that first night she slept with Liz has been a total lie. Was she ever interested in saving our relationship? Why did she put me through all that?"

Beth shook her head. "I have no idea. It's...yeah, it's beyond me." She sat next to Alex and pulled her into a one-armed hug. "I really think we need to get you out of here as soon as we can. I know you're in shock and upset, and I don't mean to push, but the quicker we do this—"

"No, it's okay," Alex interrupted. "I agree. I don't want to stay another minute here." She shuddered, and pulled away from Beth's embrace before standing up. "Let's get this done."

Chapter 18

TECHNICALLY FEBRUARY WAS SLIGHTLY WARMER than January, but as Justine trudged along the street towards Gabrielle's, she struggled to feel it. The wind that knifed her face had already numbed her nose, and her cheeks were next on its hit list. She heaved open the door to the bar in relief and rushed into its warmth. She looked down the room; her date was precisely where she'd said she'd be, perched on one of the stools at the bar, her red coat thrown across her lap in the pre-agreed signal.

Justine grinned. That arrangement had made her smile when they'd spoken on the phone earlier that week. Rose had seemed so earnest in ensuring that neither of them would be fumbling around trying to identify each other. She'd also been more than happy to meet at Gabrielle's. Justine was looking for something more casual this time round after the series of expensive—and wholly unenjoyable—dinners she'd endured in the previous few weeks.

Rose was date number eight. Number seven had not been a disaster, but equally nothing about it had set Justine on fire. The feeling had turned out to be mutual, so the parting at the end of the evening had been the easiest one yet, thankfully. She kept praying that something would change, that something would miraculously pull her out of this strange headspace she occupied. She didn't want to go back to empty one-night stands, even though she did kind of miss sex, not having had any for three months now. She knew on one level she genuinely was ready to look for something more serious. And she knew that might take time. But the way she was going, it could be years…

She shucked off her coat, scarf, and gloves and walked over to the bar.

"*Bonsoir*, Rose," she said, pulling out the stool alongside the raven-haired woman.

Rose turned, and a brilliant smile lit up her face. She was lovely—deep brown eyes with extraordinarily long eyelashes, a pert nose, and small plump lips. She looked a little older than Justine, but maybe not as old as Alex.

Stop. You swore there'd be no thoughts of Alex tonight.

"Justine, so nice to meet you," Rose said, holding out her hand. Justine shook it, smiling the whole time as Rose's calm manner immediately helped her relax.

Okay. So far, so good.

They grabbed one of the small tables and asked the waitress for menus. As they chatted idly about their journeys to the bar, the weather, and where they each lived, Justine relaxed even further. This was so…easy. Already by far the best date of the year.

"So," Justine said once they'd ordered, "tell me some more about your work. Sylvie was a little vague on just what it is you do—I mean, I know you're a surgeon, but in what speciality?"

Rose smiled. "Vascular. Anything to do with the circulation system."

"Wow, I'm impressed. So that must include heart surgery, yes?"

"Yes, quite often. Most of it is routine, to be honest, but maybe once a week I'll have to deal with an emergency."

"I bet that's tough."

Rose nodded and smiled. "It is. None of us like to lose a patient. So what do you do?" The change of subject was swift, but Justine respected it. Talking about death at the dinner table was not something she needed to pursue.

Over their starters and through their entrees, Justine and Rose exchanged more information about each other in a way that had Justine smiling from ear-to-ear. It was still easy and relaxed, and Rose was lovely company. While she was highly career-driven, and proud of what she'd achieved at her age—confirmed at forty-two—she had none of that arrogance Michelle had displayed. She was also amusing, well-read, and expressed genuine interest in Justine's life and career. It was, without a doubt, one of the best evenings out Justine had had in a long time.

As they sipped coffee afterwards, Justine checked in with her libido. While her brain found Rose attractive in so many ways, the physical attraction seemed to be taking longer to manifest. She wasn't quite sure why. Rose was definitely pleasing to look at, and her curvy body, with full breasts and long legs, should have sent all sorts of delicious signals to Justine's sexual self. Still, it wasn't happening, not entirely, although the way the light and shadows played across the cleavage Rose's shirt revealed *was* producing a subtle buzz somewhere south of Justine's abdomen.

Just after ten thirty, they said their goodbyes in the warmth of the bar rather than the chill of the street.

"I had a very lovely time tonight, Justine." Rose's smile was wide and warm.

"Me too." She paused. Should she? Yes, for once she should. Enough was going on here for her to want to see where it could take them. "Can I—"

"Would you—"

They laughed. Rose tilted her head. "Yes," she said, and Justine grinned. "I'll call you later this week, okay?"

Rose nodded. "I look forward to it." She leaned in and kissed Justine sweetly on the cheek. *"À bientôt."*

As she pondered the blank sheet of paper attached to the easel in front of her, Alex couldn't help but smile. The word *metaphor* looped through her brain and before she could stop it, her smile converted to a loud giggle.

"Everything okay, Alex?" Eleanor, the art class teacher, looked across the room at her, a confused expression on her face.

Alex got the laugh under control—just. "Fine, Eleanor. Sorry."

She picked up the soft charcoal from the tray and touched it to the paper. The model before them was a woman in her fifties, with a body that had experienced childbirth three times, and two emergency operations for breast cancer. She was slightly overweight, and scarred and wrinkled. And somehow even more beautiful as a result, in Alex's opinion. As she'd disrobed, the model had calmly explained to the group of students that for her, the opportunity to do this was a way to reclaim her body for herself. Alex had been touched by the sentiment and wanted to be able to bring some of the woman's strength and courage to the drawing she was about to start.

She'd started attending the class at the beginning of February. Art had been one of her first loves, and although she'd never quite been good enough to pursue it beyond school, she'd often sketched and painted in her twenties. It was another thing she'd lost, somehow, as she progressed through her career and relationships, and another thing she'd been keen to explore again now she was on her own, forging her new life.

So far, the new life had brought with it a balance and a calmness that both pleased and surprised her. With no one to answer to at home about just how much she worked, she found herself relaxing into her job more than she had done since the promotion. She was doing as much as she wanted each day and revelling in not looking guiltily at the clock after five thirty. Gone were the days of fretting over trying to find the right balance between the demands of her job and the demands of her partner. Her hours hadn't increased—in fact, they'd slightly decreased—but the stress of them had definitely diminished.

She was still living with Danielle and Beth but actively looking at rental properties. Being mentally ready to do that had taken her longer than she'd anticipated—especially after the trauma of the day she moved the last of her belongings out of the flat she'd owned with Terri—but her friends hadn't minded that their house guest lingered in her stay.

She'd even been out dancing again, persuading Danielle and Beth to accompany her to a club in Soho two weeks ago to celebrate her forty-seventh birthday. Getting out on the scene again had been daunting, but fun—they'd danced until one in the morning, then cabbed home and eaten a small mountain of toast while dissecting the evening's adventures.

"I confess," Danielle said, "I really did not expect to enjoy that as much as I did. Although I still cannot fathom how we used to do that three or four times a week, as I now feel as if I could sleep for a week to recover."

Alex and Beth laughed. "I know. But I had such a good time. Thank you both for going with me," Alex said, grasping their hands.

"I'd say 'any time'," Beth said, smirking, "but I'd be lying. Maybe once every couple of months."

"Oh come on, we're not that old!"

"I am," Danielle had said solemnly.

Alex swept the charcoal across the page, capturing the curve of the model's back, down over her hip to her thigh. Interesting shadows played in the folds and creases where the woman's large thighs met her rotund belly.

The March light was weak through the wide windows of the studio, but was complemented by the brightness of the ceiling lights, and Alex loved the effect it had across the woman's pale skin.

When Eleanor called an end to the class, Alex blinked; she'd been completely unaware of how much time had passed. Drawing had always done this for her, taking her to a place where the only thing she had to focus on was the movement of her hand across the paper and the essence of the image she was attempting to portray.

She stepped back from the easel. Her drawing wasn't complete, but that was okay. What was there had distinct definition and promise, and that was fine for starters.

"*Metaphor*," she whispered to herself.

"Lasagne? Again?" Christina feigned annoyance even as she reached for the serving spoon. Sylvie slapped her hand away and picked up the spoon herself.

"For that, you are last," she said, smirking as Justine and Rose laughed from the opposite side of the table. "You know it is Justine's favourite, and as this evening is in honour of her, it was an obvious choice." She served them all generous helpings that nestled alongside the salads already on their plates.

"Wow, I don't think I'll be able to make it through that," Rose said, her eyes wide as she stared at her heaped plate.

"Not to worry." Justine nudged her with her shoulder. "I'm here to scoop up any leftovers."

Rose smiled at her and leaned in to place a gentle kiss on her lips. Justine smiled and tried to ignore the little voice in the back of her head that asked why Rose's kisses still did nothing for her.

They'd been dating for about a month now. Taking it slow, as per Justine's request, which Rose seemed happy enough to oblige. Intimacy had been limited to kissing and holding each other close, an entirely new ball game for Justine, but one she almost had no choice over. Her body was still way behind her mind in the race to be fully attracted to Rose. And Rose wasn't in the same league as one of her one-night stands. Now that Justine had got to know her, she had to think of Rose as a real person with real feelings, not just a random hookup. Justine acknowledged, with a more than a little shame, that she'd managed to treat all the women she'd slept with the last eighteen months as somehow...less. She'd conveniently ignored their feelings and their lives and selfishly only focused on hers. Having started the process of moving beyond that with Alex, despite how badly that had ended, being where she was now felt good. Rose was definitely helping Justine more in that progression, whether she knew it or not. Justine had been deliberately vague with Rose on what her personal life had been like these past two years. She didn't want to see a look of disgust cross Rose's face if Justine ever confessed all that she'd done.

She couldn't deny that she and Rose had a wonderful time together. They talked about fascinating and thought-provoking subjects. They laughed. On weekends they shared wonderful walks around parks and museums and cooked for each other. While they hadn't seen each other much during the working week, due to clashes in schedules, the time they had managed to share had been satisfying in so many ways. And yet... When Justine lay down in bed at night, even if she'd kissed Rose goodnight earlier that evening, any sexual thoughts or fantasies she had did not involve Rose. The kisses they shared were...nice. But nice wasn't good enough.

"A toast," Christina said, once Sylvie had finished serving. They all raised their glasses. "To the best damn project manager in the city."

A chorus of agreement accompanied the chink of glasses as they all drank to Justine. She blushed under their attention but at the same time felt the flush of pride too. They were celebrating her latest success—a key project not only finished two weeks early but nearly twenty thousand dollars under budget. There was talk of a promotion, which was astonishing, given that RCS had only bought out her company a few months ago and normally newly acquired staff took a lot longer to appear on the radar of the parent company.

The takeover had been in November, she mused. When she'd first met Alex...

"Justine?" Rose was staring at her.

"Sorry, I drifted there. What did you say?" She hauled herself back into the conversation and desperately tried to banish the image of Alex's face from her mind.

Chapter 19

SHIT.

Alex hung her head in her hands and closed her eyes. Just when she'd made such good progress. Just when she thought she'd finally convinced herself she was over her.

Life's twists and turns never ceased to amaze her.

Or piss her off.

The e-mail from her boss had been waiting in her inbox when she'd opened her laptop first thing that morning.

Hi, Alex,

Great news, we've got the green light on the upgrade! Something else got cancelled and there's a project team available from Monday to get us underway. You'll liaise with the head of the team, Justine North, who's based in Montreal. She's relatively new to RCS, but I think that helps us—no preconceived notions of what the system should do. Her analysts are based in Montreal, but she could access some help here if required.

So let's get on with it. Please set up a meeting with her asap and start the usual feedback loop into our weekly meetings. I'd like to see this go live before the end of August, but let me know what timeframe you think is possible once you've spoken to her.

Richard

Alex let out a slow breath.

Justine.

Even seeing her name in the e-mail had sent a shiver of anticipation through Alex. For all her outward declarations to Danielle and Beth that she had moved on from the encounter in Montreal, that the only way was forwards, inwardly she'd cringed at the untruths. She still, inexplicably, craved Justine. Her smile, that twinkle in her eye, her body... And now she had to work with her directly, and somehow find a professional way to manage that. She would need all her emotional resources to pull it off.

Still, she was stronger now. She should be able to do this. Her independence had grown daily since she'd left Terri, and in a fortnight that would go one step further, with a move into a cute rented basement flat a few streets away from Danielle and Beth. A month or so after that, they should complete on the sale of the Wimbledon flat and she'd have a nice big balance in her savings account for whatever the future brought next. And no reason to have anything more to do with Terri, as communication between them was fraught and bitter while the sale of the flat went through. Thank God they'd never got married or had a civil partnership—she couldn't imagine dealing with that as well.

So much was now moving in the right direction. She just had to make sure her interaction with Justine did the same. They were simply two women who worked for the same company, and for the next four or five months, they'd be working on the same project. They were both highly paid professionals; they could do this. Surely.

Deciding there was no time like the present, and before her thoughts ran away with her and led her to chicken out, she opened a new e-mail.

Hi, Justine,

Richard Campbell has hopefully been in contact with you already. You have been allocated to us as the project manager for the upgrade of the training system. I'd like to get started on that as soon as possible, so I'll be scheduling a kickoff conference call for the middle of next week. Can you please let me know who on your team should be included in that?

I look forward to working with you.

Regards,

Alex

Well, it was nothing if not professional. Although *aloof* and *cold* were two other words that sprang to mind. Justine's heart had leapt into her mouth when she'd seen Alex's name in her inbox; contrary to what Alex had written, this Richard Campbell had *not* been in contact, so suddenly receiving an e-mail from Alex had been quite a shock. She'd opened it excitedly, more than a little alarmed at how much her heart rate increased at the prospect of contact from Alex. Then her stomach had plummeted at the content of the e-mail, and its tone.

Then the implication of the words had actually sunk in.

Oh shit, they had to work together. For a few months.

How the hell was she going to manage that? Despite everything she'd shared with Rose these past few weeks, she knew, deep down, a corner of her soul had Alex's name imprinted on it. She assumed that was one of the reasons she was still holding back from Rose, and she knew, ultimately, that was grossly unfair to Rose. She'd thought, given enough time, that the Alex corner would diminish until what she had with Rose was big enough to take it over. But she'd been seeing Rose for six weeks now and it wasn't happening.

Not by a long shot.

She groaned and her head thudded onto her desk. When Mathieu had told her the project she'd been scheduled to start on Monday had been cancelled, she'd been prepared for a dull couple of weeks until something new came up. So while having a new project so quickly was great, why oh why did it have to be Alex's?

There went the universe again with its sick sense of humour.

She needed some air. She grabbed some money from her wallet and her thick ski jacket and headed down to the ground floor. It was only five degrees out but the sun was shining, and she turned her face up to it while she waited to cross Rue McGill. The Starbucks in the World Trade Centre was busy, as always, but she didn't mind the wait. Her mind was still churning with the latest episode of the Justine-and-Alex saga. *You barely knew her*, she reminded herself. *All you had was two evenings with her. Why can't you get past this?* She had no idea. Every time she thought about it—which was more often than she'd admit to anyone—she came up blank. Her pull towards the memory of Alex was...inexplicable, yet palpable.

After paying for her latte, she made her way back out to the street. She wandered up to the square and perched on a cold wall, sipping continuously at the hot drink cupped in her gloved hands.

Whatever she thought she still felt for Alex, she had to park it. To be able to work together on this project, they had to be professional. Alex had managed it—magnificently so—in her e-mail. Now Justine just had to match that and they'd be okay.

Wouldn't they?

When she returned to her office some fifteen minutes later, she fired off a quick reply to Alex, naming names and suggesting a range of times that would suit her team for the kickoff meeting. Not acknowledging their history hurt, but it had to be done.

The neutral recorded voice that talked Alex through the login procedure for the conference call did nothing to calm her nerves. Dialling the number had made her aware of her trembling fingers and racing pulse.

This is ridiculous. She exhaled and keyed in the passcode that would open the conference line.

"Hi, this is Alex. Who's on the call?"

"Hi, Alex, this is Justine. I have the team assembled in the room with me, so we're all here."

Alex swallowed as her body responded to Justine's warm tones in ways she struggled to ignore.

"Great, that makes it easier." She was pleased her voice betrayed none of her turmoil. "Thank you all for taking the time to meet with me. Did everyone get a chance to read the project brief I attached to the meeting event?"

After the numerous noises of affirmation, Alex launched into her agenda. The meeting proceeded smoothly, despite the slight thrill that sparked through her every time Justine contributed to the conversation. Thankfully it wasn't all one-way traffic; a few of Justine's team also chipped in with questions or observations and gave Alex a welcome breather each time from the impact of Justine's presence.

If this is what I'm like on a call with her, I dread to think how I'd react face to face again. Luckily that wasn't on the cards and shouldn't need to be for a project of this nature.

"So are we agreed on next steps?" Alex asked as they began to wrap things up.

"I think so," Justine said. "Now that we've got the scope mapped out, I can get on with managing the workload and your expectations. I know it will take a few days for the team to get a test environment set up ready to configure, but I'm confident we can deliver that to you by this time next week."

"Great," Alex enthused. "Then let's meet again the same time next week and we can then start fleshing out the plan and allocating resources. Agreed?"

"Sounds perfect," Justine said, and that thrill shot through Alex again as Justine's enthusiasm also came through loud and clear. "Alex, can you hold for a second?"

"Sure."

The line went silent for a minute.

"Hey, I'm back," Justine said quietly. "It's only you and I on the call now."

"Oh." Alex didn't know what else to say. What was Justine doing?

"I just... How are you?"

Alex closed her eyes for a moment and took a deep breath. She hadn't expected this or planned for it. She'd thought they were going to be professional about this.

"I'm...fine," she muttered eventually, trying to put a lid on her irritation at being caught unprepared.

"Good. I-I'm glad." Justine exhaled a big puff of a breath. "Look, Alex, I... I guess I just wanted to say I hope we can be okay about working together. But if we're not, I won't have a problem assigning another manager to the project."

"Do you have a problem with it?" Alex asked bluntly. Was Justine trying to suggest Alex couldn't cope? Couldn't keep her professionalism in place? Alex was angry but in the next moment acknowledged it came from fear—she was scared her professionalism *had* slipped on the call with the team and that she would wobble while working with Justine.

Before she could apologise for speaking so sharply, however, Justine spoke. "No, not at all. And I wasn't suggesting you did either." Her tone was mollifying. "And," she continued after a short pause, "I genuinely wanted to make sure you were okay. I know the last few months can't have been easy for you."

Alex shivered slightly as the warmth of Justine's concerned tone seeped through her consciousness. "Thank you," she murmured. "They haven't. But I'm okay. Things are good. Or at least getting there."

"I'm really pleased to hear it."

"Thanks." She hesitated only a moment before asking, "And you? How are you?"

"I… I'm good. Thanks for asking."

They fell silent. After half a minute that threatened to drag on longer, Alex eventually broke the deadlock. "Okay, well, we'll talk again next week. Could you get that appointment set up for us all, and in the meantime, e-mail me if you have any questions?"

"Sure," Justine said hurriedly. "I will. Speak to you next week, Alex."

"Bye."

As she replaced the phone in its cradle, Alex propped her head in her free hand. She wanted to laugh, then cry, then maybe laugh some more. Just as she'd feared, everything she thought she'd forgotten about Justine, or thought she'd managed to quietly leave behind these past few months, had just turned around and slapped her with a vengeance. Suddenly she was back in Justine's apartment, with Justine's hot mouth on her skin and Justine's strong fingers buried deep inside her, and she struggled to remember to breathe.

The surge of longing, and desire, and need that ripped through her set her hands trembling again and her heart leaping in her chest.

Oh shit.

Chapter 20

"You're her project manager? You are *kidding* me."

Christina's eyes were wide, and Justine smiled despite her inner gloom. "I wish I was."

"So how does that feel? Are you two okay with each other?"

Justine nodded. "We're both professionals; we know how to play nice."

"But…?"

"Yeah." She exhaled loudly. "It's not easy."

"Do you still have feelings for her?" Christina asked solemnly.

Justine glanced out of the café window. The world outside carried on its business, seeming all calm and peaceful, while a tornado of emotions quietly ripped Justine apart from the inside out.

"Justine?" Christina's hand settled on top of Justine's.

Justine turned back to her friend and knew she didn't need to say it out loud. Christina's face fell.

"Oh, shit."

"Yep."

"I thought you'd written her off after you found out she'd cheated on her partner."

Justine sighed. "Well, after you pointed out what an ass I'd been on that issue in general, and after she took the time to explain her situation, I guess… Well, I guess I believe it wasn't as cut and dried as I thought. That it isn't who she is."

"You barely know her!" Christina threw her hands up. "How can you make that kind of call?"

"I don't know." Justine smiled weakly, knowing the phrase wouldn't appease her friend. "I just…can. Gut instinct, or whatever. I believe her."

Christina slumped back in her chair, shaking her head.

"And what about Rose?"

Justine leaned across the table and propped her head up with her free hand. "I really like her. And we have a great time together. But it's just not… I keep waiting for the spark, you know?"

"And it's not there?"

"Not yet."

"Shit."

"Yeah. I know."

They finished their coffees with small talk—Christina seemed to sense Justine wasn't able to talk anymore about the situation with Alex, or the one with Rose. But after they'd said their goodbyes and Justine walked back to her apartment in the light April rain, her thoughts spun a web of confusion centred around the two women in her life. She snorted as she let herself into the apartment and kicked off her boots. That was the thing—she didn't have two women. She had one woman she was finally realising she didn't want, at least not in a physical way. And the woman she did want in that way—and all the other ways she could possibly list—she didn't have and more than likely couldn't have.

She was supposed to be meeting Rose for a late supper at her place, but Justine wasn't remotely in the mood for it after that confession to Christina. She sat on the couch with her phone in her hand, mentally composing the message she wanted to send to put Rose off for the night. She'd arrange something face to face later in the week so that in the meantime she would have the space she needed to work out how to tell Rose she just wasn't interested in her that way. She was dreading that conversation already.

Sighing, she swiped her phone and opened a new message, her fingers tapping across the screen.

———— ◦◦◦◦◦◦ ————

Alex sniggered as she read the latest e-mail from Justine. Man, that woman could put someone in their place in the most perfect style. The idiot from IT who'd try to mansplain to Justine why her test environment would function better on another server had met his match in no uncertain terms.

She sighed.

The last two weeks had been torture of the best and worst kind. She was revelling in the amount of contact they had and the opportunities she had to share some time with Justine, however remotely. They spoke on the phone at least twice a week and e-mailed more times than Alex could count. All of which only highlighted what an amazing and accomplished woman Justine was. No wonder there was talk of her being promoted before the year was out. She was sharp, firm yet fair, incredibly knowledgeable, and clearly driven to succeed. Her e-mails oozed confidence, and some of her ideas for future enhancements or process improvements had literally left Alex speechless with admiration.

On top of all that, she was just so...lovely. Encouraging her team in all the right ways and respecting the boundaries between herself and Alex whenever anyone else was on the e-mail chain or conference call. Alex had no idea if this was something Justine struggled with because she gave nothing away. She was the consummate professional, which was exactly what Alex had said she needed.

Only...

She found herself trying to read more into what Justine was saying sometimes, more than was healthy for her. She dared to fantasise about Justine breaking down one day and confessing that she still thought about Alex as much as Alex did about her. Whenever those fantasies threatened to get out of control, she would pull herself up short, give herself a telling off, and go home and try her hardest to forget Justine for the evening.

She usually failed.

Alex sighed. Danielle had invited her for dinner at an Argentinian steakhouse tonight, and something told her that she was the one in for a grilling, not the meat. Alex had been vague with Danielle over what had been happening at work recently—she'd yet to tell her that she and Justine were working on this project together. Because she knew what would happen when she did, and she hadn't been able to face it. Tonight, however, would be different. Tonight Alex *wanted* to talk about it and wanted to hear what Danielle thought. The whole situation was driving Alex nuts, and the time for keeping it to herself was over.

She worked through until six thirty, catching up on e-mails and bulletins she should have read days ago. Satisfied she hadn't missed anything earth-shattering, she closed down her laptop finally and rubbed her aching neck.

Her phone chirped with a message from Danielle.

On my way!

She stood and retrieved her jacket and handbag. The weather was pleasantly mild as she stepped out onto the Strand, and she enjoyed her stroll up to Covent Garden. The restaurant was just off the Piazza, and she was led straight to their table, where Danielle waited.

"Hey, you." Alex smiled at her friend as Danielle stood to pull her into a close hug.

"Hello, Alex. You look very well."

They hadn't seen each other for a while due to various commitments they'd each had. Not since Danielle and Beth had helped her move into her rented flat.

"It seems rather insane that you only live around the corner, yet we haven't been able to meet up since you moved," Danielle said, mirroring Alex's thoughts.

"I know, but we're both busy women, aren't we?"

"Very true."

They ordered wine and their food as soon as the waiter appeared.

"So I need to talk to you about something," Alex said after they'd taken their first sip of the delicious Malbec.

Danielle smiled. "I am all ears."

"Um, since I saw you last, something's happened at work. I think I needed to see how things panned out before I spoke about it. And it was sort of eating me up as well, and I knew I wouldn't be able to explain it properly until I knew a bit more about what was going on. Of course, not that there *is* anything going on, but that's the problem—"

"Alex," Danielle snapped, sounding frustrated, "what *are* you talking about?"

Alex swallowed. "Sorry. It's just, I don't know how to explain it and not sound crazy."

Danielle sat still, waiting.

"I'm working on a new project, and the project manager is Justine." Alex said the words fast, as if ripping a plaster off a barely healed wound.

Danielle blinked rapidly a few times. "Justine? As in the woman you had your...dalliance with in Montreal?"

"Yep, that Justine." Alex waited to see what further reaction Danielle would have to the announcement.

"And?" Danielle's face was expressionless.

"And, well," Alex stumbled, "I've realised... I mean, I think I always knew this, deep down, but you know, being in contact again with her has only emphasised it, you know?"

"Emphasised what?"

"Oh God." She groaned, pushing her hands through her hair. "That I still have feelings for her," she blurted out. "That I'm still hugely attracted to her—and not just physically. That she's still the most amazing woman I ever met," she finished in a whisper.

"Oh, Alex," Danielle said, her tone part exasperation and part loving concern.

"I know."

"She lives in Montreal." Danielle ticked the points off on her fingers. "You only had what was essentially a one-night stand. You have no idea if she is involved with someone. She lives in Montreal."

"You said that already."

"I think it is worth repeating!"

"I know, I know. You're right, on all counts. But none of that stops me feeling the way I do about her, and about what happened with us."

"Alex, I cannot see how this has anything other than the capacity to bring you yet more heartbreak."

"I know, but I've spent an awful lot of the past few months figuring out what I do and don't want from my life and the people who share it. The woman who might yet share it. I know it sounds completely crazy, but what Justine and I had, even just for those two evenings, was incredible. The connection, for want of a better word, between us was something I could almost grasp in my hands, it had so much substance. I have never, ever felt like that with anyone."

"I remember you saying something like this at the time, and I must confess I wrote it off as just the emotional upheaval those nights caused along with the situation with Terri. But you are saying you can still feel that, even now, months later?"

"Every time I hear her voice on one of our conference calls, I feel it. Every time she writes something funny or intelligent in an e-mail, I feel it. It's exasperating, and mystifying, and so bloody wonderful all at the same time."

Danielle sat back and reached for her wine, taking a long drink before placing the glass back on the table.

"So are you saying you want to have some sort of relationship with Justine? And if so, how on earth would that work?"

"Yes, and I don't know."

"Oh, Alex…"

She stared at Danielle. The hint of disappointment in her expression twisted Alex's stomach. "You think I'm stupid, don't you?"

Danielle's eyes widened. "No, Alex. Not stupid." She smiled and grabbed Alex's hand, squeezing it tightly. "I do think you are slightly mad, however."

Alex laughed.

Rose's lips on Justine's neck were insistent, and her hands equally so as they pushed underneath the hem of her shirt. This wasn't supposed to be happening. They were supposed to have just had that light supper that had been postponed the week before, then Justine was supposed to find an opportunity to talk openly and honestly with Rose about their relationship and what it did or didn't mean to Justine.

Rose, however, clearly had other ideas. Quietly commanding Justine to leave the supper dishes on the table, she'd taken Justine's hand and led her over to the couch. The lights were already low, and the sounds of gentle, romantic piano music came from the small speakers on the far side of the room. Rose's eyes had glinted with passion as she'd swept Justine into her arms, and before Justine could engage her brain to stop her, Rose's mouth was travelling a moist path along Justine's jaw and down to her neck.

Rose moaned as her hands swept upwards to cup Justine's breasts through the silk of her shirt. Justine gave it a few moments and tried so hard to feel something. Anything. One last test. But it just wasn't there.

Slowly, carefully, she pulled away.

Rose looked confused, and aroused, which clenched at Justine's insides. Oh God, this was not going to be easy. Not now.

"I'm sorry," she whispered. "I'm just not… I really like you, Rose, I do, but—"

Rose held a hand up. "Please, don't finish that sentence." She shuffled backwards on the couch until there was distance between them. She sighed. "I thought you just needed time, but it's more than that, isn't it?"

Justine briefly closed her eyes. When she opened them, Rose was staring at her, her arms folded across her chest.

"Just tell me. Please."

"I don't actually know why myself," Justine said, knowing she was lying but unable to share the truth. She was hurting Rose enough already without bringing Alex into it. "We connect so well in so many ways, but the... physical is just not happening for me. I'm so sorry."

Rose gritted her teeth, and Justine wouldn't have blamed her if she let rip. She'd take it. She'd kept Rose waiting so long; the woman had the patience of a saint.

"I haven't ever meant to lead you on, or make you think there was more between us than there is. I honestly thought it would come, the more time we spent together. But it just...hasn't."

Rose exhaled. "If it's not there, it's not there, I suppose. For me, it has been since the first time we met. You're a very attractive woman, Justine. I was willing to take things slow and give you all the time you needed. But time isn't the issue, is it?"

Justine shook her head. "Thank you, for what it's worth. Thank you for your patience, and for not pushing."

Rose stood. "I like being with you, Justine. And maybe that's something we could do in the future. But...not for a while. *I* need time now. Time to get over you. I'm afraid you had quite an effect on me."

"I'm sorry," Justine whispered.

"I'm sure you are." Rose's tone was hard, but Justine wasn't going to protest. "I think you'd better leave."

Nodding, and knowing there was nothing else to say, Justine retrieved her coat and bag, stepped into her boots, and pulled open the front door.

She didn't look back as she left.

Chapter 21

"Hi, Justine, it's Alex."

"Oh, hey. What can I do for you?"

Straight to business. As usual. Alex let out a silent sigh. She wished Justine would relax with her, just for a moment. Just to give her some clue that this...infatuation wasn't one-sided. Something, maybe simply wishful thinking, told her it wasn't.

"Well, I just wanted to say thanks for sending over the draft testing schedule."

"No problem. I thought it made sense to start putting something together sooner rather than later. I know you still have to sort out resources at your end."

"Yeah, and I might need to firm up some of the dates once I've talked to people here, but I'll work on that and send you some amendments back once I'm done, okay?"

"Perfect." Justine's tone was still briskly polite. Alex was desperate to put a dent in it, to push the boundaries on this call just a little.

"So, how have you been?" She held her breath as she waited to see how Justine would respond.

"Um, fine, thanks. You?" Justine sounded confused and hesitant.

"You know, I'm not so bad actually. I don't think I told you, but I have my own place now. I've been there about a month. It's close to some good friends of mine, so it's nice to have a support network nearby."

"That...that sounds really good." Justine paused. Just as Alex was about to jump in, Justine continued. "I live quite near Sylvie and Christina. It helped a lot when Nadia and I split up."

Alex punched the air. They were talking. About personal stuff. The joy that gave her made her tingle all over. Never mind the effect Justine's more relaxed, casual voice had on her. Her professional persona was admirable, but when she dropped the harder edge to her voice that she used for business dealings, something warm and delicious spread throughout Alex's body. She couldn't have held it back if she tried.

"Yeah, I don't know what I would have done without Danielle and Beth," she said. Excited by their interaction, she pushed on. "I also started an art class a few weeks ago, which I'm really enjoying."

"Oh? Is this something new or have you always painted?" Justine still sounded a tad nervous, but at least she was engaging. *Keep it going, please,* Alex begged silently.

"I really loved art at school," Alex continued, "but haven't done much with it since my twenties. I've really enjoyed getting back into it."

"Are you any good?" Justine's cheeky chuckle gave bloom to an enormously wide grin on Alex's face.

"I'm not terrible," she replied, laughing. "But I won't be giving up my day job, let's put it that way."

Justine outright snorted, and Alex's heart leapt with glee at the sound.

"So, what about you? Have you been cooking much? I remember you saying how much you enjoyed it."

Justine sighed quietly. "It comes and goes. I… Yeah, I just have to be in the mood, I guess. I like cooking for my friends. Cooking for one is sometimes too depressing."

"I know what you mean." So she was still single. Alex parcelled that bit of information up and deposited it somewhere safe in the back of her mind.

An uneasy silence crept between them.

"Well, I'd better get back to it," Justine said quietly. "Some of us still have a few hours left in the day."

Alex laughed, glancing at the clock on her laptop. It was only eleven in the morning for Justine. "Yeah, I'll leave you to it. It…it was good to talk to you, Justine." She tried hard to keep the emotion out of her voice, but it was difficult. Talking like this had given her an intense glow of happy satisfaction.

"You too, Alex." Justine's voice sounded husky, hoarse almost. Alex quivered.

"Catch up with you on the team call later this week."

"Sure will. Bye." Justine hung up.

Alex stared at the phone in her hand. While the end of the call had been abrupt, and she wasn't sure what that was about, the previous few minutes had been...wonderful. And not only for the interaction with Justine. For Alex, to be that bold and free in pushing for something was uncharted territory. The changes she'd made in her life were giving her a confidence and courage to actively pursue the things she wanted, rather than the things she thought she ought to have. With the situation involving Justine, she had to acknowledge, that might not turn out to be the wisest move, but she didn't care. It felt right, here and now, and she wasn't going to hold back.

She laughed at herself. She was acting like a teen with a silly crush. Shaking her head, she stood to walk to the break room. She *felt* like a teen with a silly crush.

Justine stared at her phone as if it were a snake that might rise up and bite her. What the hell had just happened? How had they gone from super-professional to ultra-personal in the space of one phone call?

Not that she hadn't enjoyed it. Quite the opposite, in fact. But it had just come out of the blue. And on the tails of the week she'd had—ending things with Rose—it had left her reeling. Although, she realised, not necessarily in a bad way. More like in a giddy, high-school, oh-my-God-I-think-she-likes-me kind of way.

She snorted. This was crazy. Completely mad.

But completely wonderful at the same time.

Alex sounded as though she had really started to sort her life out since leaving her partner. That could only be a good thing. She sounded full of life and quietly excited about the opportunities it was presenting to her. Justine felt a warm glow on her behalf and smiled to herself. Good for her.

The wave of sadness that swept over her in the next moment wiped the smile off her face. Alex was moving on, and as far as Justine could see, she had no way of accompanying Alex in that.

She met Christina and Sylvie for dinner that night, back at Gabrielle's, and filled them in on all that had transpired with Rose earlier in the week.

"I am obviously not surprised, given what you told Christina on Sunday. But I am sad." Sylvie rubbed a comforting hand down Justine's arm.

"I am too." Justine puffed out a breath and slumped back in her seat. "Rose and I were so right in so many ways."

"But you weren't, either, were you?" Christina said bluntly, eyebrows raised as if daring Justine to argue.

Justine raised her hands. "I know, I know. Which is why I'm glad I ended it when I did. It was the right thing to do."

Sylvie nodded and drank from her wine. As she set her glass down, her lips pursed and her forehead creased into a gentle frown.

"Go ahead," Justine said, smirking half-heartedly. "Say what you need to say."

Her petite friend laughed and wagged a finger. "Okay, mind reader." She took a deep breath. "I am worried you are now pinning all of your hopes on Alex. The long-distance option. And, therefore, the unlikely option."

Justine sat back in her chair. "What are you saying?"

Sylvie shrugged. "That it is a very safe option to pine for someone who is unattainable, isn't it? Love from afar is a clever way to avoid actually being involved."

"Ouch," Justine said, staring at her. "Way to hit below the belt."

"I do not mean to hurt you, Justine. I am just expressing my concerns about what this latest turn of events means for the health of your heart." Sylvie's tone was firm but kind.

"My heart," Justine said, trying to rein in her frustration at life and not take it out on her friends, "is just fine, thank you." She grabbed her glass and took a big swig of her wine. It burned the back of her throat in her haste, and she launched into a coughing fit.

With Christina and Sylvie patting her wildly on the back, she scrabbled to reach her water glass, gratefully gulping down a few soothing mouthfuls.

"You can stop hitting me now," she mumbled as she cleared her throat one last time. "I'm okay."

Her friends chuckled as they pulled their hands away.

"Are you really okay?" Sylvie asked. "And I do not mean the coughing."

Justine sighed. "Yes and no. Today Alex and I had a wonderful phone call. Out of the blue she turned it very personal, the first time she's done that. And it was great." She smiled in remembrance. "We laughed a little, shared some info about our lives. It felt…good. Real." She looked at them, at the concern etched across their faces. "I know," she said, smiling ruefully at them. "But I just can't help it. I want her. And I don't just mean sex. I want to be around her. Share things with her. Laugh with her. Really get to know her."

"She lives in London," Christina deadpanned.

Justine flopped in her chair, as if sucker-punched. "Yeah. I know."

———————————◦◦◦◦◦———————————

"So do you own your apartment?" Alex's voice was like silk caressing Justine's ear.

"Yes. Well, me and the bank. But it is mine to do with what I will. I love it."

"That's great. I think it'll take me a while to work out when and where I want to buy. I've still got stuff I need to sort out before I make that big a decision again."

"I can understand that." Justine didn't totally get what was happening between them, but she wasn't going to stop it. Their calls—at least twice a week now—were rapidly becoming her drug of choice. Every time her phone rang, her heart rate spiked in anticipation of hearing Alex's smooth tones. They had been talking like this for three weeks, sharing more, and laughing more, and Justine was struggling to remember there was no chance for them.

God, how she wanted there to be.

It was pure torture. Listening to Alex talk and joke and not being able to touch her, to kiss her, or simply to wrap her arms around her when she sounded a little low or unsure of herself, was making Justine ache in ways she'd never imagined. While they never spoke of that infamous week in November, and they never overtly flirted, what they did share somehow had more value because of that.

"So it's nearly the weekend," Alex said. "What are you up to? Any hot dates lined up?"

Whoa. Alex had never asked anything that direct before.

"Um, no. Just dinner with Christina and Sylvie on Saturday."

"Are…are you seeing anyone, Justine?" Alex's voice was barely above a whisper, but she may as well have shouted.

Justine swallowed hard. "No. No one at the moment."

There was a brief silence. "Me neither."

"Well, I guess that would take some time for you, wouldn't it? After everything that's happened."

"Yeah. I guess."

Say it would be me, Justine thought. *Tell me when you're ready it will be me.* She dropped her forehead into her hand. God, what was she thinking? She needed to end this call before she said anything like that out loud.

"So I kinda need to get on with some things." She tried not to sound too abrupt, but the panic running rampant in her body right now had taken control. "Sorry. You know how it is."

Alex cleared her throat. "Yes. Yes, of course. Sorry, I didn't mean to keep you."

"Okay. Until next time."

"Bye, Justine."

God, even the way Alex said her name had her quivering with need. She dropped the phone back in its cradle and her head on the desk.

This was utterly crazy.

Chapter 22

SHE'D WANTED TO TELL JUSTINE. She'd wanted to just get it out there, right out there. *Justine, I can't stop thinking about you, and I want—*

What? What did she think could happen if she said something like that? They couldn't date; they lived three thousand miles apart. They couldn't arrange to meet up for a drink one night and just see how things could be, like normal people could do.

Stupid.

Ridiculous.

But oh God, how she wanted Justine. Every time they talked, her feelings consumed her. She listened to the nuances in Justine's voice, took any opportunity to make Justine laugh because she loved the husky sound of it. And whenever Justine's voice dropped a tad lower, it brought back memories of her holding Alex tight and saying, "I want to hear you come," as her fingers pushed deliciously slowly inside Alex.

She nearly moaned, and pushed herself out of her office chair. On the pretence of looking at a memo, just in case someone observed her, she paced the room, her mind in free fall. As bold as she had been these past few weeks, going that final step and really opening up to Justine had been one step too far. What if Justine didn't reciprocate? Alex had always been useless at reading so-called signals, and trying to interpret them without being able to look at Justine was impossible. And yet... Something was definitely there, between them. Something that told her Justine might be struggling with this as much as she was.

She stopped dead in the centre of her office. Unless, of course, Justine was struggling because of what Alex did in having sex with her in the first place. Justine had been abundantly clear she had no time for someone who cheated. Was Alex making her uncomfortable in this silly pursuit, in continuing to force her into conversations that were nothing to do with work? But Justine didn't sound like she was forcing answers out. Justine sounded like she was enjoying their chats as much as Alex was.

She ran her hands through her hair in frustration. This was insane. Not for the first time in her life, she wished she owned a time machine. Then she could tell Justine how she felt, and if it went tits up, she could simply rewind time and pretend it never happened.

If only.

Throwing the memo onto her desk, she forced herself to sit back down in front of her laptop and focus on work. Two hours left in the day, then it was payday drinks for the team. She laughed to herself. Yeah, a very large gin and tonic would not go amiss right now. She puffed out a breath and got back to her e-mails.

⋙◦⟨⟩◦⋘

The pub was packed. Alex shoved her way through a large—and loud—group of men in suits until she spotted Edward, her assistant, and the rest of her team wedged into a corner near the other door.

"Sorry I'm late!" She had to shout to be heard above the conversations around her. "Who's ready for another drink?"

Smiling faces and raised empty glasses told her all she needed to know, and she grinned as she took everyone's order. Fifteen minutes later, after a monumental journey back through the crowd, she emerged with a tray covered in drinks and smirked as her team descended like vultures. The first sip of her gin hit the spot perfectly and she sighed in satisfaction.

"So who else is coming down?" she asked Edward.

He leaned in so she could hear properly. "The guys from Finance said they'd be down as soon as they'd wrapped up, and a couple of legal peeps too."

"Great! The more, the merrier. It seems like it's ages since we all went out."

"True." He raised his glass to clink against hers. "Cheers, boss."

She grimaced in mock outrage. "I told you not to all me that."

He laughed. "Sorry, boss."

She glared at him, then laughed as he winked. He was on fine form tonight, and she wasn't slow about joining him in the fun zone. She took another healthy gulp of her drink and turned to involve herself in the conversation the rest of the team were sharing.

Two hours passed in a blur of fun, joking, and more gin. Alex was vaguely aware she was getting drunk. Not in a vomit-over-someone's-shoes way, but nicely buzzed, where everything was just *fun*, and she smiled a lot and wanted to dish out hugs and praise to everyone.

She wasn't the only one. Miranda, from Legal, was definitely in the same boat, and they leaned against each other slightly as they compared—bizarrely—breakup stories. Miranda was going through divorce number three, and although Alex hadn't advertised her newly single status that loudly at work, like all good office gossip, everyone knew.

"You totally did the right thing, babes," Miranda said, her drink sloshing in her glass as she waved the hand holding it to emphasise her point. "After Husband Number Two shagged that woman on our couch, there was no way I was going to stay with him." This time a large portion of her drink landed on the floor. They both stared at the puddle, giggling. "So, hooked up with anyone else yet?"

"Nah." Alex was drunk, but just enough common sense remained to hold her back from speaking about Justine. No one needed to know about her. Even Danielle and Beth didn't quite get it, and they'd known Alex for years. So she was absolutely not going to share that side of her life with someone from work. She hunted around in her brain for a change of subject, only to be saved by the director of corporate finance latching on to Miranda from her other side and hauling her into whatever conversation his group was having.

Alex stepped back for a moment, clutching her drink, vaguely aware her head was more than a little woozy. And it wasn't just from the gin, although she was surprised how only three had got her to this point already. The wooziness also came from thinking about Justine again—the minute she did, her brain turned to mush. Alex had done an excellent job of pushing her to the back of her mind since their call a few hours before. But now Justine was there again, front and centre in her mind's eye.

She sipped her drink. It was so unfair. Life and all its stupid fucked-up little twists and turns. Why couldn't anything be simple? Why couldn't she get hold of that bloody time machine? Another sip. So Justine lived three thousand miles away—so what? Modern technology was amazing. Even if there weren't time machines yet. A couple more sips. They could do that face-call thingy. And sexting. That sounded fun. She could just tell her and deal with the consequences later. She finished her drink. Just tell her, because really, who wouldn't want to hear that they were wanted? They were grown-ups, for crying out loud. Grown-ups could handle this sort of thing. No problem.

Resolute, and smiling to herself at her new-found confidence, Alex found a spot to deposit her empty glass and surreptitiously crept backwards away from the group around her. When no one called her back, she smiled triumphantly and walked rapidly, albeit not quite in a straight line, to the exit.

———————

Glancing at the clock on her screen, Justine exhaled a long breath. Nearly four, when she had one last meeting for the day and could make her escape after that. Today had frazzled her. She had three tough projects on the go, including Alex's. And, of course, that phone call between them earlier had thrown her for a loop too.

The annoying buzz of the phone had her jumping in her seat. Probably Jacques, who had already complained twice today about her timeline for his project. She picked up without looking at the caller display.

"Justine North."

"Hey, Justine." It was Alex's voice, but it didn't sound quite like Alex.

"Alex?"

"Yep." Alex let out a little giggle.

Looking at the clock again, Justine did the math. "Alex, are you…drunk?"

"Maybe just a little bit. Tiny. Miniscule. Oh, what's the word? The French one? Soupçon!" she cried, triumphant.

Justine laughed, despite her discomfort at having a drunk Alex call her at work. "Alex, what are you doing? Shouldn't you be heading home?"

"Aw, don't make me. Just wanted to talk to you."

"Well, now you have. So now you can go home."

"Don't you like me anymore?" On the one hand Alex spoke pathetically, as only someone drunk could do. But something else was there, underneath the drunk outer wrapping.

"Of course I like you, Alex. I just... You should go home. Don't you think?" God, how did she get her off the phone?

"No." Petulant. "Want to talk to you. Need to tell you something, and then I can use the time machine to make you forget."

Oh shit. Alex was seriously drunk. "Alex, I really think—"

"I really like you, Justine," Alex blurted out, her words slurring even more with the speed at which she spoke. "I mean really, *really* like you. I want... I want to be with you, Justine."

For a moment, Justine's heart faltered, then righted itself and she could breathe again. "Alex, I think—"

"Don't you want that too?"

Her mouth started to form one response, only for another to override it at the last moment. "Yes," she whispered. Alex sighed. "Now will you go home?"

"Justine—"

"No, Alex. Go home. You're gonna feel bad tomorrow morning—" and not just from the drink, Justine surmised "—and the sooner you get some sleep, the better for you, okay? Try and drink some water, take some painkillers or something."

"I like how you care for me."

"I do," she said quietly. "Promise me you'll get a cab, yes?"

"Okay. Justine?"

"Yes?"

"I can't stop thinking about you. About that night."

Oh, God.

"I know, Alex." She sighed, wondering why she was doing this. Possibly because she thought Alex wouldn't remember in the morning. "Me neither." Alex hiccupped. "Alex," Justine pleaded, "go home. Please."

"Okay. I will. Thanks for telling me."

"Sure. Be safe, Alex."

The dial tone was her only answer.

Chapter 23

Something was worryingly wrong with her head. For one thing, it was pounding so hard, she feared her eardrums would burst. For another, she couldn't seem to lift it off the pillow, which she needed to do because, oh God, did she need some ibuprofen right now. Alex whimpered as she made one last attempt to push herself upright, and at that point her lower regions joined the party.

Cramps.

Oh, deep joy. As if dealing with a hangover wasn't enough, her period had launched a surprise attack and announced itself three days earlier than scheduled.

Fuck you, universe.

Staggering into the bathroom, not daring to put on the light in case the sudden influx of illumination split her head in two, she found the ibuprofen and stumbled back to the bedroom for the glass of water she had miraculously managed to put by the bed the night before. Swallowing the tablets, her eyes adjusting to the pale light granted by the moon outside her window, she gazed at the trail of devastation beside the bed. Coat, suit, shoes, handbag. What looked like an empty packet of crisps and a taxi receipt rubbed shoulders with her open purse. A quick fumble confirmed her cards were still present, thankfully. Another search told her the cash was all gone. But, given she'd got a taxi back from the West End to home, that was probably understandable.

She groaned as she clutched her belly with one hand and her head with the other. How was this fair? And it was still only five a.m. Allegedly two hours until she had to get up for work, but right now that concept was distinctly unappealing. Maybe if she got back to sleep and let the ibuprofen do their best while she was comatose. She lay back down, rubbing her belly as if her own touch would magic away the pains.

Still, at least the appearance of her period explained to her woolly mind how only three gins had left her in this state. She'd learned over the years never to add alcohol to whatever happened to her body on the day she got her period. Of course, that was when she bothered to look at a calendar to check when she was due. Although, that didn't help in this case, given the bastard thing had turned up so early.

She lay quietly, willing her pains to dull to the point where she'd be able to sleep through them. At least she'd got home in one piece. That was always a bonus. Not that she'd been that drunk in ages. Not since long before she'd split up with Terri. And it was nice of Justine to insist on her taking a cab, making sure she'd be safely hom—*oh God!*

Bolt upright, she groaned in more than physical agony as the memory surfaced.

Oh. God.

Justine.

It all came crashing back in one horrific vision. She'd bloody drunk-called Justine last night. Oh holy mother of all things crap.

What had she said? How bad was the damage? Desperately racking her brain, she tried to piece together everything that had happened after she'd escaped the pub. She remembered tottering back to the silent offices and shutting herself in her own office. And she remembered smiling as she dialled Justine's number, desperate to hear her voice, to tell her—

Oh. God.

She'd told her.

She'd fucking *told* her.

Alex flopped back against the pillow, her hands thrown over her face. Where was a time machine when you needed one? *Forty-seven bloody years old and you drunk-called someone? How embarrassing.*

But wait. Remnants were still returning to her fogged mind. When she'd told Justine, what did Justine say? Was she annoyed? Then it came back to her as clear as day.

Justine hadn't run screaming from the call.

Justine had said she wanted Alex too.

Hi, Alex,

Just wanted to check you're okay, that you got home safely.

Justine

Justine had sent the e-mail around nine the night before, right after Alex's drunken confession. Alex stared at it for a few moments, wondering how to respond. Did she need to read anything into the fact that Justine had made no reference to the call itself? Was Justine simply being professional, given she'd sent this to a work e-mail address?

She wondered what Justine had done for the rest of her day after having to deal with Alex's bomb. She laughed—probably went out and got pissed. *That's what I would have done.* She was still trying to fathom out if Justine's confession had been genuine. Or had she just said she'd been thinking of Alex too in order to placate Alex, to get her off the phone?

Gathering her courage, knowing she'd never know unless she actually asked, she typed her response.

Hi, Justine,

I did, thank you. Thanks for insisting I get a cab.

I would like to talk to you away from work. Here is my personal e-mail address. Please would you contact me? I really hope to hear from you.

She signed her name and added her Gmail address after it, hitting Send as she held her breath. She was giving Justine all the power in this situation, and although it unnerved her, she had no choice. She couldn't force Justine to talk to her, but she hoped after what they'd said last night that Justine would reach out. If she didn't—

No, she didn't want to think about that.

Justine burrowed under the sheets until only her eyes and nose were above the covers. The dream had shaken her, but at the same time she wasn't ready to leave the comfort of her bed. It was still early, and she hadn't allowed herself the luxury of a lazy Saturday morning in a while.

She stretched out her legs, easing out a little stiffness in one knee. When she'd woken, suddenly, from the dream, one leg had been hanging off the edge of the bed at an awkward angle, and her arms were thrown over her head. It was a pose of abandon, and it mirrored her demeanour in the dream: spread-eagled, waiting with bated breath for Alex's tongue to finish its journey down her body to her clit… As much as the dream had turned her on, it had left her breathless for other reasons, as it immediately recalled that phone call on Thursday and Alex's follow-up e-mail from Friday.

Alex wanted them to talk privately. And who could blame her, after all they had shared on that phone call. The few simple words they'd exchanged had spoken volumes.

She rolled over, still aware of the dull throb between her legs and the moisture that coated her. She'd gone six months without sex now since that night with Alex. Although, she thought with a wry smile, she hadn't exactly had sex that night. She'd fucked Alex, that was all. But that made it sound so much more simplistic and crude than it was. The satisfaction she'd gained from doing what she'd done to Alex was intense, right up there with any orgasm she could have experienced herself. Just the thought of it had her groaning and her hand drifting down her body, almost as if on autopilot.

It didn't take long. A few swift strokes fuelled by images of Alex, then her hips were thrusting upwards as an almost pained cry shot from her throat. The orgasm was fierce, intense, but tinged with melancholy.

Suddenly Justine couldn't bear to be in bed with her maudlin thoughts. She threw off the sheets and strode into the bathroom. She showered as quickly as possible, not wanting her hands to linger long on her skin and torment her even further with fantasies of Alex.

Dressed in her softest pyjamas, given she had nowhere else to be this morning, she made herself eat some breakfast and drink a coffee. Her appetite was off; the week had unsettled her, and her normal healthy interest in food had escaped her. Now she ate purely because she knew she should. She pottered around the apartment for the next couple of hours, busying herself with chores, anything to try to distract her mind. She was torn between two completely opposing thought processes.

To her left, the idea that trying to pursue anything with Alex was a road to nowhere, given their history so far and the distance between them.

To her right, the undeniable connection between them, and their mutual, overwhelming desire to see what that could become, regardless of logistics.

She hadn't volunteered the latest developments to Christina and Sylvie; her friends had said all they needed to on the subject, as far as Justine was concerned. Not that she didn't value their input, but she knew their minds were set—that they believed pursuing anything with Alex was a hopeless cause. For Justine it wasn't that simple. She'd always followed her heart, or her gut instinct, whatever you wanted to call it. When she discovered Nadia's deception, she'd reacted instantly, knowing without question that she couldn't stay a minute more in the relationship. Facing up to reality with Rose had taken a bit longer, but as soon as she had, she'd acted before Rose suffered any more hurt than she had to. Justine's instincts hadn't let her down in either of those scenarios, and she truly believed they weren't disappointing her now either.

After wiping down the kitchen countertops, she walked over to the high stool at the breakfast bar, where her laptop lay. She opened it and clicked into her e-mail application. She'd already memorised Alex's Gmail address, even though she hadn't answered Alex's e-mail yesterday, nor done anything with the information Alex had given her. She'd needed time to listen to her heart, to those instincts, and to clear her mind of other peoples' opinions.

She opened a new e-mail window and began typing.

Dear Alex,

I'm sorry I didn't reply yesterday. I needed some time to think about what I wanted to say. I hope

She stopped typing. This already sounded too lame, too apologetic. It wasn't what she wanted to say, or how. She deleted it all and started again.

Hi, Alex,

I think it's fair to say your call on Thursday was a shock, but I'm glad you did it. I don't know if you regret it already, but I don't. I think you and I have been skirting around this for a long time, and it is definitely time to talk. I don't want to do it via e-mail, though. Can you send me your phone number?

Justine

She clicked Send and sat back with satisfaction. The message was as assertive as she was now feeling about this whole situation. It needed talking about, and it needed talking about soon. She still had doubts, clearly. Her hesitation was all about trust, and until they really communicated, she knew with their brief history they wouldn't have a chance at trusting each other.

Chapter 24

"ARE YOU SURE?" SYLVIE'S CONCERN was evident in her tone and her expression.

"Yes," Justine said firmly. "I know you both think this is crazy, but I will always regret it if I don't at least talk directly with her, get it all out in the open."

"I actually think that's a great idea," Christina said, and smirked as her partner stared at her in wide-eyed amazement. She gave Sylvie a quick kiss. "Yes, my darling, I disagree with you. You'll get over it."

Sylvie snorted and reached for her drink.

Amazingly, for a mild Sunday in late May, lunchtime at Gabrielle's was quiet, and they'd snaffled the best table, tucked against the window where they could watch the gay world go by outside.

Justine hadn't intended to share her approach to Alex with them, but Sylvie had asked a direct question about how things were going, and Justine wasn't about to lie outright to her friends.

She turned to Christina. "I'm surprised, I must admit. I thought you were dead set against this."

Christina shrugged. "I was. Probably still am. But it's your life, and if you feel this is what you need to do to move on, in whatever way, then it's none of my business how you do that."

"Okay, so you may have a point," Sylvie grumbled, and Justine laughed as Christina sat back with a proud grin.

Justine was home by three, and a shiver of excitement ran through her when she opened her laptop; there was one e-mail waiting for her, from

Alex. As she read it, her excitement jumped up a notch and she smiled to herself.

Alex's message was brief:

> Yes, I'd love to talk—I'm available from 3pm your time today, if
> you like? Here's my number.

Alex was free right now. Justine glanced at her phone. This was their chance to finally have whatever this was all out there. The prospect was both exhilarating and a little scary at the same time. She knew if she delayed, she'd only talk herself out of it. Letting out one slow breath, she picked up her phone and dialled.

"Hello?" Alex sounded nervous, a slight quiver in her voice.

"Hey, Alex, it's Justine."

"Hi."

"Are you okay to talk now?"

"Yes. No problem. I… Thank you for calling."

"Thanks for agreeing to a call." Justine exhaled, trying to get a lid on her own nerves.

"I know you said you don't regret my call on Thursday," Alex rushed in, "but I do want to apologise. It was incredibly unprofessional of me to call you at your office. And I also wanted to make it clear that it is very unlike me to get that drunk, just in case you were wondering."

Justine smiled. "I wasn't, but thanks for telling me. Somehow I knew that was not your normal behaviour."

"It wasn't. At all." Alex groaned. "I'm so embarrassed."

"Hey," Justine said, "please don't be. Let's face it, that call is the reason we're talking now, isn't it?"

Alex was silent for a moment. "True," she said eventually.

"So—"

"So—"

They both stopped and laughed softly.

"You first," Justine offered.

"Well." Alex paused and cleared her throat. "I guess, um, I just wanted to say, in a sober way, what I tried to say on Thursday." Her voice dropped to a whisper, and the softness of it resonated throughout Justine's body. "That I…I can't stop thinking about you. And…you said you felt the same way, but I don't know if you meant that or were just trying to get me off the phone."

Justine chuckled. "No, I did mean it."

"Oh, okay. That's…that's good." Alex paused again. "I'm… I think there is something between us that is worth exploring, you know, despite the fact we live so far apart. Is that crazy?"

"Not crazy." Justine's voice was quiet. "Not completely. But…"

"I know." Alex sighed. "There's…stuff."

"Yeah. Stuff." Justine huffed out a breath. "Can I be honest?"

"There's no point in us having this conversation if we're not."

"Yeah." She took a deep breath. "So the thing for me is, while on the one hand a big part of me understands why you did what you did with me even though you and your partner were still together, there's a part of me that, well, kind of can't let that go."

"You don't trust me." It was a statement, not a question, and Alex's tone was resigned and tinged with hurt.

Justine pushed a hand through her curls. "I don't think it's even that I don't trust you. I don't *know* you. I don't know if…cheating, if that's something you've done before, or would be something you could easily do again. I don't think that's really you, from everything you've told me about yourself, but not having spent that much time with you, to really know your character, makes me less than one hundred percent sure. Does that make sense?"

Alex sighed deeply, sending a hiss down the line. "It does. I understand. Cheating is not something I've ever done in my life before that night. I hope you can believe that, but as you say, you don't know me, so why would you believe me? All I can say is that it's the truth, and I cannot imagine a circumstance where I could do that again. But then, that's probably what I would have said before that night anyway." She was silent for a moment, just breathing softly. "I never would have imagined doing what I did," Alex continued, sounding resigned. "Not in a million years. I suppose that showed me that you can really never say never." She huffed out a sound between a sigh and a grunt. "The biggest problem with what happened between me and Terri, and why I ended up where I did with you, was because we didn't talk. If there's one thing I can promise you, or whoever I next have a relationship with, that won't happen. I'm not making that mistake again. I want to be open, and honest, even if it means bringing something to an end quickly."

"I told you what happened with my ex, Nadia," Justine said, trying to keep her voice level and calm, despite the wave of nausea the memories still stirred. "She kept her affair from me for months. I felt so…stupid, once I found out. I actually think the embarrassment of that was worse than the cheating itself. I never want to feel that again." Justine closed her eyes briefly against the remembered shame.

"I cannot imagine doing that to anyone. Ever." Alex's tone was intense. "I had…an abusive partner, before Terri. Nothing physical, just nasty mind games. I know, having been on the wrong side of that, I could never inflict that on another person."

"I realised after Nadia that I couldn't trust anyone except my two closest friends. She ruined that for me."

Alex was quiet for a moment. Then she cleared her throat. "Can I ask you something?"

"Sure."

"That night, when you took me back to your place. Was that…is that a regular thing for you? It's just, in one of our exchanges afterwards, you hinted that one-night stands were your…game."

Justine shifted uneasily on her stool. Well, they said they would be honest. "Up to that week, yes, they were. Like I said, I didn't trust anyone. I couldn't imagine giving my heart to someone again. So I just took what I could."

"So when we met in the bar after the training, and you said you wanted to spend more time with me that week…"

"Yeah, that was new for me. I was really trying to break my habit of only taking the physical from someone. Trust me, in the past, I'd have pounced on you that first night we met. But holding back from that, trying to get to know you, that was a big change. And being with you and the way you made me feel was…new for me, for the first time in over eighteen months."

"Oh."

The silence that fell between them was necessary; Justine knew they were both processing everything they'd told each other so far.

"Does that mean one-night things are no longer something you do, or need?" Alex's voice was so quiet, Justine strained to pick up her words. Her hand ached from clutching the phone so tightly to her ear.

"Yeah. Not anymore. That week...what we had...changed me. I've...I've tried dating again. I met one woman, but it didn't work out."

"Oh?"

Justine laughed wryly. "Yeah, that was just about the time I got handed your project to manage. As soon as we were in contact again, it...well, it changed things for me all over again."

"Would you still be seeing her if that hadn't happened, is that what you're saying?"

"No! No, that's not what I mean. She...she was nice, and we had some good times out together, but there was no...spark. Not like there was between you and me," she finished quietly.

"Oh," Alex breathed, and the ache the word contained sent tremors rumbling through Justine's limbs. "So are you still single?"

Justine smiled. "Yes, I am. I wouldn't be having this call with you if I wasn't. I assume you're not dating at the moment?"

"No. I haven't...since Terri and I split. I needed time for me, to deal with the aftermath of all that."

"Are you okay?"

"I'm getting there. Living on my own has helped. Lots of thinking time. I'm seeing a therapist too, once a week."

"Good for you. I should have, after Nadia, but I was too angry. I... buried it all."

"Do you think that's something you could do now? You know, see someone."

"Possibly. Christina and Sylvie have always been there for me, but even they didn't really understand what I was doing with all that...the one-night stands. Hell, I'm not even sure *I* knew what I was doing."

Alex's laugh was gentle. "Hiding, it sounds like."

The truth of it was sharp. "Yes," she breathed. "Exactly."

"Justine?"

"Yes?"

"Is...can we talk like this more often? Maybe Skype next time?"

The warmth flooding through Justine took her breath away. "I'd like that," she said, her voice husky as it dropped an octave.

"I honestly don't know if this...something is going to be possible between us. But..."

"Yeah, I know. It kind of feels like we should see, doesn't it?"

"Yes."

Chapter 25

ALEX SMILED TO HERSELF AS she dodged around the slower commuters on the pavement in front of her. The spring in her step was ridiculously corny, but she couldn't help herself. It was Friday, which meant she only had about eight hours of work to get through before she would be rushing home again to get ready for her date.

She snorted. Date. She doubted Justine thought of their Skype calls as dates, but somehow Alex had started thinking of them that way in the last week or so. They had two video calls a week now, one on a Friday and one on a Sunday. The Friday one was always shorter, as it didn't start until eleven her time, just after Justine had got home at six her time. But they would briefly talk about their week and what they planned to do for the weekend. The Sunday calls were longer, at around eight or nine her time, and on those they'd share more personal information, family history, past relationships. Anything and everything to get to know each other better, to build up a foundation of knowledge she hoped would lead to them trusting in each other. And more.

Hearing how...casual Justine had been with sex prior to their tryst hadn't been easy. It had never occurred to Alex to think about safe sex when Justine had her pinned up against that door, and she realised how naive she had been about so many things. Justine, to her credit, seemed remorseful of her past ways, acknowledging she hadn't used her best judgement at all in that awful eighteen-month period of trying to get over what Nadia had done to her.

They were taking baby steps around each other, but so far it seemed to be working. Neither had specifically talked about the future, but Alex suspected it was on Justine's mind just as much as hers. The video calls and the sharing of lives was great, but where would it take them?

She threw her bag on the floor beside her desk and started up her laptop. Before she could get too comfortable, Richard stepped into her office.

"Good morning," Alex said brightly.

"Morning. Do you have a few minutes?" He looked serious, and she toned down her beaming smile.

"Sure."

"My office, if you don't mind?"

Frowning slightly at his formality, she stood and followed him down the corridor.

He closed the door behind them and motioned her into one of the easy chairs that took up the left-hand side of his spacious office. As the global head of human resources, Richard warranted an office twice the size of her own and all the extra comforts that entailed.

Richard sat in the chair opposite her and steepled his fingers under his chin. "How's things, Alex?"

She nodded. "Good. All good, thanks."

He raised his eyebrows slightly. "Personal life too? I don't mean to pry, but…"

A hint of a blush stole across her cheeks. She had informed him a few months ago about her change of circumstances, just as a courtesy, but they hadn't talked about it since.

"Um, yes, thank you. All good there too."

"Well," he continued, shifting slightly in his seat, and it was precisely then she realised he was nervous. She didn't think she'd ever seen Richard nervous. "The thing is, I'm in the middle of some negotiations about a restructuring, and although it's early days, it seems likely it could impact you."

Her heart rate jumped up. "Oh? In what way?" Amazed that her voice came out so calmly, she folded her hands into her lap to cover their trembling.

"Well, as you know, we bought out two smaller companies last year, both Canadian. What you don't know is that we've got two more in our sights, much larger, and also Canadian. Like I said, it's early days, but if those acquisitions do transpire, it would make sense to set up a directorship over there. Essentially, the role you do here but based in Montreal."

"My role would go?" She swallowed hard against her panic.

He shook his head. "No, not at all. We would have two roles, splitting the responsibility directly down the middle, purely on a geographical basis. You'd both work together, for me, and develop processes and systems that fit regional needs but with a single global focus. Both roles would expand, but I think the one in Montreal would have the edge as we'll focus a lot more development over there in the next few years."

"Okay." Alex relaxed slightly. That wasn't as bad as she'd first thought. Her job was still safe.

Richard nodded. "Montreal will be an interesting role, I think. Much more challenging than the one you currently fill." His eyes narrowed slightly, and the corners of his mouth twitched. "And, obviously, the new post would be advertised internally before we looked for any external candidates. If anyone fancied working over there for a couple of years on a placement, for example."

Alex blinked a few times, making sure she correctly digested every word he'd just said. Was he hinting at what she thought he was? A chance for a job in Montreal, even if on a temporary basis, could radically change her life. And not just for the work.

Justine.

"Something for you to think about, perhaps," Richard said, this time breaking out into an unmistakable smile.

"Oh. Yes," she said, aware she was slightly breathless. Her mind was reeling. "When, um, when would you know how definite this all is?"

"Well, not for a few weeks yet, at the least. Maybe a month or so before we know how likely the acquisitions are to come off, but once we know that, then the restructuring will pick up pace." He paused. "That is why I was asking about your personal life, if there was capacity for you to consider a move overseas. If you happened to be interested in the role, of course."

Alex couldn't stop the grin. "Yes, there definitely is capacity."

"Good." He sat up straighter. "Now, in tandem with that, how's the upgrade project going?"

Reining her excitement back in, she filled him in on the progress, not glossing over the stumbling block they'd hit last week with some of the testing.

"Hm. I wonder if now is a good opportunity for you get back over there," he mused. "See if you can get on top of this testing issue, and meet up with some people around the restructuring ideas. I'd like you to sit down and have a good chat with a couple of the executives I've been dealing with. Help them flesh out some of the details while I work on the job description of the new role. Could you go next week?"

Bloody Richard and his last-minute trips. But she wasn't going to complain, not this time. Because it meant she would be seeing Justine again. Face to face for the first time since they'd started to see what they could be. And armed with the knowledge that Alex had a chance at a future in Montreal.

The thrill that shot through her at that thought left her flushed and on the verge of a very girly giggle.

"Seriously? You're coming over next week?" Justine's mouth opened wide in shock. She stared at Alex on the screen in front of her.

"Richard actually wanted me to fly out this Sunday, but we couldn't get it organised quickly enough. So I'm flying out late afternoon on Tuesday, have Wednesday to Friday in the office, and back again Saturday."

"Will...will you have time to meet?"

"I was hoping," Alex said shyly.

Justine exhaled slowly. This would change things, meeting again face to face. So far their video calls and e-mails had left them plateaued at a "theoretical" relationship. And that was kind of safe, almost like make-believe. Now, meeting up for real, standing in front of each other, being able to touch and...

This changed everything.

"Justine?"

She looked back at Alex's face. Alex's concern was evident even on the less-than-perfect definition of Justine's laptop screen.

"Sorry. I... I do want to see you, it's just..."

"I know," Alex said hesitantly. "It makes it...real, doesn't it?"

Justine nodded and pushed her hands into her hair. Alex let out a small indecipherable sound.

"What?" Justine asked.

Alex ducked her head and mumbled, "Nothing."

Justine grinned. "Oh no, you have to tell me now."

Alex huffed out a big breath. "I...it's just... Well, when you do that, push your hands through your hair like that? It's just...sexy." She breathed the last word and dipped her head again, and a low throb pulsed between Justine's legs. In all their calls and e-mails, neither of them had yet referenced their physical attraction. Not having done so didn't seem strange; they were trying to get to know each other beyond the physical, to understand each other without the distraction of their undeniable sexual pull toward each other. With that one word Alex had shifted their momentum again.

"Was it okay to say that?" Alex had tilted her head, and a small frown creased her forehead.

"Yeah," Justine said, blushing. "It had...a nice effect."

Alex smiled, and Justine didn't think she'd ever tire of Alex looking so adorable.

"Do you...do you ever think about me? Like that?" Justine felt like she was fifteen again, stumbling over her words in a hormone-driven mess. She was aroused and had no immediate outlet for it, and the depth of it had her quaking.

Alex nodded as she tightly grasped her knees. "A lot," she whispered.

Justine swallowed. "Me too."

They were silent for a while, staring at each other as if neither had any idea how to follow that. Justine had learned much about Alex these past couple of weeks, and her belief in Alex being a good person who'd fallen into an awful situation had only increased. She knew her feelings were heading in the right direction for something to happen between them, something more like an actual relationship. But did Alex feel the same way? Could they talk about that next week when they met in person?

Eventually Alex cleared her throat and broke into Justine's swirling thoughts.

"So could I invite you out for dinner on Thursday night? Wednesday I know I will be too tired, and this, well, it's too important for me not to give it my best."

Justine smiled. "I'm glad to hear you say that. That it's important."

"It is," Alex said firmly, and she leaned forwards slightly, bringing her beautiful face closer to the camera. "I know we haven't spoken about the future much, but there's some things I'd like, no, *need* to talk to you about. On Thursday, yes?"

Justine nodded vigorously. "Definitely. I...I can't wait to see you. Well, I know I'm seeing you now, but you know what I mean."

Alex laughed, and the sound was blissful to Justine's ears.

"I know what you mean. Me too." Alex's smile was wide.

They hung up shortly after, and Justine didn't know quite what to do with herself. It was six thirty, too early to eat, and besides, her mind was racing, which in turn had her blood racing.

In less than a week, she'd be sitting opposite Alex, talking in person. Being able to reach out and hold her hand, if she wanted to. Or stroke her face, if the mood took her.

Or kiss her.

She shook with the desire that flooded through her at that thought. How would it feel to have that closeness again, or even just the option of it? She shook her head; the idea seemed so surreal all of a sudden.

Were they crazy? How on earth could they make this work when they lived so far apart?

"But you did not tell her about the possibility of living there?" Danielle reached for her wine and stared at Alex over the rim of the glass. The look held no judgement, simply curiosity.

"No. I thought about it, but it's still only a concept. Even if I apply I may not get it. There's a fairly senior person in HR over there already—she might apply for it too. And with Justine, I'll just have to see how things go with her on Thursday as to whether I even broach the possibility." She sipped her wine. "And anyway, I didn't think it was fair to do it over a Skype call. That sort of thing should be discussed in person, face to face. If I do apply it's a pretty major step to take and it impacts both of us. Well, it could. Depending on how she feels about me."

Danielle snorted. "From what you have told me, Alex, I do not think you need to concern yourself about that," she said with a smirk.

Alex grinned. "Yeah, maybe."

"You said 'if' you apply for the role. Is there a chance you wouldn't?"

Alex sat back in her chair and sighed. "I have to be able to separate the job from the chance to be with Justine. If the job isn't really something I want, should I apply for it anyway just to be near her? My sensible brain says that's a bit risky."

Danielle frowned. "I suppose so. But given what Richard said, is it likely to be something you do not want?"

"No," Alex said, laughing. "Not at all. I guess...I guess I'm just panicking, a little. Suddenly everything I want could be handed to me on a plate, and it's a little daunting."

"But exciting, yes?"

Alex grinned. "Oh, yes."

Danielle leaned forwards and picked up Alex's hand. "I am so happy for you."

"Really? Because, you know, you thought this was all bonkers."

"Very true. But that shows how little I really know, doesn't it?" She smiled. "You never know what the universe is going to throw at you. And you are living proof of that. This time last year, where were you? And look at you now. I think you were correct all along. This was meant to be. I think by the end of the year you will be packing up and moving to Montreal, and Justine will be there waiting for you."

"God, I hope so," Alex said fervently. "I think we've still got a way to go, but I think we've learned enough about each other recently that there's a good foundation for trust there now, you know? It's obvious she's past that sleeping-around phase—she wouldn't be putting so much effort into this with me if she wasn't. And I hope I've done enough to convince her that cheating on Terri was a one-time aberration that I cannot imagine repeating under any circumstances."

Danielle nodded. "I hope so too, because I know you and I know that prospect is highly unlikely."

Alex squeezed Danielle's hand, then released it, taking another sip of her wine. They were seated opposite each other at Danielle's kitchen table, having long ago finished the simple meal Danielle had prepared for them. Beth had moved into her office to catch up on some work, leaving them alone to talk.

"What is it like working together while all of this is occurring?" Danielle asked.

"Thankfully, she's as professional as I am. She's very good at what she does, actually. So without even talking about it, we've both fallen into a good pattern of putting on a mask in front of our colleagues. I don't think anyone would guess there's anything between us."

"And would you have to maintain that if you were working in the same office?"

Alex shrugged. She hadn't thought that far ahead. Hadn't dared to. "Maybe. She wouldn't report into me, so it's not like there would be an issue over influence around promotion or anything like that. But I don't imagine we'd advertise it—I don't know of anyone having an office romance at all, never mind a same-sex one. Come to think of it, I don't even know if Justine is out at work."

"Well, although you are, you have never particularly paraded it, have you? So if she feels the need to be discrete, would it bother you?"

"Nope, I would be okay with that." She sighed. "There's still so much I don't know, and although we've been talking fairly freely, she's still been pretty tentative with me. Not holding back, as such. Just...kind of reluctant sometimes. I know you said it's obvious how she feels about me, but sometimes... I don't know. It's as if she doesn't want to give too much away. I think she feels the same way I do, but it's not really been said out loud. By either of us."

"So what is your aim for your meeting with her on Thursday? Whatever this is between you has been bubbling along for so long now, I suppose I wonder just what your next step is, apart from more sharing about who you each are? Do you think you will sleep together?" Danielle flashed her a grin.

Alex's cheeks flamed. Just the thought of being sexual with Justine again had her body flushing hot and cold. Sometimes on their Skype calls, Alex had found herself drifting from the conversation as she stared at Justine's face, the lips she remembered feeling so soft against her own, the body that had pinned her so deliciously against that door...

Danielle chuckled. "I did not mean to make you blush."

"Sure you didn't." Alex smirked when Danielle guffawed. "I have no idea about Thursday." She threw her hands up. "All I could think of when I asked her to meet was just to see her again, to talk to her." She laughed.

"It's kind of bizarre to think about, that it's going to finally happen after all this time."

"I can imagine. So perhaps that is a good thing, then. No preconceived notions about what the evening will bring, other than a chance to reconnect, in whatever form that takes."

Nodding, Alex smiled. "But I can't lie—if there's a chance of things progressing, I won't say no." She shivered at the thought. "Underneath all the drama and the talking and the getting to know each other, that spark is still there. With bells on."

Danielle threw back her head and laughed. "Look out, Justine," she said, her eyes sparkling, "you have no idea what is going to hit you."

Chapter 26

It was a mad dash to get out of the office on time to get to Heathrow as—typically—suddenly everyone wanted something from her right as she started to pack up her desk. Edward fielded as much as he could, but even so, Alex was still carrying on a conversation with one of the senior finance managers as she wheeled her case down the corridor towards the lifts.

"E-mail me, Annie, and I'll look at it as soon as I get to Heathrow. But I really have to go. Now," she said, thumbing the button for the lift multiple times in the vain hope the action would make it arrive faster.

Moments later she was cocooned alone in the lift as it descended, and she allowed herself a slow exhalation. Work wasn't the only thing that was frantic; her thoughts were spinning and had been ever since she'd woken up far too early that morning. In just over forty-eight hours she would see Justine. They had arranged their dinner venue over e-mail; neither of them had been able to rearrange their Sunday plans to be able to have a Skype call, so they hadn't actually spoken since Friday.

Justine's hesitancy at Alex's news of her visit had been awkward to witness, but the rational part of Alex understood where Justine's concerns lay. She herself was finding the whole concept utterly surreal and was expending a lot of energy trying to keep herself calm. Even meeting up on Thursday didn't mean anything would be resolved between them—it was just another stage of this strange process they had found themselves in.

She bundled her case into the waiting taxi and slouched back gratefully in its comfy seat as the driver swung them westwards towards the airport. While London shot by her window, Alex tried to organise her thoughts once more. She was nervous, there was no doubt about that. No matter how much she and Justine had shared these past two weeks, no matter how strongly she felt an attraction—and that was such a tame word for what she felt for Justine—the path they'd travelled to this point had been bumpy, to say the least. Too bumpy to continue? That was what they had to figure out. Would she still feel the same strong desire for Justine when in her presence again, or had she unwittingly built it up to be more than it was due to their distance? And would Justine be willing to give them a go, to take a chance? She had been so hurt by Nadia; Alex could see how gun-shy that would make her. But surely, Alex reasoned, before panic set in again, Justine had to try again sometime, didn't she? And who better to try with than someone who wanted her as deeply as Alex did?

Stop looking for her; you know she's in meetings.

Justine's silent admonition to herself pulled her gaze back to where it needed to be—directly in front of her so she didn't trip over her own feet on her way to the coffee room. This was her third walk down the corridor in less than ninety minutes, and she shook her head. She knew what she was doing—hoping for a sighting, a brief greeting, anything. Pathetic. But it was tortuous, knowing that Alex was in the building now, probably on the very same floor, breathing the same conditioned air.

Alex had messaged Justine the previous evening, just checking in after she'd arrived, making small talk about her flight but already planning an early night to get over her travels. Justine had respected her need for rest and held back the suggestion on the tip of her tongue to meet for a quick drink. She was glad she had, as a wave of uncertainty had swept over her shortly afterwards. Even now she was torn between wanting to lay eyes on Alex, and wanting to run a mile in the other direction.

She was scared. Two years ago Nadia had handed Justine the biggest embarrassment of her life, and she wasn't entirely sure the scars from that had completely mended. To discover she'd been living a lie for six months hurt like hell, and she was still making her way back to normal from that low point of her life. She knew Alex could help with that. If Justine let her. But that would require her to conquer her fear of being hurt that badly again, and she vacillated between thinking she could do just that and not remotely thinking it was possible.

She had arranged to meet up with Sylvie for a drink after work, ostensibly to keep her mind off Alex, but she knew she would more than likely spend the entire evening talking of nothing *but* Alex.

She reached the coffee room and stared at the machine. Why was she even pretending—two cups were her limit on most days. Sighing, she closed her eyes momentarily. This was crazy. Turning abruptly, she marched back to her office and shut the door. Immersing herself in reports, test plans, and resource scheduling, she willed her day to sprint to its end.

By the time she joined Sylvie at Hugo's, pulling out a tall stool at the bar and ordering a large glass of the Pinot Noir, she was exhausted. Her brain had been on overdrive, filling itself with anything and everything work-related to keep images and thoughts of Alex at bay. Now, sitting close to her friend with a glass of wine in her hand, she let everything she'd bottled up spill out into the air between them.

"One minute I think I'm crazy to consider it," she said, after filling Sylvie in on everything that had happened and what she thought about it. "The next I think I'd be crazy *not* to do this." She hung her head and Sylvie rubbed comforting circles on her back.

"You are getting ahead of yourself, Justine," Sylvie said in her soft accent. "You are trying to figure it all out before you have even seen her. *That* is crazy."

Justine raised her head and couldn't help smiling at Sylvie's calm expression. "You're right. As usual. God, this is just...so hard, Sylvie. So hard."

"I know you are scared," Sylvie whispered, "and I do not blame you, not after what that...*bitch* did to you."

Sylvie rarely used profanity, and the sound of one falling from her lips had Justine giggling uncontrollably. Sylvie shrugged.

"Eh, I made you laugh. This is progress."

"Yeah, I think I needed that. *Merci, mon amie.*"

Sylvie touched her glass to Justine's and sipped, her eyes sparkling.

—◦◦◦◦◦—

"We've ordered lunch in, if that's okay with you, Alex?"

"Lovely, thanks." She wasn't about to tell the global head of finance operations that she'd rather take a walk at lunchtime. She'd spent all of

Wednesday, and now Thursday morning too, ensconced in a conference room with three members of the executive committee, discussing the expansion plans and the restructuring that would follow. She was tired, but it had been worth it—the plans for the new directorship based in Montreal had considerably firmed up since her arrival, and it was clear the role was going to be as challenging and interesting as Richard had suggested. They had confirmed the terms too—a two-year contract if it went to anyone other than a Canadian resident. So she'd have two years to prove herself and see where her career took her after that. Or where her personal life took her in the same amount of time, because two years with Justine could decide the rest of their lives together... Setting aside all thoughts of Justine, as far as she could, she listened to the committee describe what they envisaged for the role and knew she wanted a crack at it.

It was exciting and nerve-racking. Moving to another country would never have been something she thought she would seriously consider. Having no real commitments back in the UK meant she had the freedom to play with the idea. Although, having turned her life around one way in the last year because of a failed relationship, the rational part of her questioned why she'd want to turn it around another way for yet another relationship. Especially a relationship that hadn't really even got off the ground.

Baby steps. Just try and take it slow, see what tomorrow brings.

Their lunch arrived, and laptops and piles of briefing notes were pushed to one side while they ate. She made small talk as best she could with the three other people who shared the table. These were people she would work closely with, if she got the role, and whether she liked them or not, she needed to get on with them.

She racked her brain for an opening into a conversation she wanted to start, and suddenly remembered that one of the committee members had mentioned being from Toronto, and only moving to Montreal recently to take up his position here.

"So, Simon," she said, wiping at her mouth with a paper napkin, then smiling warmly at him across the table. "How did your move here go? Did you find it easy to find somewhere to live?"

That set off a lively discussion around living in Montreal that lasted throughout the remainder of their forty-five-minute lunch break. It gained her some valuable information, as she'd hoped, and she scribbled copious notes as her colleagues battled with good-natured rivalry over the best—and worst—areas to live in metropolitan Montreal.

I liked the area where Justine's apartment is, close to the Gay Village.

A small blush coated her cheeks as she recalled that night—the walk to Justine's place hadn't taken long from the bar, although she had no real idea which direction they'd gone. And when she'd left, doing the walk of shame, she'd wandered blindly until she found a cab. If they were to make something of their connection, if they were going to see what they could be, then maybe living near each other would be a help. Especially as Alex wouldn't know anyone else in Montreal.

At that thought, she mentally pulled up short. In the rapidly evolving situation, she hadn't stopped to consider that. If she got the job, she'd be putting all her eggs in one basket in relying on Justine to be her one and only connection in the city. True, there was Sonia, but she wasn't in Montreal all year. Although at least part of the year was better than nothing.

Alex excused herself to the washroom at the end of the lunch break and sat for moment in the cubicle, pondering this latest train of thought. If she got the job and she and Justine didn't work out, she'd be in a very lonely place until she built up a social network. And while she didn't have a huge list of friends back in the UK, she could always rely on a good handful to be available when she needed. In Montreal, that would all change, and the thought of it unnerved her. Was she crazy to consider this move? Wouldn't it be easier, and safer, to stay in the UK, forget this notion of exploring what she and Justine could have, and move her life on in a different way back on home soil?

As she washed her hands, she looked at herself in the mirror. The confused face staring back at her wasn't a surprise.

Chapter 27

THE RESTAURANT WAS PROBABLY BEAUTIFULLY decorated, but Alex barely took in her surroundings as her gaze swept the room. She was focused on only one thing—seeing Justine.

"*Bonsoir, Madame.*" The woman at the desk smiled widely as Alex pulled her focus back to the welcoming face.

"Hi, I'm here to meet Justine North. A table booked for two?"

The woman ran her finger down the printed sheet in front of her, finally stopping about halfway.

"Ah, *oui*. This way, please."

Alex followed her through the room to an empty table in the middle of the large dining area. She glanced at her watch; technically she was exactly on time, so she was a little surprised not to see Justine already at the table. Alex allowed the woman to pull out a chair for her, choosing the one facing the door.

"Can I get you something to drink while you wait?"

"Just some sparkling water, thank you."

A waiter brought the glass a couple of minutes later, and Alex took a few sips, simply to have something to do. She tried hard to breathe evenly, but her nerves were all over the place. And Justine being late wasn't helping. Had she changed her mind? Got held up at work? Alex checked her phone once more; no messages.

Fifteen minutes later Alex had almost talked herself into leaving, her heart close to breaking at thinking Justine had given up on them before they even got started. Then Justine pushed through the door.

She was every bit as gorgeous as Alex remembered; a Skype screen hadn't done her justice.

Striding purposefully across the room, Justine looked serious and intent and...hot. Alex shifted in her seat, arousal darting through her. Justine's face wore a frown of frustration and she gushed her apology as she pulled her chair back from the table.

"Alex, I'm so sorry. I got held up at the last minute. Did you get my message?"

Numbly shaking her head, completely in a daze at the glorious vision before her, Alex struggled to find her voice.

"I... No," she managed eventually.

Justine's frown deepened. "That's odd, I sent it half an hour ago." She sat and exhaled sharply. "I'm really sorry, I don't know what's happened there."

Alex shrugged. "That's okay. I was just getting worried, I'll be honest. But you're here now."

"Worried?"

"That...that you'd changed your mind." Alex's voice was small.

Justine closed her eyes briefly. When she reopened them, her gaze was intense. "I wouldn't have left you sitting here, even if I had changed my mind. Please know that."

"Okay." Alex smiled, and Justine's face relaxed in relief. Alex took a moment to drink her in. Her beauty was still mesmerising.

"I...I can't believe you're here," Justine said quietly, her gaze roaming over Alex's face.

"I know." Alex chuckled. "It's actually surreal to be sitting here, looking at you. You...you look good."

Justine inclined her head slightly. "Thank you. So do you. Amazing, in fact."

Alex's cheeks tinged with heat, and Justine grinned.

The waiter appeared, offered Justine some water, and deposited menus in front of them.

"How are you feeling?" Justine asked as he departed. "Have you been in meetings constantly?"

Alex nodded. "I have. It's been pretty draining, especially on top of the long travelling day on Tuesday." She lifted one shoulder. "But it's okay. We've got a lot done."

"You didn't actually explain what you were doing over here, other than catching up with me around that testing mess. More training too?"

Alex reached for her water and took a healthy gulp. Technically she couldn't tell Justine anything about the restructuring, as much of it was still confidential. She'd gone back and forth about this earlier, as she dressed for the evening, and decided all she could do was couch it in terms of the change in her role, but not the reason it was happening.

"Well, there are some changes being made to our team, and I needed to meet with some people to go through that." She knew it sounded vague, but she wasn't ready, so early in the evening, to talk about the possibility of moving here. "What about you?" she continued. "Had a busy week?"

If Justine noticed the swift turnaround, she didn't comment. "Average for me. I know we have the team meeting tomorrow on your upgrade, but I can tell you I think I've made progress today on that block in the test program."

"That's great!"

They talked more about the project either side of ordering their meals and a glass of wine each. Alex wanted to watch her alcohol intake carefully—she didn't need any hint of drunkenness colouring their conversation.

Their main courses arrived; neither had bothered with a starter. For Alex, even being able to make it through one course was going to be a struggle with her stomach in knots, and she wondered if it was the same for Justine. Small talk fell easily from their lips while they ate, but she could definitely feel tension building up between them as the meal progressed. With hindsight, and ever-increasing discomfort, Alex wondered if dinner had been such a good idea, especially in public. Might they have been better off meeting in her hotel room, where they could talk freely? Here in the restaurant, she was aware of the other patrons within earshot, the music that forced them to talk just a little louder than normal to be heard, and the background hum of other conversations.

"Are you okay?" Justine asked suddenly.

"What? Oh, yes." Alex flushed, realising she had drifted from their conversation. "I'm sorry. I... It's just I'm finding this a little difficult."

"Being here with me?" Justine's voice cracked.

"No, not that. No," Alex said, reaching out a hand without thinking, then pausing just before it came to rest on top of Justine's. She stared at her hovering hand. It had been pure instinct to want to reach out and comfort Justine, to show, in some physical way, that she wanted to be with her. Glancing up, she saw Justine staring at her hand too, a longing in her eyes that sent a shiver down Alex's spine. She lowered her hand onto Justine's and held back the gasp of pleasure that tried to escape her throat at the simple touch.

Justine's smile seared through her. It lifted Justine's natural beauty into another realm, and left Alex breathless and aching in ways she'd never experienced, yet always yearned for.

She found her voice again, despite her throat closing up from the piercing emotion of the moment. "Being somewhere so public, I'm struggling to be able to talk to you about what really matters." She waved her free hand. "There are too many people, too much noise..."

Justine nodded and turned her hand to hold Alex's in her palm, her thumb rubbing tantalising circles over Alex's knuckles. The softness of the touch, and the warmth of her fingers, set off a quivering deep down in Alex's belly.

"Then let's get out of here. Find somewhere quieter." Justine smiled and squeezed Alex's hand.

Chapter 28

THEY STEPPED OUT INTO A delightfully mild June evening. A soft breeze wafted their hair away from their faces as Justine gestured them across the street. The restaurant they'd just left was near Notre-Dame, and Justine led them back in the direction of Alex's hotel.

"How about a quiet bar in a cute hotel not far from here?" Justine asked as they wove their way through the many pedestrians enjoying the night air. It was still relatively early, only eight thirty. "It's tucked away down one of the side streets here, so it doesn't tend to get packed out."

Alex smiled at her. "Sounds perfect." She knew the bar back at the W, where she was staying again, was normally busy and loud. The last thing they needed right now. And somehow, with this hesitancy between them, inviting Justine back to her hotel room seemed far too presumptuous.

They walked in silence, zigzagging through the narrow streets until Justine took the two steps up to the ornate entrance of the boutique hotel. The bar was just off the lobby, and they were soon settled in two small armchairs alongside one of the windows.

"Wine?" Justine asked. Alex caught the nervous tremor in her voice and knew her own voice would sound the same when she spoke.

"Yes, but just a small one, please. Red."

Justine nodded and caught the attention of the bartender. Having placed their order, by unspoken agreement they waited until their drinks had been served before speaking again.

"So," Alex began, knowing she had to be the one to take the lead, even though it sent her stomach free-falling yet again. She sat forwards slightly;

the importance of what they were about to discuss made a relaxed posture next to impossible. "I wanted to talk about us. Well, about the possibility of us." She shook her head. "God, I'm not sure that came out right."

Justine smiled. "It did. Just because we've kind of started talking about how we feel about each other, it's…well, it's never been anything particularly solid, has it? Kind of theoretical, really."

"Yes!" Alex nodded, glad they seemed to be on the same wavelength about that, at least. "As much as those Skype calls gave us a better way to communicate, it still felt a bit odd trying to figure this all out without actually being in the same room as each other. I guess that's what I hoped we could do on this trip. Tonight."

"We can certainly start," Justine said quietly.

There it was again, Justine being…reticent. Maybe she was still unsure, but maybe she just needed more from Alex to know where she stood. Which meant Alex had to be brave and get it all out there. The thought was frightening, but she hadn't spent the last nine months re-evaluating her life, her desires, and her own nature not to do this now. Not when the woman who stirred more in her than anyone had ever done was sitting so close to her, potentially only one conversation away from being in her arms. In her life.

"I know we, and maybe our friends too, think this is a little crazy." She shrugged. "We had one amazing evening that ended very badly, and since then, this weird rollercoaster of events that conspired to bring us together again." She gazed into Justine's eyes, held them captive. "But I meant what I said on that silly call a few weeks ago. I cannot stop thinking about you. And that's only increased with all the calls we've shared since. I love talking to you, sharing details of our lives with each other. And the physical attraction… Let's just say the memories—" she cleared her throat at the rush of desire that swept through her "—of being pressed up against your door, with you kissing me…touching me, have kept me awake so many nights."

The flush that pinked Justine's cheeks told her those sleepless nights had been mutual.

"Sitting here now," Alex continued, leaning further forwards, "looking at you, all I want to do is know you. Be with you." She paused, took a deep breath. She felt bold and terrified all at once. "I know you have trust issues from what Nadia did, and you're going to be hesitant about getting involved with someone like me, who did cheat on her partner." Her voice cracked. "But all I can do is repeat what I said on one of our calls. I cannot imagine ever being in that position again. I'd like you to give me a chance to prove that. Because I think what you and I have has the potential, already, to be the best thing that's ever happened to me."

It was her best pitch. She had to know if Justine reciprocated at this depth before she brought up the possibility of being here on a more permanent basis. She reached for her wine and took a slow mouthful, waiting.

Justine watched her, her gaze travelling over Alex's face, down to Alex's hands wrapped around her wine glass.

"You don't hold back, do you, when you need to get it out there?" Justine's voice was husky, and her hand quivered slightly as she reached for her own wine.

"It's too important," Alex said, tilting her head. "Why, now, would I not be honest with you? Isn't that what this is all about?" She sighed, her frustration at Justine's slowness to respond threatening to spill over.

Justine held up a placating hand. "It wasn't a criticism. I'm simply in awe. After all you've been through, I guess I didn't expect you to be so...bold."

"I've had a lot of time to think. About me, about my relationships. About what I do and don't want. And working with my therapist has made me realise how my past timidity had led me into situations that weren't good for me at all. Doesn't mean this is easy. You have no idea how many knots are currently tying up my stomach."

Justine smiled warmly and reached out to stroke Alex's hand. The touch thrilled her.

"Then I can only try and match your bravery," Justine said as she continued to play with Alex's hand. "It would be grossly unfair of me not to. But understand that this isn't easy for me either."

"I know."

Justine looked away for a moment, dropping Alex's hand, then looked back at her again. "Nadia doing what she did, it...it just about killed me, Alex. I didn't know who I was for quite some time after that. And I said it gave me trust issues, but it did more than that. It made me scared. Scared to let anyone else in, just in case. Scared to risk my heart again, because I don't think I could take being that hurt again. So it's easier, right, not to get involved in anything serious?" She paused. "At least, that's what I kept telling myself. Then we had those two wonderful evenings, and with you it was all different again. For a while I forgot I was supposed to be scared, and not interested in knowing someone further. I don't know how you did it, in such a short space of time, but that's what you gave me that week."

She took a quick sip of her wine and Alex stayed silent, knowing there was more to come.

"But learning that you had a partner back home… God, Alex, that was just too much. Everything came back. All the embarrassment, the bitter memories. The fear. And yes, I've clawed back from that since then, and I've also done my own thinking. But—" she swung her gaze up to meet Alex's "—I still have my doubts. Not necessarily about you. I think I do believe you when you say that was a one-off. Maybe the doubts are more about myself. About whether I think I can truly commit to someone. The fear is still there, and it's holding me back. I know that. But I can't seem to stop it."

Alex swallowed, knowing she had to tell her it all now. Last throw of the dice.

"There is something else I need to tell you, that may make a difference. I hope."

Justine's eyebrows quirked. "Yes?"

"It's difficult to give you details because it's still confidential. But one of the main reasons I'm here to meet with the executives is because there are some changes being proposed to my role. Specifically, there is a high possibility a new directorship will be opened up here in the Montreal office. It would be a two-year contract if it went to someone not from Canada." She took a deep breath. "And Richard has made it very clear to me that he would be happy for me to apply for it, if I was interested." When Justine didn't visibly react, she added, driving home the point, "If I got it, I'd be living here, Justine."

Justine stared at her, her face giving nothing away. Then she huffed out an extended breath and sat back in her chair, her eyes wide.

"I…I don't know what to say." She shook her head. "That's… Alex, that's huge. Are you interested in the role?"

Alex nodded slowly. "Yes, I am. It's a great opportunity."

"And if…if I said I didn't want to have a relationship with you?"

Alex's heart lurched, but she answered honestly. "Then I would probably still go for the job, but if I got it, you and I would have to work out how we'd…deal with seeing each other in the office. I wouldn't want there to be anything awkward between us threatening either of our careers."

"I'd like to think we'd be adults about it." Justine ran her hands through her hair, and Alex admonished her libido for reacting to that tantalising image.

"So would I," Alex said, more calmly than she felt. "I didn't mean we wouldn't. But it could be difficult, in the beginning. Knowing all that we did about each other, knowing that we'd had this conversation and then not made that leap forwards into…something."

Justine looked away, staring across the room, her hands twisting around each other in her lap.

After a couple of minutes, Alex couldn't bear it any longer. "Justine, please talk to me. What are you thinking?"

Justine slowly turned her gaze back to Alex. "I…I don't know what I'm thinking. The idea that you could be living here, that that could give us a real opportunity to see what we can be… Well, that's something big I need to get my head around. It confuses things, even more. Gives my head yet another strand to try and separate."

"What do you mean?"

Justine sighed, and shook her head. "Alex, I'm trying, I really am. I know it probably doesn't seem like it to you, because I'm being so vague. But I'm trying to sort through all of what I know to get to the underlying feelings. To understand whether I truly want to be with you, because I care for you, have feelings for you, or if I am chasing a ridiculous dream."

Alex's anger was quick and sharp and she didn't feel the need to filter it. "Well, I know *I* care for *you*! I know I have feelings for you, Justine. Real ones. Deep ones. I look at you and, God, my heart just wants to beat out of my chest. Is that crazy, based on what little we've shared so far? I don't know, and I don't care." She tried to tone it down, to rein in the passion burning in her veins. It wasn't easy, not when this gorgeous yet frustrating woman sat so close to her. "I only know that wanting to be with you, *wanting* you, is the biggest, most honest feeling I've had in my life. It is torture sitting across from you now, like this, when all I want to do is pull you into my arms, and kiss you, and do everything I can to make you believe me." She stopped abruptly, the emotion overwhelming her.

Justine's stare was wide-eyed. "It's not that I don't believe you, Alex. Truly," she said, her voice cracking with her own emotion. "I just don't think I'm as brave as you are. No matter what I feel."

Alex threw her hands up. "Well, that's one of the problems. I don't know how you feel, because you've never told me."

"I do have feelings for you," Justine said heatedly. "I do! It's just…"

Alex leaned forwards and grabbed Justine's hand, linking their fingers and squeezing tight, desperation eating at her insides. "If you need more time, I will give you that. But please don't write us off before we've even had a chance to get started. That's all I want—a chance."

Justine looked confused and scared, her glance darting back and forth but never settling on Alex's face for more than a moment.

Alex let go of her hand and reached for the last of her wine. Justine wasn't ready, that was the message Alex was getting. She didn't know if Justine would ever be ready, but she knew she needed to walk away from this now. She'd said her piece and staying any longer to try to get a decision out of Justine would lead to nothing but heartache.

"I didn't mean to push you," she said, setting the empty glass back down. "I…I'll back off, give you some time, okay?"

Justine nodded. "I…I don't mean to be awkward, or upset you."

Alex's smile barely lifted the corners of her mouth. "I know you don't." She stood. "I think I'd better go." She picked up her handbag and slung it over her shoulder. "Call me, or message, or…something. I'd like to see you again before I leave on Saturday, but if that's too soon… Well, just let me know, okay?"

Justine wandered aimlessly through the narrow streets of the Ville-Marie, no idea where she was heading but forcing her feet to keep moving because the walking was helping to calm her down.

Alex had left the bar half an hour ago. Thirty minutes of emotional torture that had dug its claws deep into Justine's mind and mercilessly tormented her.

214

What on earth was she doing? Alex had laid her soul bare, shared the stunning announcement of her potential move to Montreal, and Justine had let her walk out of the bar thinking...what? That Justine didn't care for her? Didn't want her? Neither of those were true. She'd shared Alex's sentiments, sitting across from her in the bar, her body going crazy with desire for Alex, but her mind... Her mind kept blocking all her attempts to just go for what she wanted.

Fear. Such a powerful force. Good at protecting, at keeping her out of situations that weren't right for her. Now the fear was holding her back from something that could be so good for her. Something that could bring her happiness, and joy, and—maybe—love.

No matter what Alex had done when cheating on Terri with Justine, she was obviously in a different place now. Her time alone had done wonders, helping her come to terms with so much about herself and what she wanted from life.

And she wants you.

There was no doubt about that. Her impassioned speech had sent the hairs on the back of Justine's neck skywards, and huge cracks had appeared in her armour. Why was she still working so hard to keep that armour in place? Hadn't being with Rose taught her that what she really wanted from a partner was everything Alex was offering?

And now Alex could be living in Montreal. Okay, maybe only for two years, but that was a long time. Certainly long enough to find out what they could be. Together. The thought of it made her quiver. She let her mind wander, thinking of all the places they could explore together, all the things they could do together. The possibilities excited her, had her yearning for them.

She thought back to Alex's words when talking about her cheating incident. She'd said she couldn't imagine ever being in that situation again. She hadn't actually promised she wouldn't ever do it again. Although, wasn't asking for that a bit unrealistic? Who could ever promise anything? You never knew what life would throw at you. You just had to get on with it when it did and deal with the consequences. Life wasn't perfect. No one was perfect.

She stopped short, earning her a disgruntled tut from the person behind her, who had to veer sharply to avoid bumping into her.

Was that what she'd been holding out for? Perfect? Thinking that would avoid all hurt she could possibly experience in the future?

She shook her head, her epiphany lighting up her mind. Stupid. No one was perfect—she only had to look in a mirror to know the truth of that.

Alex wasn't perfect. But Alex *was* gorgeous, intelligent, caring, warm.

And Alex wanted Justine, just as she was. Alex wasn't looking for perfect. She was just looking for a chance to show Justine how good they could be together, with all their faults and doubts. Because she believed that all the good things they had outweighed all the not-so-good, and that made them worth exploring.

And she's right.

Justine snorted out a laugh, earning her some wary glances from an older couple walking by.

I'm an idiot.

Chapter 29

ALEX DRANK THE LAST OF the herbal tea and placed the cup back on the tray. The tea had done a little of what she needed it to do; she had at least ceased pacing around the room. But the hot drink hadn't soothed her inner turmoil that much and she needed further distraction. It was only a little past ten and she couldn't possibly sleep yet.

Leaving Justine at the bar earlier had been one of the hardest things she'd ever done. She walked out of the hotel wondering if she would ever be able to spend time with Justine in anything other than a professional capacity. It hurt. Ached deep in her bones and her soul. But she'd thrown everything she had at it, tried her hardest to convince Justine to see what they could be together was worth a try. If it failed, at least she would know she had given it her best shot.

But it would still hurt—and for a very long time, she suspected.

She sat on the bed and opened her laptop. Work. She always had work to do that could help take her mind off her troubles. She dealt with the handful of e-mails that had appeared in her inbox since she'd left the office earlier, then opened one of the restructuring strategy papers they had been discussing that afternoon. Five minutes later she closed it—the focus of the document was the proposed new role, and thinking about that did nothing to take her mind off the situation with Justine.

She knew she would have to think about the role, though, and soon, so that the minute the application process started, she'd be ready. She had to be able to make the decision on whether to take it or not based purely on the job and not what it meant about being close to Justine. And she was sure she would—the job sounded like a huge step forwards for her. But having said that, could she cope with being based here if she and Justine weren't together? How painful would it be to see her regularly in an office setting and not have that connection between them? They still had to get through the rest of the upgrade project too, regardless of whether Alex went for the new role or not.

She closed her eyes and groaned. God, why couldn't it be easier?

Her mobile phone pinged with a message notification. Justine's name appeared on the screen, and her heart rate increased. She opened the message, then slumped. It was Justine's inexplicably delayed message from earlier letting her know she'd be late for their dinner. God, that seemed so long ago.

Sadness washing over her, she flung the phone back beside her on the bed, only for it to chirp again as she did. She picked it up—another message from Justine.

> Please, if you are still awake, can I come up?

She was here?

Her heart pounded as she typed out her response. *Where are you?*

> Down in reception. They won't let me in or call you. Please, can I come up?

Grabbing the phone beside the bed, she called reception.

"Good evening, Ms Saunders. This is Helene. How can I help you?"

"Hi, Helene. There is a visitor for me in reception, Justine North. Would you please let her up to my room?"

"Of course, Ms Saunders. Have a good evening."

Alex tidied the room frantically, throwing her discarded clothes into the wardrobe and shoving her laptop back into its bag. She dashed to the bathroom mirror to check her hair, pulling a brush through it anyway just for something to do. Her mind was racing. Justine was here. What did she want? Had she made a decision that quickly, and if so, which way?

The knock at the door was firm and Alex's heart skipped a beat. She exhaled two huge breaths and walked slowly to the door.

Justine smiled weakly as they came face to face. "Hey," she whispered.

"Hey yourself." Alex's voice trembled, matching the quiver that had taken over her whole body.

"Can I?" Justine motioned to the room behind Alex.

"Oh, God, of course. Sorry," Alex mumbled, stepping aside to let Justine walk past. She caught a hint of Justine's perfume as she did, and it stirred something low in her belly.

She closed the door and leaned against it for a moment, looking at Justine looking at her.

"Are you okay?" she asked eventually, fearing the answer but she had to know.

Justine nodded and smiled, a deeper smile than before, one that reached her eyes and lit up her entire face. God, she was beautiful when she smiled.

"I'm an idiot," Justine said, shrugging. "A very big idiot."

Alex stared at her, blinking rapidly. *What the hell?*

Justine stepped closer, and Alex's breath caught in her throat. She'd seen that look only once before on Justine's face, and the last time it had weakened her knees just as it was doing now.

"Wh-what do you mean?" It was hard to find words, to construct even the shortest of sentences with her heart beating so loudly in every cell of her body.

Justine stopped a pace away. "I was about to believe that I couldn't have this. That I couldn't have you. Us. That somehow my life would be better without you in it. I don't think," she said, closing that last bit of distance between them until her face, and her warmth, were mere centimetres away, "that I've ever had a more stupid thought in my entire life."

The kiss was like nothing Alex had ever experienced. It wasn't hard, but it wasn't soft. It wasn't just a meeting of lips, or of tongues, but somehow contained every ounce of both of them in their entirety, inside and out. It utterly consumed her, drained her mind of all thought, sent wildfire scorching through her blood. When Justine's tongue swept across hers, when her hands cupped Alex's face and pulled her in even deeper, Alex wanted to laugh and cry and shout for joy. This was a kiss that claimed, that said—loud and clear—*you are mine and I am yours*. And so she gave it everything she had, everything she was and hoped to be. Her arms snaked around Justine's waist, her palms pressing into Justine's back as she pulled her in even closer, as if such a thing were possible when they were already fused at every single touch point along the length of their bodies.

Minutes later they had to break for air; they stared at each other, chests heaving for breath, eyes shining.

"I'm sorry," Justine said quietly. "Sorry for not realising this earlier. Sorry for making you doubt, in any way, what I feel for you."

Alex shook her head, still numb from the turnaround in events, yet at the same time feeling more alive than ever.

"It doesn't matter," she said. "Not now. None of it matters."

Justine nodded slowly, a wide smile splitting her face again. "Will you apply for the job? Please? I want you here. With me."

Alex laughed in delight. "Oh, honey, right now that's a no-brainer—and I'll do my very best to get it."

Then she gasped as Justine swooped in, her mouth plundering Alex's in ways she didn't even know were possible. Now Justine's kisses were hard, her tongue thrusting, her arms wrapping tightly around Alex's shoulders. The fire it sparked was intense, curling up from her toes and in from her fingers to meet well and truly dead centre between her legs.

"Justine," she gasped in between more searing kisses. "Bed."

Justine lifted her head, her grin sinfully playful. "Yes?"

Alex didn't bother answering. She pushed Justine backwards, earning a throaty groan from her soon-to-be lover. The old Alex, the timid version of herself, no longer existed; in her place was a woman who knew exactly what she wanted and was more than happy to make it clear. They reached the bed in a tangle of arms attempting to undo buttons and remove clothing.

"Wait," Alex breathed. "Let me." She pushed Justine's hands away from her shirt and reached to finish what Justine had started. She took her time, revelling in Justine's gaze sweeping hotly over every inch of skin that was revealed. She pushed the shirt back from her shoulders and let it fall haphazardly to the floor. The black bra she was wearing wasn't her sexiest, but the hint of lace that edged the cups seemed to meet with Justine's approval. Although Justine appeared far more concerned with what the cups contained, if her heated stare was anything to go by. Alex reached behind herself to unclasp the satin. As the cups fell away, Justine let out a small whimper, a sound that packed a powerful punch in the quiet room. Alex met her gaze and licked her lips. Her nipples hardened as Justine reached out slowly, her fingertips barely grazing the outside curves of Alex's breasts.

"So beautiful," Justine whispered, keeping her touches soft and teasing, glancing up at Alex as her breath hitched with each pass of Justine's fingers across her areolas. This was agony of the sweetest kind. Such a contrast to their first intimacy all those months before, but just as arousing, albeit for different reasons. This was not just about passion and need. This was about emotion, and connection, and...love. It was already the undertone for every touch, every caress and kiss, even if Alex knew it would be some time before she said the words.

She cradled Justine's head tenderly as Justine bent and placed the softest of kisses on Alex's nipple. When her tongue lapped at the hardened nub, Alex moaned, sweet and low, and Justine's hands clenched at Alex's waist. Justine's lips pulled at the nipple, the sensation connecting directly with Alex's clit in the most exquisite way.

"Yes," she whispered, running her fingers into Justine's hair and clasping tightly. "Oh..."

Justine sucked, and nibbled, and pulled, first with lips, then with teeth. Wetness flooded between Alex's legs, and her pussy ached with an intensity that bordered on painful. She wasn't going to ask Justine to hurry, however. This had been months in the making and she wanted it to last. Soberly, she realised she didn't know when they'd see each other again once she left on Saturday, so the connection they made tonight and in the next thirty-six hours had to last them for however long it took to get the job application sorted out. And if she didn't get the job... Justine's hands were on the zipper of her trousers, and Alex banished all thoughts of time apart to focus solely on the sensation of Justine stripping her.

She stood before Justine, nipples rock-hard and the evidence of her arousal obvious at the tops of her thighs. She'd never been so wet. She didn't actually know it was possible for her body to produce so much. Justine's breathing was ragged as she stared at Alex's nudity, her gaze roaming over every inch.

"God, Alex, you're..." Justine looked up at Alex and leaned forwards to kiss her. "You are so gorgeous I can't even find the words to properly tell you how I feel."

"Then don't." Alex smiled, her body throbbing. "Show me."

Justine's groan was animalistic. She lunged in, her mouth claiming Alex's once more. She held Alex close, her hands wandering over Alex's skin, trailing goose bumps and warmth wherever her fingertips landed. Alex pulled back from their kiss, desperate to feel Justine's equally naked skin against her own.

"Undress. Now," she said, twirling her finger in a head-to-toe motion the length of Justine's body.

Justine grinned. "Yes, ma'am." And she laughed outright as Alex quirked her eyebrows and allowed her most salacious smile to paint her face.

God, they were so in tune with each other. What if they hadn't taken this chance? What if they'd let this go by? Alex shook the thoughts off. They were here, now, and that was all that mattered. That and the fact she was about see Justine naked for the first time, and the anticipation of that, building from Justine's slow strip, was driving her insane. Justine's shirt was off now, revealing a plunging turquoise bra that cupped and lifted her breasts deliciously.

"Oh, God," Alex murmured. She raised her eyes to meet Justine's gaze. "Faster. I want to see you."

Justine's breath hitched and her fingers fumbled with her zipper. Finally she got it and pushed the trousers off her hips to the floor. She stood for a moment in her matching turquoise blue bikinis, dazzling in their sexiness, and Alex drank in the sight. This was something she'd dreamed of, so many times over so many months.

"Do the rest for me?" Justine asked, her smile cheeky even as her chest heaved with her desire.

Alex didn't need asking twice. She stepped forwards and reached for the clasp at the front of Justine's bra. "Hm, front-fastening. How convenient."

Her blood roared in her ears as she unsnapped the fastening, and she groaned as Justine trembled when Alex's fingers pushed the bra way. Alex took a moment to observe, to think about exactly where she wanted to plant her mouth on the curves on offer before her. Justine's small but beautifully formed breasts had Alex's mouth watering at the prospect of tasting them. Staring into Justine's eyes, she cupped a breast in each hand. They sat perfectly in her palms, the pale pink nipples, hardening by the second, pushing between her fingers.

"Oh, Alex," Justine murmured, and her eyes fluttered shut.

Alex dipped her head and took one breast into her mouth, devouring it. Justine gasped and pushed against her, offering her more. Alex took it all, swirling her tongue around the nipple before tugging it with her teeth.

"Jesus!" Justine's voice sounded strained, and Alex understood her torture. It was all she could do not to throw Justine onto the bed behind her and dive in.

She pulled back from Justine's breast and reached for her bikinis. Justine quivered as Alex's fingers pushed at the fabric, guiding it over Justine's hips, then bending to help pass the discarded briefs down her legs to the floor. She caught the scent of Justine then and moaned. Kneeling, she let Justine step out of the briefs before pressing her forehead against the soft skin of Justine's abdomen, just above the trimmed patch of curls at the apex of her thighs.

Justine held her head as Alex breathed her in, running her hands up Justine's legs, up the backs of her thighs to her ass, where she clasped lightly at the soft, yet muscular globes. She tugged on the curves where Justine's ass met her thighs to indicate that Justine should open her legs. Once Justine had obeyed, without any hesitation Alex ran her tongue down over the crisp curls to the wetness that awaited her. Justine's gasp rent the air, and the throbbing in Alex's clit increased tenfold.

Justine tasted so sweet. Oh, God, so, so sweet. Alex lapped at her, Justine's gasps and small cries adding to Alex's arousal by the second, along with the sensation of coating her lips and tongue in the delicious moisture flooding out of Justine.

"Alex, I-I can't stand up anymore," Justine said, her voice a ragged whisper.

Alex lifted her head, swiping one more long lick over Justine's clit before smiling at her. "Then why don't you lie down and let me carry on?"

Justine stumbled backwards and Alex crawled across the short distance to the bed to sit between Justine's legs, which were draped over the edge of the mattress. She took a moment to look up the landscape of Justine's beautiful body, aching at the view, before dipping her head between Justine's thighs.

"Oh, *God*," Justine moaned as Alex resumed exactly where she had left off, only this time with significantly easier access. Her palms pressing against the insides of Justine's thighs, she pushed Justine's legs as far apart as she could, then pressed her face against the deliciously wet folds of

Justine's pussy. She sighed into the touch. This was perfect. Being here, right here, was everything she wanted. Slowly, teasingly, she truly tasted Justine, learning what she liked, and didn't like, doing everything she could to bring this woman the most pleasure she possibly could. Finally, when she judged Justine couldn't wait any longer—if the arch of her hips was any indication—Alex moved her focus to Justine's swollen clit. Taking it between her lips, as Justine cried out above her, she licked at it with firm strokes that had Justine's fingers digging into Alex's hair.

Justine's orgasm, when it hit a few moments later, caused Alex's thighs to clench in semi-release. But her joy at bringing such pleasure to Justine overrode her own arousal and need. Justine held her close, keeping their connection while her aftershocks, of which there were many, shuddered through her.

"Come here, please." Justine sounded…emotional. Suddenly worried, Alex clambered up the length of Justine's body to lie on top of her. She gazed into Justine's eyes.

"Are you okay?"

Justine nodded and pulled Alex down for a tender kiss, her tongue only just reaching for Alex's before she moved away and her head flopped back against the bed.

"That…I…" Justine swallowed. "That was incredible."

Relief washed through Alex. "I agree," she said, smiling widely. "You felt incredible. And tasted amazing."

Justine grinned and her eyebrows hiked up her forehead. "Mm, and what do you taste like, huh?"

Alex's clit twitched at the question, but before she could respond, Justine flipped her over onto her back. Deceptively strong arms pinned her to the bed as Justine's mouth went on a journey. She started with the sensitive spot just below Alex's ear, kissing and licking until Alex squirmed beneath her. It was wonderful, the feeling of Justine's naked body on top of hers, Justine's mouth working its magic on her skin. And when she revisited Alex's breasts, teasing and licking at her nipples, Alex knew her orgasm wouldn't take long.

"Justine," she pleaded. "Please, I can't wait any longer."

Justine lifted her head from Alex's breast and smiled. A smile filled with tenderness and desire in an intoxicating combination that had Alex's heart soaring. Then Justine was moving, rapidly, down Alex's body to lie between her thighs, nudging Alex open further with her shoulders.

The first touch of her tongue, licking delicately at her entrance, wrenched a deep groan from Alex. She anchored herself to the bed with her fists, clutching at handfuls of sheet. She'd never felt like this. Never felt so consumed by desire for one person that the merest of touches had the capacity to make her weep with joy. She tried to hold it back, tried to make it last, but the softness of Justine's tongue on her swollen lips and clit, just the visual of her between her legs—when she could force her eyes open to take it in—blew every circuit in her brain. Two more firm licks across her clit and she was gone, the orgasm spiralling outwards across her thighs, her belly, and turning her limbs to liquid. Her hips lifted off the bed; she was vaguely aware that Justine rose with her, grasping her thighs, riding her pleasure together.

The laughter came then, rippling up out of Alex's throat. The sheer joy of release, and overwhelming relief that they were here. Finally.

Justine chuckled from between Alex's legs. "Please tell me the laughter is not a reflection on my love-making skills."

Alex giggled. "Come here. And no, it isn't." She waited until Justine was on top of her again, their bodies pressed tightly together from head to toe. She kissed her, trying to express with her lips all that she felt in the moment, because somehow words wouldn't do it justice.

Justine pulled back slightly, enough to be able to look in Alex's eyes. "Sure you're okay?"

"Definitely. Everything about that was just so perfect. I laughed because the happiness kind of overwhelmed me for a moment."

Justine beamed. "Well, I'm glad it wasn't just me who felt that way."

Shaking her head, Alex pulled her back down for another kiss, this one deeper and longer.

This time when Justine lifted her head, she looked serious.

"What?" Alex asked, rubbing her thumb along Justine's jawline.

"You leave on Saturday." Justine looked like a kicked puppy.

"I know," Alex responded quietly. "But you know I'll be back, yes? I don't know how long it will take, but I'll do whatever I can to make it happen. Okay?"

Justine kissed her. "Will you come to mine tomorrow, for dinner? Stay the night? You can go to the airport from there on Saturday. I know the company's paid for this room until then, but—"

Alex cut her off with a finger pressed against her lips. "I don't care if they take the cost of it out of my salary. I'm definitely spending tomorrow night with you at your place. It'll be nice to see beyond the hallway," she said with a smirk.

Justine's eyebrows shot up. "You… I can't believe you said that! Right, that deserves a very special response," she said, laughing as she once again pinned Alex to the bed. "Very special…" And she dipped her head and kissed Alex hard, her tongue demanding, firing up Alex's desire in a millisecond. In the next moment she released one of Alex's hands to rapidly sweep her fingers down Alex's body and between her legs.

"The last time you were in my apartment, I did this to you," Justine rasped, and she pushed a finger swiftly inside Alex, making her gasp with pleasure. "And I want to do it again." She pulled out, and re-entered her slowly. "And again." She repeated the words over and over as she fucked Alex to a slow, deeper-seated orgasm that stripped her mind of all thoughts except those centred on just how much pleasure they could bring each other in the next thirty-six hours.

Chapter 30

THE SMILE WOULDN'T LEAVE HER face, no matter how hard she tried. Alex had even caught herself giggling at one point, much to the confusion of the two people working in the cubicles nearest her. She apologised as she blushed. She just couldn't help it, though—a combination of a distinct lack of sleep, a sexual satisfaction the likes of which she'd never known, and the promise of whatever else she and Justine would share in only a few hours' time meant she was walking on air.

Although she did need coffee to counteract the first of her symptoms. She scooped up her mug and headed for the coffee machine down the hall. Being based on the executive floor for the week had its perks, including access to proper coffee brewed at regular intervals by the CEO's executive assistant. As she stirred the hot liquid, her mind drifted with the swirling motion of the spoon, wondering what Justine would cook for them tonight. Would they even get as far as dinner? They'd both been insatiable for each other the night before. But equally it would be lovely to simply spend time together—cook a meal, talk, plan ahead. She tried not to dwell on the fact she'd have to leave Montreal in twenty-four hours, or that it would be who-knew-when before she could be with Justine again, and kiss those soft lips, and make love to that beautiful body.

She smiled as certain parts of her own body responded to the thought— yeah, dinner might have to wait awhile. She hoped Justine could still finish on time. As today was Alex's last day, she merely had a wrap-up meeting at four, which she fully expected to be walking out of at five. If Justine couldn't finish her day by then, Alex had no idea what she—

"Hey." The whispered word made her jump and her spoon clattered to the floor. She whipped her head round to find Justine's grinning face only inches from her own.

She laughed. "Oh my God, you scared me." She flicked her gaze around the room; it was empty. "What are you doing creeping up on unsuspecting women?"

Justine's grin widened. "If you hadn't been so far away, you would have heard me walking over. Just where had your mind gone then, hm?"

Alex blushed but held Justine's gaze. "To last night. And tonight." She was delighted at the slight flush that crept across Justine's cheeks. She smirked. "I was wondering what you planned to cook and whether we'd ever eat it."

Justine sniggered. "Okay, fair point." Her expression softened, and she sucked in a big breath. "Alex…" She stopped, swallowed. "I cannot stop thinking about you. About us."

Alex shuddered as waves of intense emotion washed over her. "Me too," she whispered, aching to reach out, to touch.

"Tonight, I want us to just…be, you know? To talk, and share, and imagine other nights like that in the future. Nights where we have all the time in the world to just…be."

Alex nodded, not trusting her voice, and her hands trembled by her sides.

Justine glanced over her shoulder before turning back to Alex. "God, I want to kiss you so badly right now."

Alex was scorched by the heat in Justine's gaze and took a step back simply to avoid the temptation to pull Justine in for a long, deep kiss.

"Sorry," Justine said, "I didn't mean to—"

"No, it's okay. I…I like hearing you say that, but I'm afraid I'm about to act on it, and we can't do that here."

Justine exhaled, then smiled. "Yeah, that was probably more than a little mean of me."

"It was," Alex said, nodding, "but in good news, I totally forgive you."

Justine reached out a hand, and—

"Ah, Alex, there you are," said a loud male voice, and Alex nearly guffawed at the terrified expression on Justine's face, thankfully hidden from their intruder. She neatly sidestepped Justine and moved behind her to greet the head of the legal department.

"William, I was just making a coffee before joining you. Would you like one?"

"No, that's fine. I was just coming to say we've moved rooms—we're now in conference room two."

"Lovely, I'll see you there in a moment."

She waited until he'd left the room before she turned back to Justine, whose face had relaxed somewhat during Alex's exchange with William.

"Oh, honey," Alex whispered, laughing, "your face was a picture!"

Justine snorted. "Yeah, lesson learned—don't ogle your girlfriend at the coffee machine."

"I don't mind being ogled," Alex murmured, smiling.

Justine grinned. "Well, I'll save it for later, shall I? Although, I think I can promise a lot more than just ogling…"

It was Alex's turn to blush again. "I'm counting on it," she said, "so you'd better deliver." Before Justine could respond, she winked, picked up her mug, and strutted out of the room.

———— ⚬◦🙠🙡◦⚬ ————

Justine could feel the warmth of Alex's body behind her as she slid her key into the lock.

"Does it feel odd to be back here?" Justine asked, mindful of the memories of their last time in her apartment.

"A little," Alex whispered. "But I'm hoping we're going to make some new, better memories here in a few minutes' time."

Justine turned to look at her and grinned. "A few minutes? So we're definitely not eating first?"

Alex's smile was wicked and sent a flash of want careening through Justine's body. "We will be eating. Just not food."

Justine pushed the door open with such force it crashed back against the wall.

"Steady," Alex said, smirking. Then she was pushing Justine through the door, kicking it shut with her foot as she less than gently shoved Justine up against the wall. Her mouth was fierce on Justine's, and Justine was almost overwhelmed by the need it engendered. The need for skin, and tongues, and fingers.

"God, today has been torture," Alex murmured as she halted her mouth's progress across Justine's jawline. "Especially since our little run-in at the coffee machine. Sitting in meetings all day and all I could think about was this." She cupped Justine's breasts. "And this." She took Justine's mouth in another searing kiss.

"Bedroom," Justine panted as their lips parted, grabbing Alex's hand and pulling her down the hallway.

"What, no tour?" Alex asked impishly.

Justine laughed. "Later," she said as they crossed the threshold to the bedroom. "Much later."

In less than three minutes she had Alex exactly where she wanted her. Naked, spread-eagled on her bed, with her fingers enveloped in the hot wetness of Alex's pussy and her lips wrapped around an engorged nipple. Alex's cries were soft but coloured with her desire, a desire Justine shared, a powerful expression of all they were coming to mean to each other. It was intense, and intoxicating, and, she had to be honest, a little terrifying. She didn't want to lose this now.

"Faster," Alex groaned, and Justine obliged happily, plunging harder and deeper and overcome with emotion as Alex came beneath her, clutching at Justine's shoulders, fingers digging so deep, Justine was sure they would leave bruises. She didn't care; carrying the marks of Alex's passion would be an honour.

Slowly, she pulled out of Alex and rearranged herself on top of her, kissing her neck, her face, her lips.

No, she didn't want to lose this now, and if Alex didn't get that job, then they needed an alternative plan to give them a chance at this.

"Can I ask you something?"

"Anything," Alex murmured, leaning up to kiss Justine.

"So don't be offended by this, but how likely is it that you'd get this job?"

Alex smiled. "Not offended. That's a perfectly reasonable question." She sighed and clasped her arms tighter around Justine's body. "There's only one other senior person who would apply, I believe. She's based here and came in from that other company we took over last year. So she knows Canadian regional law and processes, but she doesn't really know RCS. Whereas I know RCS like the back of my hand but less than she does about Canadian employment law or culture. I know a fair amount, though, because I had to learn it to help with the acquisitions." She shrugged. "I'd like to think I'd be the frontrunner, because of my longevity in my current post. But it isn't a walk-in. I have to be honest about that."

Justine nodded, trying not to worry too much about how fragile their situation still was. "So what will we do if you don't get it?"

Alex looked haunted, just for a moment, and Justine almost regretted asking. But they needed to be honest—that was what they'd agreed, and that meant asking awkward questions and not hiding from the answers.

"I don't know. It's all so new I haven't really got my head around it." Alex wore a sad smile. "So maybe we should work on that, throw some ideas around, think about what each of us wants and how it might fit together."

"Yeah, okay." Justine smiled, relieved Alex wasn't trying to sweep it under the carpet. "But maybe not right now," she said, winking. Not now, not when they were warm, naked, and had so little time together before Alex flew back tomorrow.

Alex giggled. "Hm, agreed. I think," she said, rolling Justine onto her back and sliding herself seductively on top of her, "we should save that for another day, don't you?"

"Oh, yeah. Definitely," Justine whispered, then she moaned as Alex's teeth pulled at one of her nipples.

⊰⊱

It was hours later. The sheets were a tangled mess over their half-exposed bodies, but Alex wasn't cold. The heat of the passion between them had left their skin burning, a sheen of perspiration coating them. Alex had come more times than she thought possible in one night. She gazed down at Justine dozing in her arms, and her heart swelled with the love that sight sent coursing through her. It was just under the surface, but it wouldn't take much more for it to break free and be verbalised. And something told her it would be reciprocated, whenever she did say it.

She leaned down and placed a tender kiss on Justine's forehead. She was sated and simply content to hold this incredible woman in her arms until sleep claimed her. Given the energy she'd expended in the last few hours, she was surprised it hadn't yet. She glanced at the clock. Two a.m. Oh well. Her flight was at nine in the evening, so she only had to get back to the hotel to pack and check out, then she could stay here until it was time to

231

leave. Justine had already mentioned taking her somewhere amazing for lunch, but as she gazed down at the beauty in her arms, she wondered if they'd even leave the apartment once she got back from the hotel.

Sunday, she'd be back in London, with no idea when they could be together again. It hurt, pulled at her heart with a low ache she couldn't shake, no matter how tightly she held Justine or how many times they made love.

She frowned. Now that they'd finally found each other, the need to ensure they'd didn't lose each other was consuming her. She needed to get working on her job application. It would probably be a given for her to get an interview, but she'd have to impress some fairly senior people for them to want to offer her the role. The easiest option for them would be the woman already based in Montreal. Alex would need to work hard to convince them that easiest wasn't necessarily best.

And the sooner this could happen, the better, she thought as she looked down at Justine again. Time and distance were everything now, and both needed to diminish.

Fast.

Chapter 31

Interview is Thursday at 2! xx

ALEX HIT SEND ON THE message; knowing Justine would see it the moment she woke gave her a much-needed tingle of joy.

The last seven weeks had been so hard. They'd thought saying goodbye at the airport that Saturday evening had been tough, both clinging to each other until the very last moment before Alex had to get to her gate, but it hadn't prepared them for the reality of being apart. As Alex had suspected, the application process had been straightforward, once the job had actually been advertised—but that had taken considerably longer than she'd anticipated. Justine had tried to mask her disappointment at each delay, and Alex had done her best to soothe her, but they'd both struggled.

The intimacy they'd shared on her last trip had left them both desperate for more. They'd tried phone sex, and Skype sex, but neither had really satisfied. They both craved the physical touches that were impossible down a phone line. Which had led them into many convoluted discussions about what their alternative plans could be if Alex didn't get the job in Montreal. Justine was checking with her family as to their ancestry, to see if she had any chance of getting UK residency status. Alex had spoken to Richard to see if there were any other opportunities in Montreal, or even New York, as that was at least only a ninety-minute flight away from Justine. Richard had smiled and told her to bide her time. Thankfully, he hadn't pried into her reasons for suddenly wanting so badly to move across the Atlantic.

Now, finally, she had her shot at the Montreal job. The interview would be a combination of face to face and video—Richard and she in a conference room here in London with a video link to two executives in Montreal. She had been told that, as expected, the woman in Montreal had also applied, so both of them were being interviewed this week, and if neither of them were deemed suitable, the job would be advertised externally in Canada.

Alex wasn't letting herself think of that, though. Every evening this week she had plans for preparing for her interview, probably the most important interview of her career so far. She had spent hours already researching and reading up on Canadian employment law and culture, finding online seminars that discussed various aspects of both, and surfed through web pages of TED talks to find anything relevant. Yes, she really wanted this job on its merits alone—it would shift her career up another level, and after two years in this role, she would be in a strong position to take on something at Richard's level, if it came up, either at RCS or elsewhere. It was definitely the best career move she could make right now. But she had to be honest with herself—knowing how she felt about Justine, and how much Justine felt for her, it was the best move she could make for *her*, not just her career. It was a chance to have everything, and she was going for it with everything she had.

Two hours later, after she had immersed herself in the preliminary work for next year's budget—a task that always took her by surprise in the middle of August—she smiled as her phone beeped with a message from Justine.

Yes! At last! Oh God, such good news. Call me later? Xx

She glanced at the time and grinned. Six a.m. in Montreal, so Justine had indeed seen the message as soon as she woke. Alex hoped it had put a smile on her face.

With a warm glow in her chest, she returned to her budget papers, grinning as she allowed herself to wonder if she would be looking at a different set of budget papers this time next year.

———————◦◦⊂⊃◦◦———————

"Well?" Justine didn't even bother with hello as the Skype call connected, and Alex smiled.

"It was good, I think." She exhaled slowly. "I really felt like I'd shown them how much I can offer, and how much I know already, as well as demonstrating that I'm willing to learn more. I think they were impressed."

"Yes!" Justine fist-pumped and did a happy dance in her seat, which had Alex guffawing.

"Honey, calm down, please," she said, waiting for Justine to catch her eye. "Please, don't get carried away. I don't want you—"

"Hey, I know. Don't worry. I know it's not a given." Justine smiled wanly. "But I'm still going to hope with every little cell in my body, okay?"

Alex grinned and her heart beat a tad faster at how adorable her girlfriend was being right now. "Okay, I can understand that. Me too."

"So." Justine huffed out a breath. "What now? How long until a decision?"

"Well, the other applicant's interview is tomorrow. I imagine they'll all take the weekend to think about it, probably have a meeting early next week to discuss both of us. I guess, maybe, a decision around the middle of next week?"

Justine groaned. "I don't know if I can stand the wait."

"I know, I know. God, I miss you, Justine." The words had emerged without thought; she did miss her, physically and mentally. Talking like this just wasn't enough. They needed to be together.

"Oh, I miss you too." Justine slumped back on her sofa, her face crestfallen. "Can I suggest something?"

"What?"

Justine sat forward again, her face looming large in the screen in front of Alex. "If, God forbid, you don't get the job—" Alex shuddered at the thought "—can we at least then book a trip? One of us come to the other, or we meet somewhere like New York? Have you got enough holiday to do that?"

Alex was nodding before Justine had even finished asking. "I do, and yes, I think that's a great idea. But let's hope it doesn't come to that."

The days crawled by. Alex did all she could to keep herself busy, to keep her mind off the situation. She and Justine spoke nearly every night, but somehow these calls were even harder now. With the decision about the job hanging over them unresolved, their conversation was sporadic and full of silences where they simply stared longingly at each other. Alex ached to be with Justine; she wished they were waiting this out together, where they could hold and comfort each other. The distance was agonising.

On Wednesday Alex was a little late into the office after some problems on the Tube and rushed to get her laptop booted up and her working day started. She was engrossed in playing catch-up when the sound of someone clearing his throat caused her to look up from her screen.

Richard was leaning against the door to her office.

"Hi," she said, her heart pounding. *Was this—*

Richard, his voice serious, his face expressionless, said, "Do you have a minute? My office?"

Chapter 32

JUSTINE WAS WAY TOO EARLY, but that couldn't be helped. She'd been twitchy all day, which was understandable, but it was driving her nuts. So, at five, she'd given up trying to find things to keep her occupied and jumped in her car. It was a new purchase, one bought with the future in mind, and the thought made her smile as she headed out of the city. The roads were surprisingly clear, given the snow that had fallen in the last few days.

Traffic was lighter than she'd anticipated; she was still getting used to Montreal's patterns of ebb and flow, and Saturday at five was clearly an ebb.

By the time she'd parked up and made her way into the building, it was only just past six. Crazy—she had, in all likelihood, ninety minutes to kill. But at least here there was plenty to distract her. She took her time getting a coffee and sipping it slowly, people-watching as she did. Then she wandered past the cheesy tourist shop and, on impulse, bought a cute Mountie bear and an "I love Montreal" key chain. She even got the cashier to gift-wrap them, because why not?

She meandered through the small shopping area, taking nothing in as her mind was focused elsewhere. She reached the end of the arrivals hall and checked the time: nearly seven. Then she glanced up at the board and her heart leapt.

BA95 LONDON HEATHROW: LANDED

She made her way back to the barriers that separated the greeters from the travellers arriving. It was packed with people along its full length, but she knew she had time to wait it out and find her spot at the front as people came and went.

Thirty minutes later and she was there. Front and centre. She had a perfect view of one set of doors and an oblique view of the other set. Of course, the universe would probably choose the other set of doors, but hey, she'd roll with it.

Another twenty minutes went by and her stomach churned. So close...

It had been more difficult than they'd imagined to bring this day about, since the decision four months ago. But, suddenly, in the last three weeks it had all come together and now, right now, Alex was only minutes away from arriving for her two-year placement in the newly announced position of director of HR training and development (global) at RCS.

Two years. It wasn't forever, but it was enough for now. They'd made plans, talked endlessly about what they wanted, what they didn't want, what they dreamed about. Since that night the last time she was here, when they'd first laid bare their souls, everything between them had simply fallen into place. Alex had apparently romped the interview, clear daylight between her and the other candidate. They'd offered her the job without hesitation; no need to see external candidates.

It was as if the universe was simply waiting for them to each just be open and honest with each other before granting them their ultimate wishes.

Two years. It would fly by, but she knew—they both knew—that by the end of that period, they'd know exactly where they were and what they were. She hadn't mentioned it to Alex, but she'd already been researching how easy it would be for Alex to get residency if they got married. It was crazy thinking, when so far they'd only spent two nights together, four months ago. But they'd spoken nearly every day since then, in one way or another, and although they weren't physically close, the emotional connection between them was iron-cast. Tonight, if Alex wasn't too tired, the physical would be resurrected, and Justine shivered at the prospect.

The doors in front of her glided open and a steady stream of people flooded through, pushing trolleys piled high with luggage, obscuring Justine's view now and then. She knew not to look for a big trolley; Alex was arriving with two suitcases only, containing simply clothes and toiletries. Everything else had been crated up a couple of days ago and sent via air, paid for by the company as part of the relocation deal. Alex had spent the last two nights staying with Danielle and Beth, who were already booked to come out for Alex's birthday in March. The idea made Justine nervous but pleased that Alex's friends had got behind her so emphatically with her life-changing move.

And now, here it was, two days before Christmas and she and Alex would be spending it together. It was beyond her wildest dreams of a year ago…

The doors opened again, and Justine's breath caught in her throat.

Alex.

She was here, and she was smiling from ear-to-ear even as the tears poured down her cheeks. She almost jogged over to Justine, dropping the handles of her suitcases as she came to a halt, then her arms were tight around Justine's shoulders, and their lips were pressed together in a fierce kiss.

"You're here," Justine whispered as their lips parted, gazing into the shimmering green eyes of her beautiful lover.

"I am." Alex sniffled and wiped at her eyes. "God, it's so good to see you."

"And you." Justine pulled back slightly. "Come on, come to the end so I can hold you properly without this damn railing in the way!"

Alex chuckled and picked up her cases again, wheeling them along the walkway in parallel with Justine on the other side of the now relatively empty barrier. Alex skirted round the end of it and dropped the cases again, throwing herself fully into Justine's arms, her mouth seeking Justine's instantly.

They kissed, unhurriedly, their hands in each other's hair, or cupping each other's faces.

"Justine," Alex said as they pulled apart slightly for air. Her eyes were shining and her breath came in ragged gasps. "I… God, I've missed you."

"I know. Me too." Justine gazed at her, and suddenly, here in the arrivals hall at Montreal's airport, she was ready. They were words she'd never spoken to Alex—somehow saying them on a phone call or a Skype session hadn't ever felt right. Alex hadn't said them either, and Justine suspected for the same reasons as she; the miles between them made it seem almost impersonal, no matter how strong her feelings. But now, even with scurrying passengers pushing past them and the noise of the tannoy above them, it felt utterly right.

The words that had been lingering, waiting for their perfect opportunity, came tumbling out.

"Alex, I love you."

"Oh!" Alex's hand flew to her mouth, then away again. "Oh, honey, I love you too."

Justine pulled her close, noting how perfectly they fit together, with not a hair's breadth between their bodies.

Nothing between them anymore; not miles, not misunderstandings, not doubts.

Nothing except a future.

About A.L. Brooks

A.L. Brooks currently resides in London, although over the years she has lived in places as far afield as Aberdeen and Australia. She works 9–5 in corporate financial systems and spends many a lunchtime in the gym attempting to achieve some semblance of those firm abs she likes to write about so much. And then promptly negates all that with a couple of glasses of red wine and half a slab of dark chocolate in the evenings. When not writing she likes doing a bit of Latin dancing, cooking, travelling both at home and abroad, reading lots of other writers' lesfic, and listening to mellow jazz.

CONNECT WITH AUTHOR
Website: www.albrookswriter.com
E-Mail: albrookswriter@gmail.com

Other Books from Ylva Publishing

www.ylva-publishing.com

Dark Horse

A.L. Brooks

ISBN: 978-3-95533-785-8
Length: 272 pages (99,000 words)

Sometimes, going back is the only way forward. Punished for a crime she did not commit, Sadie is sent away to rebuild her life. Several years later she returns home to visit her terminally ill mother and face up to the past. In the midst of family turmoil Sadie meets Holly and falls in love for the first time. Can Sadie overcome the lies of the past to build a brighter future?

Flinging It

G Benson

ISBN: 978-3-95533-682-0
Length: 376 pages (113,000 words)

Midwife Frazer and social worker Cora have always grated on each other's nerves, but they have to work together to start up a programme for at-risk parents. Soon, the unexpected happens: they tumble into an affair. However, Cora is married to their boss, and both know it needs to end. But what they have might turn out to be much more than just a little distraction.

Rewriting the Ending

hp tune

ISBN: 978-3-95533-503-8
Length: 286 pages (107,000 pages)

A chance meeting in an airport lounge and a shared flight itinerary leaves Juliet and Mia connected. But how do you stay connected when you've only known each other for twenty four hours, are destined for different continents and each have a past to reconcile?

Hold My Hand

AC Oswald

ISBN: 978-3-95533-686-8
Length: 187 pages (66,000 words)

When Bethany and Savannah split up, Bethany is heartbroken. But a year later they meet again and their feelings are as strong as ever. So why did Savannah leave her?

Bethany is devastated by the answer and realises she will lose Savannah again—to cancer.

In a world where time is fleeting but love lasts forever, Savannah and Bethany can only hold each other and live their dreams.

Coming from Ylva Publishing

www.ylva-publishing.com

Who'd Have Thought

G Benson

When Hayden Pérez stumbles across an offer to marry Samantha Thomson—a cold, rude, and complicated neurosurgeon—for $200,000, what's a cash-strapped ER nurse to do? Sure, Hayden has to convince everyone around them they're madly in love, but it's only for a year, right? What could possibly go wrong?

The Art of Us

KL Hughes

When Charlee met a leggy brunette with a valedictorian medal hanging from her rear-view mirror and an attitude as biting as a Boston winter, it was love. For four years, she and Alexandra were unbreakable...until they weren't. A chance meeting years later sweeps them up in a whirlwind of heart-rending history. Is it too late? Or should the past remain the past?

Miles Apart
© 2017 by A.L. Brooks

ISBN: 978-3-95533-866-4

Also available as e-book.

Published by Ylva Publishing, legal entity of Ylva Verlag, e.Kfr.

Ylva Verlag, e.Kfr.
Owner: Astrid Ohletz
Am Kirschgarten 2
65830 Kriftel
Germany

www.ylva-publishing.com

First edition: 2017

Credits
Edited by Gill McKnight and JoSelle
Proofread by Amanda Jean
Cover Design and Print Layout by Streetlight Graphics

www.ingramcontent.com/pod-product-compliance
Lightning Source LLC
Chambersburg PA
CBHW031218020726
47499CB00002B/634